A SURPRISING INTRODUCTION

The man had raven-black hair, and dark slashes over his deep blue eyes. The structure of his face was strong, with a firm jaw and chin, and a nose that was as aristocratic as any in England. Then he smiled, and Emma wondered if any woman had ever been able to resist him.

Emma became flustered under his intent regard. "I have come to find my husband," she blurted out.

Lord Melbourne was both intrigued and amused. "I don't believe there are any misplaced husbands here at present," he said. "But you may search for yourself."

Emma was embarrassed by her reaction to this man. Every morning she reminded herself of Richard's deception, and vowed she would spend the rest of her days alone rather than shackled to a man, no matter how charming he appeared to be. But instead of treating the first attractive man she met with icy contempt, she was acting more the green girl than a married woman—albeit one without a husband in attendance.

The silence was stretching on far too long and the earl sought to break it. "I am Richard Tremayne, Earl of Melbourne," he said by way of introduction.

"Richard Tremayne!" burst out Emma. "You cannot be Richard Tremayne!"

The earl saw the distress in her face and reached out to steady her, but she jerked away from his hand as if burnt.

"And why not, madam?"

"Because Richard Tremayne is my husband . . . ."

BOOK YOUR PLACE ON OUR WEBSITE AND MAKE THE READING CONNECTION!

We've created a customized website just for our very special readers, where you can get the inside scoop on everything that's going on with Zebra, Pinnacle and Kensington books.

When you come online, you'll have the exciting opportunity to:

- View covers of upcoming books
- Read sample chapters
- Learn about our future publishing schedule (listed by publication month *and author*)
- Find out when your favorite authors will be visiting a city near you
- Search for and order backlist books from our online catalog
- Check out author bios and background information
- Send e-mail to your favorite authors
- Meet the Kensington staff online
- Join us in weekly chats with authors, readers and other guests
- Get writing guidelines
- AND MUCH MORE!

**Visit our website at
http://www.zebrabooks.com**

THE PHANTOM
HUSBAND

Alana Clayton

Zebra Books
Kensington Publishing Corp.

http://www.zebrabooks.com

To the greatest cousins imaginable,
Virginia and John White
and
Mildred Inez Wilson,
with appreciation for their boundless
love, encouragement and support.
I return them all tenfold—
but especially love.

ZEBRA BOOKS are published by

Kensington Publishing Corp.
850 Third Avenue
New York, NY 10022

First Printing: November, 1998
10 9 8 7 6 5 4 3 2 1

Printed in the United States of America

Chapter One

" 'Heaven has no rage like love to hatred turned, nor hell a fury like a woman scorned.' "

The words cut Emma to the quick. Perhaps because they bore more than a smidgeon of truth to which, of course, she would never admit. "Mr. Congreve's words are not at all appropriate in my case, Laura."

"They're from his work *The Mourning Bride,*" replied Laura. "That seems to be fitting."

"I am neither scorned nor mourning," snapped Emma.

"Then why are we haring off on this shatterbrained chase?" asked Laura, hoping her bluntness would knock some sense into Emma.

Emma fought the surge of resentment that threatened to burst from between her lips with a rancor her friend did not deserve. It was Richard who had brought her to this state, and it was Richard who deserved to feel the sharp edge of her tongue.

"I feel I should make an effort to find my husband," she replied, her emotions under tight control.

"Why? Do you actually want to find a man who deserted you at your wedding breakfast and hasn't been seen since? You should count yourself lucky to have gotten off so lightly."

"Something dreadful might have happened to him," responded Emma, even though she could not bring herself to believe it. "And if he has just turned tail and run, then I'm shackled to a phantom husband, who will prevent me from marrying until he is pronounced legally dead—and that will not be for seven years. No, I'll not let Richard ruin my future. I'll find him, and when I do I'll discover what is behind his strange behavior. Then I'll unearth a way to get him out of my life for good."

"At least write before descending upon his home with no notice," pleaded Laura.

"And give him time to get away if he is intent upon avoiding me? I think not. He was man enough to court me, and rush me into a marriage which he swore would be forever; he should be man enough to explain why he left before the ink was dry on the church registry."

Laura studied the young woman she had helped raise. Emma was attractive, with reddish highlights in her brown hair, and hazel eyes that now glowed golden with outrage in the early morning light. She should be raising children of her own, or at least have nothing more taxing to think about than what gown she was going to wear to the next soirée. Instead, she was left wondering where her bridegroom was and why he had left her so precipitously.

But worry was nothing new to Emma. She had lost her mother when she was only nine years of age, and had immediately attempted to step into her shoes. No one thought to tell the child she was far too young to do so, and she never considered it herself. Her father, accepting he would never have a son, began taking her about the estate with him, teaching her everything she should know in order to carry on after he was gone.

Now Emma's father was dead, and trouble had begun to haunt her soon after. Laura wished she could be of some help, but Emma was stubbornly independent, and insisted upon taking all the responsibility directly upon her shoulders.

Laura decided to make one more attempt to change her mind. "Then why not wait a few days longer to depart? Surely he'll return and we'll be saved this tedious journey."

Emma's expression softened as she studied the other woman.

Laura Seger had been her and her sister's governess. She had been called away for two years to nurse a sick relative, but had returned after their father's death to lend countenance to two young women living alone.

Emma, her sister Charlotte, and Laura had begun a trip to the Continent some months earlier, but Laura had fallen ill when they reached Dover and was just now recovering her strength.

"I know you're not completely well, Laura, but I promise, we'll travel slowly. We'll stop whenever you need to rest. I don't want you to suffer a relapse."

Laura breathed a heavy sigh, accepting that further discussion would make not one whit of difference to Emma's decision. Once she had made up her mind, she seldom changed it.

"Now where is Charlotte?" asked Emma impatiently.

"Most probably in the church praying you will come to your senses. She is even less pleased with this excursion than I am. She wants to go home, Emma, and you are doing her a vast disservice in not taking her," scolded Laura.

"You know the cause of her dissatisfaction as well as I do. If we go home Albert will be living on our doorstep. And unless I lock Charlotte in her room, I cannot be assured of keeping them apart."

"Perhaps if she got to know Albert better, she might not admire him so. What is forbidden is always attractive to the young."

"Albert could convince her to elope or could compromise her before she comes to her senses," argued Emma. "No, I cannot risk that she will fall into his hands."

"But why was it necessary to slip away in the dark of night, merely to discourage an unacceptable suitor who is dangling after Charlotte? Surely an admonition to him would have served as well."

"You know that I had politely requested he leave her alone more than once," Emma reminded her. "I had also demanded and threatened; all to no avail. He ignored my every plea. I had no choice left but to remove Charlotte from his reach."

Laura sighed. "And perhaps you were right in doing so. I cannot say I was pleased with his attentions to her. There is something about him that I cannot like."

"He is a libertine who will stop at nothing to provide for his decadent desires. Unfortunately, he sees Charlotte as an easy way to do so."

"But she will have no control over her funds for years," Laura pointed out.

"Albert would depend upon my good will. He knows I would never let Charlotte suffer."

"I can accept what you say about Charlotte; it is not so unusual to remove a young girl from the influence of an older man. But I still do not understand why you insisted upon rushing into marriage with a near stranger."

Emma stared out the window, her lips compressed into a tight slash. She would like nothing better than to share her burden with someone else, but Laura was always hard pressed to think ill of anyone. She was also more peacemaker than soldier, and would most likely counsel Emma to appease her enemy instead of opposing him.

Her impulsive marriage was not a love match as she had led Laura and Charlotte to believe, but was instead intended to solve her problem. With a man in the house, Emma felt Albert would be leery of pressing his suit with Charlotte. However, all she had achieved thus far was to further complicate her life.

At all events, if she ever got free of this coil, she would never again tie herself to another man. Although her experience was not extensive, with the exception of her father, she had not yet found one male worthy of her trust.

"You see what this has brought us to, don't you?" asked Laura, when it was obvious Emma was not going to answer. "We have been stuck in Dover for months; I nearly died; you married a stranger whom we are preparing to chase across the countryside; Charlotte is pining for home; and we have yet to reach Paris."

Emma could not refute Laura's remarks, and realized she was being much milder with her rebuke than many would have been under similar circumstances. Charlotte, for example, had become increasingly quarrelsome the longer Emma refused to return to their home. Neither she nor Laura knew the entire reason for their journey and Emma's subsequent marriage, and she could not tell them. Voicing her suspicions without proof would only drive Charlotte further away, and convince Laura that she was all about in the head.

A sense of failure swept over Emma. It was important that she handle her problems alone. Her father had trusted her to take his place as head of the family, and she had worked hard to live up to his expectations. There was nothing more Emma could say without revealing the entire story to Laura, and she was not convinced she should do so. Instead, she took a deep fortifying breath to regain the confidence that had sustained her thus far.

"I can't imagine what is keeping Charlotte," said Emma, rising and pacing the length of the room to stare out the window. "She knew I wanted to make an early start. Ah, there she is now." Emma watched her sister approach along the dusty road that led into the village. Her steps grew slower as she neared the house, and Emma made ready for the inevitable argument.

Emma forced a smile to her face. "We had almost given you up," she said, when her sister appeared in the doorway.

"I wish you had," Charlotte mumbled sullenly. "Then I could have returned home."

"We are not going to discuss this again," said Emma. "We have made our plans and we will stick to them."

"You mean *you* have made *your* plans. As far as I know, Laura and I had nothing to do with them."

Emma's confidence weakened beneath Charlotte's indignant words. She wondered again whether she had done the right thing in leaving home. But it was far too late to turn back now. She must resolve this farce of a marriage before her life could return to normal.

"Charlotte dear, I know you're unhappy, and that you don't understand or agree with what I'm doing. But if you'll be patient just a little longer everything will come right."

"You've been telling me that for months, and nothing has changed. I want to go home!" Charlotte demanded, stamping her foot in childish rage.

"You know we can't until I find out what has happened to Richard," reasoned Emma.

"He came to his senses, that's what happened," cried out

Charlotte, her face twisting into a bitter mask as tears rolled down her cheeks. "He found out what a . . . a tyrant you are and got out while he could. Otherwise you would have him under your thumb just as you do the rest of us." She turned and ran out of the room, her skirts swirling around her ankles. Her sobs were audible as her footsteps sounded on the stairs.

Emma's belief in herself had taken a beating this morning. "Is she right, Laura? Have my decisions only complicated what should have been simple?"

Laura sympathized with the young woman who had had too much responsibility thrust upon her from an early age. "You have done what you thought was right, my dear. No one can be criticized for that. It's too early to determine whether your judgments were right or wrong. But whatever the case, they were done with the best interests of your sister in mind."

Laura rose and straightened her skirts. "Now, I will go help Charlotte ready herself for our journey. We shouldn't be long."

"Thank you, Laura. I don't know how I could have gone on without you."

"You would have managed, Emma. You have a strong constitution."

"Or as Charlotte says, I am a despot," replied Emma bitterly.

Laura moved to her side and laid a hand on her shoulder. "You mustn't think that. Charlotte is a green girl, barely out of the schoolroom. She has been pampered and given her every wish all her life. Now she is being denied for the first time, and it only makes her yearning the more keen. As soon as she finds a young man who will flatter her, she will forget all about Albert."

"I pray that you're right," said Emma.

"I am. Now, I must go to Charlotte or we will never be gone from here." When Laura reached the door, she paused. "If Richard is not at the estate," she asked gently, "what then?"

Emma turned to face her. "Then I shall track him down with whatever means are available." Her voice was hard and unyielding.

Laura shuddered at the fire that flashed from Emma's eyes. She did not envy Richard Tremayne when Emma found him.

* * *

Richard Tremayne, Earl of Melbourne, stood in front of the house that until very recently had belonged to his uncle. It was a Palladian style manor house, but it had not received adequate care for the last seven years of his uncle's life. Ivy crawled over the brick walls, covering even the windows in its effort to swallow the building. It sat amidst a wild growth of bushes, trees, and grass that had at one time been an attractive park. The scene exuded a feeling of desolation, and the earl was happy to be spending only one more night in the house.

Lord Melbourne turned to the man at his side. David Whitney was as much his friend as his steward, and had accompanied him to oversee the repairs on the house and grounds. "I'm not at all certain that Uncle Charles did me a service by making me his heir."

"It will take some work," admitted Whitney, "but the estate will be tolerable again. The inside already looks much better. I have men arriving tomorrow who will begin work on the park and the outside of the house. Give me a fortnight and you won't recognize it as the same place."

"You have never failed me yet, so I will take you at your word. I'll admit, I won't be sorry to see the last of this place," said the earl, eyeing the house once again with distaste.

"I'm sure your uncle wasn't pleased at seeing his home fall into such disrepair."

Lord Melbourne nodded in agreement. "Uncle Charles was confined to his bed the past few years and wasn't able to see the toll that neglect had taken on his property. For that I'm grateful.

"Indeed, it's my cousin Edward who should shoulder most of the blame for this," he said, gesturing toward the house. "Edward thought of nothing but his own enjoyment. He bled every penny that he could from his father, and then disappeared. Toward the end of his life, Charles gave up on ever seeing him again, and made me his heir."

"A sad turn of events," commiserated Whitney.

"Yes," agreed the earl. "Uncle Charles did nothing more than love a son who did not return his regard, and it ruined his life.

When I last talked to my uncle, he asked that I bring the property back to its former state of prosperity, and to see that his people did not continue to suffer for his son's folly.

"Charles had always been my favorite uncle, and I would have done anything in my power to ease his mind. He seemed at peace after I assured him I would do as he asked; he passed away in his sleep a few nights later." Lord Melbourne stopped speaking and stared off into the distance.

"You did all that you could," Whitney solemnly assured him.

The earl heaved a great sigh. "I suppose I did. He was a proud man and would not accept help even though I offered it. But I fully intend to fulfill my promise to him and restore this forsaken place to its former—"

Lord Melbourne frowned as his conversation was interrupted by the sounds of a coach making its way toward the house.

Emma, Charlotte, and Laura were holding on for dear life as the coach jolted down the disreputable excuse for a drive. Tall weeds and grass crowded against the sides of the coach as it followed the barely distinguishable twin ruts that served as a guide to the house. The coachman's curses were clearly discernible as he fought the branches that were nearly knocking him from his seat.

If this was Richard's home, Emma thought, then it had surely been abandoned long ago, just as he had abandoned her. She lifted her chin, determined not to become as neglected as the estate because of one man.

"How are you?" Emma asked Laura. The woman's face was pale and a thin film of perspiration dotted her forehead.

"I'll be fine as soon as I get my feet on solid ground," replied Laura through gritted teeth.

Emma was beginning to doubt her hasty decision to follow Richard to his home. Laura was clearly not up to the travel, and Charlotte—completely devastated that they were not going home—had been silent during most of the trip.

It was a relief to everyone when the coach finally came to a halt. The three women sat for a moment, grateful for the cessation of movement. Emma shifted tentatively, wondering how many bruises she had obtained on the ride from the main road to the house, when suddenly the coach door opened and a wickedly handsome face appeared.

The man had raven-black hair, and dark slashes of brows over deep blue eyes. The structure of his face was strong, with a firm jaw and chin, and a nose that was as aristocratic as any in England. Then he smiled, and Emma wondered if any woman had ever been able to resist him.

Emma became flustered under his intent regard. "I have come to find my husband," she blurted out.

Lord Melbourne was both intrigued and amused by the thought of a woman so blatantly pursuing her husband. "I don't believe there are any misplaced husbands here at present," he said. "But if you would care to step down you may search for yourself."

Emma was embarrassed by her reaction to this man. Every morning she reminded herself of Richard's deception, and vowed she would spend the rest of her days alone rather than shackled to a man, no matter how charming he appeared to be. But instead of treating the first attractive man she met with icy contempt, she was acting more the green girl than a married woman—albeit one without a husband in attendance.

The man looked the consummate rake, but if she wanted to learn whether this was her husband's home, and whether he was here, she must gather her wits and accept his invitation.

Lord Melbourne helped the ladies down, and they stood looking around them. Emma's spirits dipped even lower as she observed the shabby state of the house and the area surrounding it. If this was her husband's home, no one had lived here for a very long time. Her hope of a rapid end to her search was quickly turning into despair.

The silence was stretching on far too long and the earl sought to break it. "I am Richard Tremayne, Earl of Melbourne," he said by way of introduction. "And this is my steward, David Whitney."

"Richard Tremayne!" burst out Emma, before anyone else could speak. "You cannot be Richard Tremayne!"

The earl saw the distress in her pale face, and reached out to steady her, but she jerked away from his hand as if burnt.

"And why not, madam?"

"Because Richard Tremayne is my husband," replied Emma, her hand pressed to her chest.

Lord Melbourne inspected the three women once again. Perhaps they had escaped from Bedlam and thought this was the perfect place to conceal themselves until the search for them ended. However, their clothing was far too superior for institutional garb, and except for the one claiming he could not be who he was, their behavior was unexceptional.

"You undoubtedly have the wrong Richard Tremayne," replied the earl, although he knew of no other but himself. "If I were married, I'm sure I would remember it." He smiled, hoping to lighten the atmosphere, but his charm did not work on the termagant standing before him.

"My husband claimed this was his home," protested Emma.

Lord Melbourne was unaccustomed to explaining his personal affairs, but he considered it might be best in this instance. "I recently inherited the estate when my uncle, Charles Tremayne, died. He was an elderly man, confined to his bed these past three years."

The look of confusion on the woman's face prompted a sudden surge of compassion on the earl's part for her and her companions. They appeared tired from what had evidently been a long day in a coach traveling over poor roads.

"Why not come in for some refreshments? We've had a few weeks to work on the house, and I can assure you it looks better inside than out."

Emma's first inclination was to refuse his hospitality. He had ruined her hopes of finding Richard, and either settling their differences and beginning their life together, or completely severing the connection. Instead, she had arrived at an estate which appeared to be in ruins, with an earl in residence who claimed to be Richard Tremayne. Emma wanted nothing more than to bury her head beneath a pillow and give herself over to a fit of the dismals.

"You have not yet given me your name," said Lord Melbourne, breaking into her thoughts.

Emma pulled her wits together and attempted to contrive a calm facade. An introduction would be proper since he had offered his hospitality. "I am Emma Randolph."

"I understood you to say your husband's name was Tremayne," commented the earl.

"I prefer to keep my own name for the time being," she said shortly.

"I see," said Lord Melbourne, although he actually didn't; but it wouldn't be polite to question her reasons on such a short acquaintance. Moreover, he had enough on his plate at the moment, and didn't want to be drawn into Emma Randolph's problem of a missing husband.

"This is my sister, Charlotte, and our companion Miss Seger," said Emma completing the introductions.

The earl acknowledged the women, and escorted them into the house, while David Whitney excused himself to oversee the work going on around the estate.

Emma was relieved to see that the house was, indeed, in better condition inside than out. While the furnishings were worn, they were clean, with no air of mustiness invading the rooms. A substantial tea was served, for which Emma was thankful.

"The coachman," she said as she lifted her second cup of tea, ashamed to have forgotten him until then.

"In the kitchen with cook fussing over him. She dotes on anyone who shows obvious approval of her meals."

"Which I'm sure he did," said Emma ruefully. "I'm afraid we're taking advantage of both you and your cook. None of us have eaten since breakfast."

Lord Melbourne was glad to see her hostility seemed to be lessening. "The best compliment you can pay her is to eat hearty."

The ladies had taken a few minutes to refresh themselves, and the tea and food had restored color to their faces. Altogether, they looked in far better spirits than when they had arrived.

They made an attractive group around the table. Charlotte, the younger sister, had dark hair with eyes to match. The pink and white striped gown she wore brought out the blush of youth on her cheeks. Once she developed the strength of purpose her sister possessed, she would be quite a challenge for any man.

During the conversation, he had learned that Miss Seger was recovering from a lengthy illness. And, although she did look better than when she had first climbed from the coach, he had to admit she did not appear to be in the best of health. Her gray gown hung from her shoulders as if it had been made for someone at least a size larger. Her pale blonde hair was dull and pulled back into a simple knot at the nape of her neck, while her blue eyes looked entirely too large for her thin face.

Finally, there was Emma Randolph. She was the smallest of the three women, but made the most lasting impression. Her dark brown hair was gathered in a cluster of curls at the back of her head. Even after the dust of travel, it gleamed like silk, and looked as if it might slip through his fingers just as smoothly. Her eyes were hazel, changing from green to gold according to her disposition. If they had met in London, without all the foolishness of a lost husband, he would have no doubt been attracted to her.

"Is there by chance another Richard Tremayne in your family, my lord?" she asked, pulling him from his reflection.

"I cannot think of another one, madam. I have a brother named Adam, but he is on the Continent with Wellington at present, and has been this past year and a half."

"Then my husband could not be your brother."

Lord Melbourne thought of Adam and smiled. "No, Adam is not the marrying kind. At least, not the last time I saw him.

"The rest of our family is sparse. That's not to say that somewhere in England there is not another Richard Tremayne. It's simply that I know of no other."

Emma sighed and set down her cup. Her appetite had vanished along with her hopes of finding her husband. He had lied about this estate being his family home. Had he lied about everything else, too? Why had he insisted they marry so quickly if he was going to desert her as soon as the vows were said? There had to be a reason, but Emma could think of nothing he had gained by such a machination.

"Mrs. . . . er . . . Miss . . . I'll admit, madam, I'm at a loss as to how to address you."

"Miss Randolph will do nicely," Emma replied shortly. Thus far, her marriage was on paper only. She and Richard had barely shared a meal together after their wedding ceremony, not to mention a bed. Since the marriage had not been consummated, Emma did not feel as if she were truly wed. And from Richard's havey-cavey actions, she was even beginning to question the legality of their vows.

"Miss Randolph, may I make a suggestion?" asked the earl.

"Of course, my lord."

"The day grows late. The village inn does not have adequate lodging for ladies, and it is far too late to reach the next village of any size. Why not spend the evening here, and begin your travels again tomorrow morning when you are better rested?"

Emma looked at Charlotte and Laura. Charlotte was tired, but her youth would carry her through. However, Laura was obviously not strong enough to continue much further without seriously endangering her fragile health.

"There will be no impropriety," Lord Melbourne assured her. "You are a married woman, and you also have a companion, so your reputations will be safe."

Emma hesitated a moment longer.

"You needn't worry about unsatisfactory chambers; the staff has just finished cleaning the rooms," he added with a smile.

"Please, Emma," pleaded Charlotte. "I cannot abide climbing back into the coach today."

For once, Emma was in agreement with her sister. She was too tired and discouraged to refuse such a convenient refuge. "We will be grateful to accept your hospitality, my lord. We are all weary, but I am most concerned for Laura."

"Don't worry, my dear," said Laura. "I shall be fine after a good night's rest."

"Good, then it's settled. Supper will be at seven unless you would rather have a tray in your room. If that is the case, you need only advise the maid."

Emma, Charlotte, and Laura all appeared downstairs for supper that evening. Emma would not lose any chance, however small, to solve the puzzle behind her husband's disappearance. Although Lord Melbourne had denied any knowledge of another Richard Tremayne, it was possible he had merely forgotten a relative far removed.

As they took their seats around the table, Emma observed that the cook must be as excellent as Lord Melbourne had claimed, for she had done a remarkable job of preparing supper with little warning there would be guests.

Cornish hens stuffed with rice, braised rabbit, fish, and beef were offered, all cooked to perfection. An array of vegetables filled the table, followed by pastries and custard.

It was the best meal Emma had eaten since she had left home. "You did not overpraise the cook, my lord. Your uncle was lucky to have her," she said, helping herself to several spears of tender asparagus.

"Yes, he was, but I wonder how content she will be without anyone in residence."

"You don't mean to turn her off, do you?" asked Emma.

"No, I promised my uncle that none of his people would suffer after his death. I haven't decided what to do with the estate yet. I have no interest in living here, but the house has been neglected and the fields idle for too long. If I can't find a relative who desires to take it in hand, I will need to hire someone to oversee it."

The mention of relatives brought Emma's mind back to her problem. "I suppose you haven't thought of another Richard Tremayne in the family since we spoke earlier, have you?"

"I'm afraid not, Miss Randolph."

"Is there anyone else I might ask?"

"There's my mother, of course, and several uncles, but I wouldn't place a great deal of confidence in the belief that they will be able to tell you any more than I can."

"I'm not questioning your memory, my lord, but if there is the slightest chance they might have knowledge of a distant relative, then I must investigate."

Lord Melbourne was beginning to become irritated with Miss Randolph's single-mindedness, and opened his mouth to deliver a mild set-down when Miss Seger intervened with a question about London shops. By the time he had answered, he was back in good humor.

The remainder of the meal passed uneventfully. David Whitney had joined them for supper and directed a great deal of his attention to Laura. Since their numbers were uneven, Charlotte was left without a dinner partner, but she did not seem to mind. She had been largely silent since their arrival, and even now stared morosely at her plate while eating little.

A burst of laughter from David Whitney and Miss Seger drew Lord Melbourne's attention again. He had become acquainted with David in London years ago. He was a few years older than the earl; a younger son from a good family who had no chance of inheriting. Yet he loved the land and yearned to spend his time planting and harvesting rather than fritter away his life in the military or be sequestered in an office.

David had been with him for quite a few years now, and Lord Melbourne had never considered his steward's single state. He had never complained, but his life must be a lonely one caught between master and tenants. He needed a wife and family, thought the earl, and briefly contemplated how to bring Whitney together with an acceptable woman who would welcome his suit. Lord Melbourne smiled to himself. He had never regarded himself as a matchmaker, but neither did he did want to lose such an excellent steward.

At some point in his life, a man needed a mate. Not only to furnish an heir—which seemed to be all he heard about from his mother these days—but for the intimate companionship that can only come from two people joined as one.

Lord Melbourne imagined that in the perfect union there would be a sharing that would transcend mere words. His own parents had seemed to have had such a relationship, and he wondered if he could find the same contentment. By George, he sounded like the veriest schoolgirl rattling on about true love, he thought wryly, turning his attention back to the supper conversation.

Chapter Two

The next morning Lord Melbourne rose early, taking pleasure that the day would be a fine one for traveling. He was anxious to return home to see whether any word of his brother had arrived during his absence. Adam had gone missing in the battle at Orthez back in February, and though he had not been listed as dead, his whereabouts were unknown.

While his mother put on a brave front, he knew she was suffering, wondering at the fate of her youngest son. Not knowing was far worse than actual knowledge, but Adam had been swallowed up in the confusion of the war, and there was no trace of him as yet. Lord Melbourne prayed that they would soon receive some news of him.

The earl hesitated only a moment, then shrugged and continued preparations for his journey. He had answered every inquiry Miss Randolph had put to him. Since he could be no further assistance to his guests, he decided to keep to his original plan of returning home.

He went downstairs to the library and sat behind the massive desk. Pulling a sheet of paper from the drawer, he reflected a moment before beginning to write.

After Miss Randolph had ceased questioning him about his

relatives, the past evening had been quite pleasant. He and Whitney had joined the ladies in the drawing room for a short time before the women, pleading fatigue, retired.

The ladies would, no doubt, be abed later than usual this morning after their long day of travel. Unwilling to wait until they arose, the earl quickly penned a note to Miss Randolph inviting them to stay until they were rested and able to take up their journey in good health again. Relieved to be out of the situation, he left David Whitney in charge of the restoration of the estate and began his journey home.

It was nearly noon by the time Emma descended to the breakfast room. She had finished a substantial repast and felt much the better for it by the time Charlotte and Laura joined her.

"We have made this trip for nothing, and Lord Melbourne has been unable to help us. Can we not return home now?" asked Charlotte as she settled into a chair at the table.

"I haven't decided what to do yet. I want to speak with the earl again. Perhaps he has remembered something that will help."

"Of course, it must always be what *you* want," complained Charlotte. "I am tired to death of living in rented rooms when we have a perfectly good home to go to."

"You only feel that way because our plans have gone awry," explained Emma. "You would have liked Paris had we reached there."

"I'm sorry," apologized Laura. "This is all my fault."

"It's nothing of the sort," objected Emma. "Any one of us could have taken ill."

"But it was me," Laura argued. "And that caused us to stay in Dover, and allowed you to meet Richard and be rushed into a marriage that should have never happened."

"You cannot blame yourself for something I did of my own free will," protested Emma. "In truth, it's too late for any of us to be dwelling on what has already been done. We should focus on the future."

Charlotte had filled her plate with ham, buttered eggs, and a muffin, but had not tasted any of them. "Then I think we should return home," she repeated, her lower lip protruding in a childish pout.

Emma reminded herself of her sister's youth before she answered. "Charlotte, I still must find out what happened to Richard. Surely, you understand that I cannot just go home and pretend nothing has changed, don't you?"

"I suppose," mumbled Charlotte grudgingly.

"Good. Then let us finish breakfast, and as soon as I speak with Lord Melbourne, we shall decide what to do next."

"Good morning, ladies," said David Whitney as he stepped into the room.

Engrossed in learning all she could from Lord Melbourne, Charlotte had not noticed the night before what a well set-up man David Whitney was. He was tall, with broad shoulders which were covered this morning by a dark brown jacket. Tan breeches encasing muscular legs met black topboots with brown turn-over tops just below his knees.

His skin had been darkened by the sun, which made his blond hair and light blue eyes even more arresting. Altogether, David Whitney was an attractive man, and she wondered how he had remained single so long.

"You are all looking well rested today," he said.

"Thank you," said Laura. "I cannot speak for anyone else, but a good night's sleep has done wonders for me."

"Then perhaps you should consider staying for a day or two until you're completely recovered," he suggested, smiling at her.

"I'm afraid that's out of the question," said Emma. "As soon as I speak to Lord Melbourne again, we must be on our way."

"That brings me to my reason for being here," said Whitney, pulling a square of paper from his pocket. "Lord Melbourne asked that I give this to you."

A foreboding of what the note contained made Emma hesitate in taking it from Mr. Whitney. When she finally accepted the paper, she held it tentatively as if expecting it to snap at her fingers any moment.

Meanwhile, Mr. Whitney had moved closer to Laura and they were conversing in low tones, while Charlotte—the sullen expression remaining on her face—continued to rearrange the food on her plate without taking so much as a bite.

"I must go," said Mr. Whitney, his voice startling Emma out of her reverie.

"Thank you so much for putting up with us," said Laura, as if he were the owner of the estate.

"It has been my pleasure. Miss Seger, will you walk with me to the door? I will point out the folly we discussed last night. You might want to visit it before you leave."

"I would be delighted," said Laura rising from her chair.

"Miss Randolph. Miss Charlotte," he said with a small bow. "I hope we may see one another again."

"Thank you, Mr. Whitney," answered Emma.

Whitney stood aside, allowing Laura to precede him through the door. The two left the room without a backward glance.

Emma's apprehension had proven correct. "He is gone," she said, after reading the note the earl had left for her.

"Who?" questioned Laura, having just returned to the breakfast table.

"Lord Melbourne." There was a sinking feeling in the pit of Emma's stomach, as if she had stepped off an impossibly high cliff and was plummeting rapidly toward the ground below. "He invites us to remain as long as we wish, but he pleads business at home for his departure this morning."

"It was pleasant of him to offer us such hospitality," commented Laura.

"It is not hospitality I need, but help in finding Richard," Emma complained. "I was depending upon Lord Melbourne to remember something which would guide me in the right direction."

"He told you when we arrived, and again at supper, that he

was not acquainted with another Richard Tremayne,'' Laura reminded her.

''I know, but I thought perhaps overnight he might have recalled a distant relative. I'm beginning to think that Richard and our wedding were just a dream since he disappeared so quickly and completely after we said our vows. I must confess, I'm at a loss for what to do.''

''Then let us go home,'' pleaded Charlotte.

Emma ignored her sister. Rising, she paced the floor deep in thought. ''We shall follow him,'' she exclaimed suddenly.

''But we are, and have found nothing,'' said Charlotte.

''No, we shall follow Lord Melbourne,'' clarified Emma. ''I shall get directions from Mr. Whitney, and we shall follow the earl to his estate.''

''Emma,'' said Laura, doubt plain in her voice. ''Do you think it wise to pursue his lordship? After all, he has been more than generous with his hospitality, and has said he knows nothing more to help you.''

''Perhaps he needs to be urged to think harder. It's difficult to believe that he knows nothing of a man who must be a part of his family,'' she insisted stubbornly. ''If not, he might be able to introduce me to one of his relatives who would remember more.''

Lord Melbourne had not looked like a man who would appreciate being urged to do anything but what he wanted to do of his own free will, thought Laura, but she doubted Emma would listen.

''Possibly we should consider Charlotte's suggestion and return home,'' suggested Laura. ''We could make inquiries from there, and if we find a lead to Richard, then we could have your man of business look into it.''

''That is a splendid idea,'' agreed Charlotte, looking at her sister hopefully.

''No one would pursue the search with as much dedication as I will,'' replied Emma. ''I would end up this time next year with no more knowledge than I have now. No, I must continue until there is no further hope that I can find Richard.''

Her face took on a stubborn look that told both Laura and

Charlotte further entreaty would be useless. They were on their way down the rutted drive less than an hour later, the coachman cursing all the way.

Due to the lateness of their departure, the ladies did not arrive at Lord Melbourne's estate until the following day. Emma was grateful the distance was no further, for they had spent an uncomfortable night at an inadequate inn, and Laura was not bearing up at all well with the traveling. Her head was resting against the back of the seat, and her eyes were closed as the dusty coach rolled between the stone columns on the main road that marked the entrance to Melbourne Park.

There could be no greater contrast between this drive and the one leading to the earl's latest acquisition. The ground beneath the coach's wheels was smooth and free of even the slightest imperfection, while the drive itself was broad enough for two coaches to pass without crowding. A well-kept park fell away from each side of the road, and the limbs of the huge trees that marked the way to the house were trimmed so as to remove all hint of threat to the coachman.

When they reached the end of the drive, Emma was nearly overwhelmed by the immensity of the house. Melbourne House was three stories, and built of brick which had mellowed to a rosy hue over the years. Wings stretched away to either side; tall arched windows broke the monotony of the facade and sparkled in the afternoon light. A columned portico forming a shallow bow marked the entrance where the door was already being opened to greet them.

The three ladies were welcomed into the marble-floored entrance hall by the butler. The hall was huge; a carved fireplace, flanked by two William and Mary chairs, dominated the wall. Additional chairs and small tables were placed at intervals around the walls, while a larger, round table holding an arrangement of flowers adorned the center of the spacious foyer.

Directly across from the entrance, a graceful staircase rose halfway, then separated before continuing to the next floor. A double mahogany door opened to the right, and it was toward that threshold the butler led them.

The ladies were shown into the drawing room, which was decorated in pastel shades and filled with the graceful lines of Queen Anne furniture. The earl's mother sat in a wingback chair looking every inch the countess she was.

Lady Melbourne was a slim, erect figure whose face was as aristocratic as her son's, only much more finely drawn. A few strands of silver showed in her dark hair, but her eyes—which were a shade lighter blue than Lord Melbourne's—were as curious as a young girl's. She wore a lilac gown, but had chosen to ignore the wearing of a widow's cap, which many women in her position affected.

There was something about her that Emma immediately liked, and she hoped that Lady Melbourne would be as accommodating as she looked. Emma took a chair across from the countess, while Charlotte and Laura chose a settee nearby.

"Lady Melbourne, I am Emma Randolph. This is my sister, Charlotte, and our companion, Miss Laura Seger. I want to thank you for receiving us."

"I'm very pleased to meet all of you," the countess responded graciously. "Richard's friends are always welcome here."

"In truth, I believe our acquaintance is too short to be called a friendship. You see, we met only a few days ago at his late uncle's estate."

A hint of amusement gleamed in Lady Melbourne's eyes. "Yes, he told me about your encounter. I understand you livened up his days while he was away from home."

"Well, one day at least," admitted Emma. "He left too early the next morning for us to speak further."

"And that, of course, is why you're here."

"I don't know whether he told you my story or not . . ."

"He said you were looking for your husband, whose name happens to be the same as his."

Emma nodded. "That's correct. My husband had also described his family home, and that is where we met Lord Melbourne. He explained that he had recently inherited the estate from his uncle. I admit, I'm at a loss. I thought that perhaps, after some consideration, Lord Melbourne might have remembered something more that would be useful to me in my search for my husband.''

''I doubt that he would know any more than I do about the family,'' replied Lady Melbourne kindly. ''I have searched my memory since Richard related the story, but I'm afraid the other Richard Tremaynes who were in our family have long since departed this earth.''

Emma visibly wilted. She had counted more than she should have on Lord or Lady Melbourne being able to help her. Now she had nowhere to turn. Perhaps Laura and Charlotte were right; perhaps they should go home and hire someone to continue the search.

The tea tray arrived, and they discussed the weather and the poor condition of the public roads while Lady Melbourne poured and passed plates.

''You do not travel well, Miss Seger?'' asked the countess.

''In the normal course of events it does not bother me,'' replied Laura. ''But I've been ill, and my constitution is not as strong as it should be,'' she confessed.

''You need to rest and regain your strength,'' advised Lady Melbourne as her son entered the room.

''I understood that we had visitors, but I never expected to see you again so soon,'' said the earl abruptly, directing his last words toward Emma. His sleep had been interrupted the night before by visions of Miss Randolph. Her slim figure had run through his dreams calling out his name, or more likely, her husband's name, until she had driven him from his bed at an earlier than usual hour. He had not welcomed the intrusion; that, and the lack of sleep, had made him irritable.

''Richard! Your manners have gone begging,'' reprimanded Lady Melbourne. ''Miss Randolph has come asking for our help.''

The earl dropped into a chair across from Emma, irritation creasing his brow. He had been amused at her mission to find her husband when they first met. But now she had encroached on his privacy after he had made it plain he could not help her.

"I have told you all that I know. I assume that my mother has done the same," he said, with little grace.

"I'm afraid I could add nothing new," admitted Lady Melbourne.

A satisfied smile curved the earl's lips. "So, Miss Randolph, that should settle the matter once and for all. Your Richard Tremayne is not one of our family. You should look elsewhere for him."

The earl's obvious gloating depressed Emma's spirit even further. She would find no help here. "You are right, my lord. I apologize for our intrusion." Setting down her cup, she turned to Lady Melbourne. "Thank you for your hospitality, my lady. I hope we haven't disturbed your day beyond all redemption." She attempted a smile that only succeeded in stirring Lady Melbourne's compassion.

"Of course not, my dear," replied the countess. "My days sometimes grow dull. You have merely enlivened this one for me."

The three ladies rose, and Lord Melbourne stood, eager to show them out the door and out of his life.

"Wait a moment," said Lady Melbourne, stopping them as they turned to leave. "Why not spend a few days here? Miss Seger looks worn to the bone. She would benefit greatly from a few days' rest, and I would welcome the company."

The earl could not believe his ears. Just when Miss Randolph was finally convinced that she should search elsewhere for her husband, his mother invited her to break her journey at Melbourne Park.

"I'm certain the ladies are anxious to be on their way," said Lord Melbourne.

"Oh, surely, you are not in such a hurry." Lady Melbourne was amused at her son's discomfort. Clearly, Miss Randolph had a disturbing effect on Richard. It was too bad she was already married. Richard was seldom disconcerted by a woman, and finding that he wasn't above such a common failing might encourage him to seek a bride and furnish the family an heir, a dereliction of duty she had brought to his attention numerous times with no success.

Lord Melbourne's reaction irritated Emma. She had done nothing to the man except to ask for information, and he could not get rid of her fast enough. Perhaps he should learn he could not order the world to his liking.

"Your invitation is most kind, my lady. I'm certain Laura would enjoy a few days' respite from the coach."

"Good," said Lady Melbourne before Richard could add anything further. "I'll have you shown to your rooms where you can rest and refresh yourself."

"What," demanded the earl, after the women had left, "inspired you to issue that invitation?"

"It seemed the courteous thing to do," said his mother. "They were all worn out by the travel, but Miss Seger was suffering the most. I don't know if you're aware that she almost died during her illness, and if she doesn't get some rest, I'm sure she will worsen again. Considering the situation, I would have been remiss not to have made the offer."

Lord Melbourne felt a bit guilty, as she had intended him to; but it was overshadowed by a sense of foreboding that promised this would develop into far more than a few days' rest for three weary travelers.

Their first day at Melbourne Park proved uneventful. Emma and Charlotte slept late, while Laura kept to her room the entire day. Lord Melbourne was away from home and did not return until late in the evening. Despite Lady Melbourne's excuses, Emma was convinced it was their presence which kept him away.

The next morning Emma sat with Laura while Charlotte went riding with the earl. At noon she left Laura with a tray full of appetizing food and went downstairs for luncheon.

The others had already reached the drawing room, and Emma hurried forward ready to apologize for being late. Lord and Lady Melbourne were listening to Charlotte rattle on about how much she had enjoyed the ride that morning.

The three looked up as Emma entered. "I'm sorry to be

late," she apologized. "I was with Laura and didn't realize the hour until her tray was brought."

"And how is she?" asked Lady Melbourne.

"Much better. She wanted to get up, but I urged her to stay abed another day."

"A wise decision, I'm sure," Lady Melbourne agreed.

"Would you like a sherry before luncheon?" asked the earl.

"I wouldn't want to cause a further delay."

"Another few minutes will not matter one way or the other," he said, pouring Emma a small glass of the amber liquid.

Emma took a seat across from Lady Melbourne. As she leaned forward, reaching for the glass Lord Melbourne offered her, a locket swung free from her gown, catching the bright light coming through the tall, multi-paned windows.

Lady Melbourne gave a gasp and turned as pale as Laura had been when they first arrived.

"What is it, my lady?" asked Emma, concerned at Lady Melbourne's expression.

"That locket," she replied weakly. "Where did you get it?"

"Why, my husband gave it to me when we were betrothed. It's the only thing he left me," she said wryly.

"May I see it?" the countess asked.

"Of course. Just let me undo it."

Lord Melbourne moved behind her to help with the clasp. His hands were warm against her neck, and she was surprised to find that despite their being at loggerheads with one another, she quite liked his touch. She reminded herself that she had sworn to forsake men for the rest of her days, and crushed the pleasurable feeling that insisted upon surfacing.

"Here it is," said the earl, handing the locket to his mother. His voice remained normal, even though he had felt an unexpected urge to caress the soft skin his fingers had touched a moment earlier.

Lady Melbourne took the locket into her trembling hands. "I wore such a locket for years," she said to Emma. "When my younger son, Adam, left for war, I gave it to him. I told him as long as he had it, he would be safe."

"Don't fret," soothed Lord Melbourne. "There must be more than one locket like this one."

Lady Melbourne opened the locket and stared at its contents before holding it out toward Emma. "This is Richard, and this is Adam," she said, pointing first to one side, then the other. A tear slowly tracked down her cheek and dropped unnoticed onto her gown.

"But that is my husband!" exclaimed Emma. Relief flooded her; the mystery had been solved at last. Adam Tremayne was the man she had married.

"It cannot be," Lord Melbourne declared harshly.

"But it is," she insisted. "He gave it to me himself. He told me about having the likeness done. How difficult it was to sit still long enough, and how his mother scolded him."

"It's true, Richard," interjected the countess. "I remember it well. You were so very patient. You sat for as long as needed without a single complaint, but Adam was an altogether different story."

The earl smiled. "He always was. He had an intolerance for remaining in one place more than a few minutes. But anyone could guess that, for it's a common enough reaction in a young boy."

"And it could have been Adam recounting the memory," maintained Emma.

"Adam has been missing since the battle at Orthez, some four months ago, Miss Randolph. We have no idea where he is." He did not speak the obvious: that Adam could well be dead. "But I do know that he was not in Dover marrying you or he would have contacted us. He would never let us worry about him if he could do otherwise."

Lord Melbourne was angry that Miss Randolph had upset his mother. It was a daily struggle for her to keep her spirits up, and now this stranger had barged into their lives destroying what little peace she had found.

Emma remained silent, her mind spinning with what she had learned. Was Adam Tremayne her husband? And, if not, how had her husband come to possess the locket?

"Perhaps it is Adam," said Lady Melbourne. Her cheeks

were flushed and her eyes were bright with hope. "He could be on a secret mission for the government, and under orders not to let even his family know his whereabouts. Adam is impetuous, Richard, you know he is. He could have met Miss Randolph and fallen in love. It would be just like him to decide to marry quickly."

Lord Melbourne moved to his mother's side. Taking her hand, he said, "That is just wishful thinking. Adam would have let us know he was safe even if it went against orders."

"You can't know that," argued the countess. "Adam has been away for some time now, and war makes a man out of a boy. I'm sure he has changed since we last saw him."

"Why is it so impossible to think your brother might have married me?" asked Emma, wanting to believe Lady Melbourne's arguments.

The earl swiftly appraised Miss Randolph, from her dark rich curls to the tips of her slippers peeping out from beneath the blue flowered muslin gown she wore. Although Adam usually flirted with flighty young women who would listen to the nonsense he spouted, he had—as their mother had pointed out—no doubt changed since he had left home. Perhaps it was not inconceivable that Adam would form a *tendre* for Emma Randolph, Lord Melbourne admitted reluctantly, but that was a long way from marrying the chit.

"What did your husband look like?" he asked.

"He had blond hair and blue eyes. He was not quite as tall as you, and he was slighter in build."

"That sounds just like Adam," said Lady Melbourne, her hands clasped tightly in her lap, and tears still brightening her eyes.

"It could also describe an unlimited number of other men," countered the earl. "Did he have any distinguishing features?"

"You mean such as scars?" asked Emma.

Lord Melbourne nodded in the affirmative, not taking his eyes from her.

"No, none that I could see," she mused, attempting to visualize Richard's appearance.

The earl stared at her a moment too long after her answer.

She blushed when she realized her reply indicated she had little intimate knowledge of her husband. She felt demeaned that he had not desired her enough to stay even one night to claim his bride.

"Was there nothing else?" the earl demanded. "Did his ears stick out? Was his nose crooked? Did he have all his teeth? Good God, woman, think! There must be something beyond what you've told us."

Emma was tired of his bullying. He had no right to treat her like a criminal. "His ears lay perfectly against his head. His nose had never been broken and did not have even a bump to disfigure it. And while I did not pry open his mouth and inspect his teeth, they looked as intact as yours, my lord. Indeed, his features are remarkably similar to yours," she shot back, anger causing her voice to be sharper than usual.

"It is possible that it's Adam," said the countess, breaking into their acrimonious exchange. "You both have the Tremayne look about you."

"And why would he use my name if he meant to marry?" Lord Melbourne asked his mother gently. "Or, if he did, why did he not also use my title, nor claim Melbourne Park as his home?"

"Oh, I had forgotten that," said the countess, her body sagging back into the chair and hope leaving her face.

Lord Melbourne turned from his mother, his face dark with anger. "And you, Miss Randolph, do you have an explanation?"

"I do not know where my husband is, my lord, or even why he left me as soon as we said our vows. How could I hope to know whether your brother and my husband are the same, and if they are, what motivated his disappearance?"

Lord Melbourne held back the scalding words that begged to escape. It would not serve to overset his mother further by being at daggers drawn with a guest. He did not yet know the true purpose behind Miss Randolph's appearance on his doorstep, nor her continued intrusion in his life, but his suspicions were rising, and he meant to find out the truth before much more time passed.

"Then, if Adam is not Miss Randolph's husband, perhaps they know one another, and that is why he had the locket," suggested Lady Melbourne. "I cannot understand why Adam would give the locket to someone else, but it is possible, isn't it?"

The earl could not kill the slight hope that showed in his mother's face. "Anything is possible with Adam," he agreed. "Would your husband present you with a gift that did not belong to him, and say it was a family heirloom?" he said to Emma.

Emma was totally exhausted with the emotions that had run through her in the short period of time since Lady Melbourne had recognized the locket. "I do not know what my husband is capable of, my lord," she confessed. "The more I learn about what he is not, the less remains of what I thought I knew. Soon there will be nothing left and I shall be convinced that he never was."

"I know that he actually existed," Charlotte reminded her. "He spent a great deal of time with us, and I did not imagine him."

It was the first time Charlotte had indicated any sign of interest in the search for finding Richard, and Emma's spirit was buoyed by her support.

Emma ignored the earl who was still glaring down at her. "I'm so sorry, my lady," she apologized. "I would not have worn the locket had I known it would bring you pain. But my husband claimed to be the boy in Adam's picture, and I had no reason to question it."

"There's no need for an apology," replied Lady Melbourne. "I'm confident you did not do it on purpose."

But the earl was not so certain. To him, it appeared to be contrived that Miss Randolph had worn the locket and had seated herself so that his mother was in just the right position to notice it. However, he could not confirm his suspicion, and it would do no good to make the accusation without proof.

"There is probably a simple explanation for all of this," said Lord Melbourne. "Adam was forever misplacing his belongings. It is most likely he merely lost the locket. Perhaps even before he left England.''

He did not attempt to explain how it could have gotten into Miss Randolph's mysterious husband's hands, or why he would have lied about its origin, but the idea that she accidentally found her way to his door while searching for her husband was becoming highly suspect.

As much as it went against his wishes, he determined he would get to know Miss Randolph better; perhaps he could find the real reason behind her insistence that she might be a part of his family.

Chapter Three

Luncheon had passed in an uneasy fashion, marked by fits and starts of conversation punctuated by stretches of silence. Lady Melbourne ate little, and retired to her room soon after they left the table. Emma was relieved when it was over and she could escape for a walk in the garden. She was staring into an ornamental circular pool, watching the flashes of darting fish, when the earl joined her.

"I think it's time we had a talk, Miss Randolph." His voice was courteous, but tightly controlled.

Emma had been expecting and dreading that very thing. "Indeed, my lord, and what would you have us discuss?"

"Your husband," he replied shortly.

"My husband is my affair," she said, immediately regretting her choice of words.

"You made him mine when you wore my mother's locket," countered the earl.

"I did not know it was hers," objected Emma. "I would not have caused her distress on purpose."

"I'm not suggesting you did, madam. I'm merely asking you to relate the circumstances surrounding how it came into your possession."

"I've already told you. My husband gave it to me when we became betrothed. He said it contained a likeness of himself and his brother. I know nothing else." She began walking away, but he followed, matching his stride to hers.

"Normally, I wouldn't delve into your personal life, Miss Randolph, but I need to know about your husband. The fact that he has my name, and the locket that Adam carried, is too much to be considered a coincidence."

Emma paced silently along the garden path, considering his request. She agreed with his conclusion; there must be some connection between her husband and Lord Melbourne's family. While she was wary of telling her story to anyone, she also understood Lord Melbourne's concern. If Charlotte were missing, she would pursue every line of inquiry to find her. And if there was a chance Adam was safe, rather than being lost at war, his family deserved to know.

"Why haven't you contacted the war office about your brother?" she asked, curious why he hadn't pursued the obvious line of inquiry.

"Do you think I haven't? I've haunted the halls of every department in government that might be able to help. They all tell me they have no information on him. As you might well guess, the situation in France is chaotic. It's my understanding that over 40,000 men were involved in the Battle of Orthez. Thousands were killed and more were left wounded. They tell me it isn't unusual for men to go missing in such a melee."

She did not want to ask the question, but she had a stake in his answer and needed to know. "Are they ever found?"

Lord Melbourne stared straight in front of him. His brows were a dark slash above his eyes, and his mouth compressed into a firm line before he answered.

"Some are found in the hospitals; some on the battlefield. Some . . ." he paused to swallow, "are never found at all."

"Adam will be located. I'm certain of it," she said gently, touching his arm in commiseration.

"Thank you, Miss Randolph." His words were stiff, but held none of the acrimony she had come to expect from him.

''You can see why I'm anxious to learn anything I can which might shed a light on where he might be,'' he continued.

Telling the earl about Richard would do her no harm, decided Emma, and his inquiries might help her to locate the blackguard. If she hoped to find her husband, Lord Melbourne would undoubtedly be only the first of many who would need to hear her story.

''I do see, my lord, and I will tell you what I can, but I doubt whether it will help you discover the whereabouts of your brother.''

''Allow me to be the judge of that,'' he said brusquely, their brief moment of empathy over.

Emma dropped her hand, and took an imperceptible step away from him; she would not make the mistake of attempting to console him again. They walked in silence for a moment while Emma considered how to begin. She could tell the earl was beginning to grow restless, and decided to match his bluntness in her speech.

''As you have most likely assumed, I did not know my husband long before we wed,'' she began. ''He did not talk much of his past life, but led me to believe it was because of his involvement with the government. He hinted at secret trips, and important documents he carried. He never told me anything of substance, and I did not insist he relate more than he was willing.

''When Richard first disappeared, I thought he might have been called away on another assignment, but quickly realized he could have taken a few minutes to have made some kind of an excuse for such an immediate departure. He had told me enough that he knew I would understand. It is for that reason that I now question his claim of serving the crown, and must seriously doubt the veracity of the small part of his life he did relate.''

''Whatever he said, be it truth or not, should tell us something,'' commented the earl.

''Then I shall relate all I remember.'' Except for the parts that did not pertain to his problem, she decided, before beginning her story.

''I should first tell you that Laura has been with us since I was nine and Charlotte was four but, at one time, she was gone from us for the better part of two years, caring for an invalid aunt. Her aunt passed away a short time before our father, and when Laura heard of our father's death she wrote asking if we would like her to return. Of course, we were thrilled she was free to come home, for she had been with us long enough to become one of our family.

"Since we had all experienced the illness and death of a loved one, we decided that once the mourning period for my father was over, we would travel to the Continent to lift our spirits. Besides, Laura is overly fond of shopping, and there is no better place than Paris," she said with a small smile which she did not expect him to return.

"During our trip to the coast, we ran into several days of chill, wet weather, and just as we reached Dover, Laura was taken ill. When I realized her convalescence would be a long one, I rented a cottage which was much more comfortable than the rooms at the inn. We had not been there long when . . . when I met Richard." Emma paused, and found it almost impossible to begin again.

"I know this cannot be easy for you, Miss Randolph, but after it is said you might feel the better for it," encouraged Lord Melbourne. The words might have been helpful if they had been uttered in anything but such a cold tone as he affected.

Emma wondered how she could feel better in recounting the mess she had made of her life. She stopped and stared up at the earl, searching his face for any sign of compassion. His expression was stern; his eyes a hard, cold blue. She could not detect so much as a hint of softness in his countenance.

Emma suppressed a sigh; she would not allow herself to feel belittled. No matter what his opinion, it was far too late to change the facts. If he thought the less of her for what she was about to say, then she would accept it with as much forbearance as possible.

"Forgive me," she said, "but I must call him Richard. It is the only name I have for him."

Lord Melbourne nodded. "For all we know it could very well be his name." Taking her hand, he placed it on his arm.

Emma was too astonished to pull away. His gesture was completely opposite of what she had come to expect from him, and her reaction kept her silent as they continued across the park toward a small lake. She should reclaim her hand, Emma thought, but the warmth of his arm beneath her fingers gave her a sense of security she had not experienced since her father's death. She admonished herself for being such a weakling.

They reached the lake, and Lord Melbourne indicated a bench under a tree near the water's edge. There was a profusion of cattails growing close by and, when the breeze blew, the air was filled with their downy fur. It was a glorious day; one to be savored and stored in the memory until the middle of winter when the dream of summer called, yet reality held it back. Then, it could be taken out and examined in detail until the cold gusts of the northern winds lost some of their chill.

"Miss Randolph?"

"I'm sorry. I became caught up in the beauty of the day."

"My brother and I swam here when we were children," he said, looking out over the glistening water. "We were very close."

"As were Charlotte and I until we became involved in this unsavory affair. Now, all she will do is repeat that she wants to go home. Not exactly a brilliant beginning for a conversation."

"She's young yet; she'll come around."

"I hope you're right. Now I suppose I had better finish my story," said Emma, reluctant to give up the few minutes' peace she had enjoyed.

"As I said, we had not been in Dover long before I met Richard," she began, taking up her story where she had left off. "I had gone into the village. There was a small bookshop, and I thought to find a novel to occupy Laura. She was confined to bed at that point, and becoming more restless every day, even though she was still too weak to get up and about.

"Richard came into the store while I was there and struck up a conversation. I know it was imprudent, but his manners were impeccable, and his address unexceptionable. It wasn't long before he was calling on us, lifting us from our doldrums by telling outrageous stories, and *on-dits* about London society."

"Where did he come about his information from Town?"

Emma frowned, attempting to think back. "He would sometimes say a friend told him, and other times that he read it. I never thought to question him any closer.''

"There was no reason to do so at the time," agreed the earl. "What kinds of stories did he tell you?"

"Stories of his home and boyhood experiences. He also spoke of places he had visited. When he found we were traveling to Paris, he told us what we should see while we were there. He seemed to know the city well, and I assumed he had spent more than a little time there. When I inquired further, he indicated his activity there was secret and, at the time, I concluded it was in service to the crown.''

"We'll go over the childhood stories he told later," said Lord Melbourne. "For the present, continue with how you came to marry him.''

Emma resented his curt commands, but was determined to control her temper. "There's not much more to tell. Richard became an integral part of our daily life. Charlotte liked him well enough; he kept her amused when she became homesick. However, Laura did not accept him as wholeheartedly. She said we knew too little about him to completely trust his good intentions. Her wariness certainly proved to be valid. If I had listened to her, I would not be in such a fix now.''

Although Lord Melbourne doubted her regret was genuine, he could not allow her to discover his distrust. "I have no firsthand experience, Miss Randolph, but I have seen many of my friends smelling of April and May. In my observation, love makes an ordinary person do all manner of things he would not normally do. You are far from being the first person to listen to your heart rather than your mind.''

Emma wondered what he would think of her if he knew love had not entered into her marriage at all. That instead it was a well thought-out plan far removed from the romance a woman expected from marriage. But she could not tell him that, for it would lead to his questioning her as to the reason behind such a rash decision, and some things she must keep to herself.

"Thank you for being so generous, my lord, I'm not sure I deserve it," she said, before commencing her story again. "Richard made quite a few trips before our marriage. He claimed it was business, making it sound very mysterious. He indicated that he would soon be finished, then he could devote his entire attention to me. Since we had met at Dover and he had an intimate knowledge of France, I believed him when he said that he worked for the government. What a fool I was!''

Lord Melbourne kept his disbelief hidden behind an impassive expression. He would play her game until she tripped herself up. ''Don't judge yourself too harshly. The situation in which you found yourself was an unusual one. You were away from home and your friend was seriously ill. I'm sure that Richard offered you comfort and security. Besides, we cannot rule out that he is involved with the government in some way. You were not foolish to accept what you considered to be a gentleman's offer under the circumstances; merely unfortunate that the gentleman you chose seems unworthy of your trust.''

And who would have been worthy? thought Emma. Would the earl have offered his assistance if he had met her in Dover? Perhaps, but it would not have included marriage. She quickly chided herself for thinking of him in that manner. It was clear Lord Melbourne was not searching for a wife, and if he had been, she was certain there were candidates aplenty in the *ton*.

''I had known Richard only two months when he asked me to marry him,'' Emma said, in order to halt her wayward thoughts.

''Why did you agree to such a hasty marriage?'' asked the earl. ''Surely he could have offered you his protection and accompanied you anywhere with Miss Seger as your companion. There would have been no gossip attached to such an arrangement.''

Emma could not tell him why she felt she had to marry so swiftly. That was one of the secrets she must keep for the time being.

''I suppose I was merely caught up in the moment,'' replied Emma fatuously. ''Richard insisted that we marry immediately, and I saw no reason to wait.''

''How long after the wedding did he leave?'' asked Lord Melbourne.

Emma hesitated. She was not proud of the fact that her

husband found her so undesirable he had not wanted to claim his bride.

"Miss Randolph?"

"During the wedding breakfast," she answered shortly.

Lord Melbourne thought he had misunderstood her. He had concluded from her earlier comment that she had not known her husband well, but her answer had caught him completely unawares.

"You mean the next morning?" he asked.

"No, I mean we were married and went to the local inn for a wedding breakfast." As hard as it was, Emma succeeded in holding her voice emotionless; she wanted to get this over with as quickly as possible. "We had barely begun when Richard excused himself. He said he would be back before I had time to miss him. You can see, he was wrong," she said wryly.

"He just disappeared without leaving word for you?"

Emma nodded. "Without even stopping to pack his clothes or personal belongings, or to pay his bill at the inn."

The earl was astonished; how could she expect him to believe her husband had left before consummating his marriage? Even though they were at odds with one another, Lord Melbourne could not deny the fact that Miss Randolph was an extremely attractive woman. One that he would pursue if circumstances—and her character—were different.

"Are you comfortable, Miss Randolph?" he asked.

"Yes, my lord. This is a very pleasant place indeed."

"Good. We will go over what you have told me again."

"I am keeping to my rooms today," declared Emma rebelliously.

Laura had come to see why Emma had not appeared at breakfast, and found her staring out the window. "And what am I to tell Lord and Lady Melbourne?" asked Laura.

"Tell them I have the megrims, that is always a convenient excuse."

"If you want to deceive our host and hostess, you must do

it yourself. I will not be a party to it unless there is good reason.''

"Good reason! Is it good reason that I have been hounded by Lord Melbourne these past days? He has attempted to poke and prod into every corner of my life. I have repeated again and again every word Richard spoke about his background. When I finish, his lordship only looks at me in that arrogant manner of his and asks the same question a different way. Well, I will not endure another day,'' she finished, clenching her fists in anger.

Laura had been aware of Lord Melbourne's nearly constant attendance on Emma since she had shown up wearing the locket. The company was too small not to notice. And, although she did not approve, Laura had watched over Emma too long to refuse to protect her privacy. "I shall say you have decided to keep to your room and rest today then."

Emma nodded and returned her gaze out the window. It was a beautiful morning and she yearned to be out of doors. Instead, Lord Melbourne was forcing her to stay inside, hiding away like a thief.

Suddenly Emma's backbone stiffened. She had spent the last few months hiding, and her nature rebelled against continuing. She would not allow the earl to keep her quaking in her room.

"No, Laura, I should not involve you in this. Give me enough time to change and call for a mount. Then, if anyone asks, you may tell them I have gone for a ride. But try to delay until you are certain I'm well away from the house and Lord Melbourne cannot catch up with me." She gave an impish smile and went to the armoire to collect her riding habit.

"I'll stay and help you dress," offered Laura. "Then I'll give you sufficient time to make your escape."

The morning was as fine as it had looked from inside the house, thought Emma as she closed the door behind her with a sigh of relief. She walked quickly to the stable where she made the acquaintance of George Barton, the head groom.

"Are you an experienced rider, Miss Randolph?" he asked, when she said she wanted a mount.

"My father had me on a horse before I could walk. From the time I got my first pony, there's been seldom a day I've missed riding. I understand Lord Melbourne has some fine bits of blood."

"That he has," agreed George. "And I suppose you'd be wanting to try one?"

"Perhaps not his best, but one that will at least not put me to sleep," she agreed, smiling.

George barked an order, and a few minutes later a mare that had been brushed until she shone like black satin was led out.

"This is Devil's Lady," said George.

Emma studied the animal, liking what she saw. "And, from the look in her eye, the name is probably appropriate."

"She's a spirited one," agreed George. "But if you're the rider you say you are, you'll be well satisfied with her."

George tossed Emma into the saddle, and she guided Devil's Lady out of the stableyard. She held the mare back until they reached the open stretches of the park, then loosened the reins and gave the animal her head. The mare surged forward, enjoying the opportunity to gallop across the thick green turf as much as Emma did. The groom who accompanied her trailed so far behind that she easily forgot he was there.

Emma shrugged aside the slight pang of guilt she felt at slipping away. Each of the last days had become successively more tiring with Lord Melbourne's constant questioning. At first, she answered readily for she, too, had wanted to get to the bottom of the mystery surrounding her husband and his connection to the locket. Until there was actual proof otherwise, she could not ignore the possibility that Adam could indeed be her missing husband.

His brother's actions might seem extremely peculiar to the earl, but Adam could have suffered an accident which caused his unusual behavior. Emma had heard that a blow to the head could result in complete or partial loss of memory. Perhaps Adam could remember his brother's name, and some of his past, but nothing more. He could have been similarly afflicted after the wedding, and might even now be wandering about with no knowledge of his true identity.

Emma attempted to clear her mind of such an alarming picture. She needed to keep her wits about her if she was going to find Richard, or Adam, or whatever his name turned out to be. However, enduring endless questioning from Lord Melbourne had not been productive. It was apparent that she had no additional information to help them solve the puzzle.

But the earl had not given up so easily. He had gone over again and again every word Richard had said to her concerning his home and family. He seemed nonplussed that the stories her husband had told proved true. In Emma's mind, it only served to add weight to the theory that Adam and Richard were one.

Last night, after supper, Lord Melbourne had again approached her, but she had quickly excused herself and fled to her room much earlier than usual.

Now she had slipped out of the back of the house like an errant schoolgirl. Well, this would be the last time. She had done nothing wrong, and had been more than patient with the earl. She did not owe the man one word of explanation concerning her life, but had humored him because of his mother's grief for Adam.

But now she had given him every bit of information she possessed about the Richard Tremayne who was her husband, and had done so for the final time. When next they met she would tell him of her decision and be done with slipping about.

As she pulled the mare to a walk, hoofbeats sounded behind her and she silently groaned. They would not be from the groom's mount, for he would never approach her unless she were threatened. Only one person, other than herself, would ride with such abandonment. It seemed Laura had not waited long enough after all. Perhaps it was just as well; Emma and Lord Melbourne could have their conversation away from Lady Melbourne, where they would not cause her any further distress.

The earl slowed his mount to match her mare's stride. "Miss Randolph. You should have told me you wanted to ride. I would have gladly accompanied you."

His words held the merest hint of reproof, but it was enough to reinforce Emma's resolve to make her discontent known.

"The beauty and solitude of the morning do wonders for my spirits," she replied shortly.

"Would you rather continue on your own?" he asked smoothly.

Emma was irritated he had chosen to be courteous just when she had determined to voice her dissatisfaction. "You have never once asked whether I would welcome company. Why begin now?" she snapped.

"Because my mother has been ringing a peal over my head this morning. She reminded me you were a guest in my home, not a prisoner to be constantly questioned no matter what the motivation." He reached over and took hold of the mare's reins, pulling the animal to a stop.

Emma was wearing a dark green riding habit trimmed with black braid. A small hat tilted forward over her dark hair, with a single black ostrich plume curling down to brush the ridge of her cheek.

Her gaze, as green as the riding habit, settled on him, and he could readily understand how a man might be rash enough to rush her into marriage. If that were her only claim, he could have believed her; but he could not accept that she was married to Adam. Lord Melbourne would do what he must to keep his mother happy, but that did not include taking Miss Randolph's story as truth, and welcoming her into the family.

"I'm afraid my concern over Adam has caused me to forget my role as host, and I apologize," he said, without so much as a flicker of an eye to betray his true feelings.

Emma could not break from his gaze. He seemed entirely sincere, and she could do nothing else than forgive him. "If I could tell you anything more that could help, I would. I want to unravel this mystery as much as you do, my lord."

The earl did not like falseness in his dealings with others, but his mother had forced him into a situation where he had no other choice.

"I seem to have lost sight of that in my eagerness to find out how your husband came to possess the locket," he said.

"We have not proven that Adam and Richard are not one and the same," she pointed out.

Lord Melbourne was unable to allow her to think he believed it to be true, no matter how much he wished to remain in charity with her until he discovered the motivation behind her story. "It is highly unlikely that Adam is Richard."

"You discount the possibility that he could have been ill or injured and forgotten who he was?"

"That rarely occurs except in novels," he scoffed.

"Then, if you have no belief in the possibility, it appears that neither of us can help the other," said Emma, strangely sad that she spoke the truth. It meant that there was no longer any reason to stay at Melbourne Park. "We have encroached on your generosity far too long as it is, my lord. We shall leave first thing in the morning."

She had spoken the words that would have made Lord Melbourne extremely happy if they had been uttered before his mother had discovered the locket. But the situation had changed, and if Emma left he would lose all contact with her and might never find the answer to his questions concerning Adam.

While he did not believe Adam had married Miss Randolph, the locket confirmed that their paths might have crossed at one time or another. Although it went against his best inclination to urge her to extend her visit, there was nothing else for him to do at present.

"Why rush off, Miss Randolph? As I mentioned, I have not been the best of hosts. Give me the opportunity to rectify that oversight. I would not like you to leave thinking me a curmudgeon."

Emma opened her mouth to decline his invitation, but then he smiled at her. She had not seen that particular smile since the day he had opened the coach door at his late uncle's estate. It affected her even more strongly than it had then. A warmth invaded her body, reducing her refusal into an answering smile.

"I suppose Laura could benefit by a few more days' rest."

"I'm certain it would be for the best," he agreed before she could change her mind. "Now," he said, releasing his hold on her mare, ''if you are up to it, I would be happy to show you more of the estate.''

''That would be pleasant indeed, my lord.'' Emma could not believe her foolishness. She was a married woman, yet her heart was tripping over itself simply because an attractive man was by her side. And, by his own admission, he was only there to make amends for treating her poorly. Emma vowed to strengthen her resolve never again to think of men in a romantic sense, and attended to Lord Melbourne's comments about the estate.

''You are in much better spirits,'' said Laura, when Emma returned from her ride. ''Lord Melbourne must not have found you.''

''No, he did, but we've come to an understanding. He apologized for his behavior, and urged us to continue our visit so that he might make up for his poor manners.''

''And you accepted?'' asked Laura, unable to keep the astonishment out of her voice.

''It would have been churlish of me not to.'' Emma removed her hat and began unbuttoning her jacket. ''Besides, I need a few days to consider what we should do next. As usual, we crossed swords as to whether Richard and Adam are the same, but he did not belabor the point, so his resistance to the possibility could be weakening. For all I know, he could know even more than he's telling.''

''Why would he withhold information from you?'' asked Laura. ''I should think the more you knew the more likely you would be able to prove Richard is not Adam.''

''Unless he believes it to be true,'' answered Emma. ''Then he might want to find Adam and pretend his marriage never happened, particularly if he's suffering from some illness. I cannot see Lord Melbourne accepting me as his sister-in-law when he thinks I'm scheming to trap his brother and insure my future with his fortune.''

Laura's face was a mask of disbelief. ''I cannot accept that the earl actually accused you of such treachery.''

"Oh, he didn't, not in so many words. He didn't need to. I have seen it in his face and heard it in his voice as he questioned me. There's no doubt he believes I'm capable of doing so. And if it turns out that Richard is not Adam, then I'm certain his lordship will consider that I have gotten all that I deserve."

"If the man you married is not Adam how could he have known so much about the Tremayne family?"

"Lord Melbourne speculates it could be anyone who has known the family over the years. Or he could even be an acquaintance of a friend to the family, who has heard the stories secondhand. The Tremayne family is well known, so you can see the possibilities are endless."

"It seems the more you find out, the more confusing and hopeless this all becomes," said Laura.

"I cannot think that way. I am determined to find Richard. I will not allow him to ruin my life in this manner."

Laura helped Emma out of her habit and into a yellow striped gown with a deep flounced hem. "I cannot imagine why Richard would deceive you."

"It's a complete puzzle to me," replied Emma. "He had little to gain. While he would be able to live well at my expense, he would not have control of either the estate or my funds. But he was aware of that, and acted as if it was of no concern to him. And if he is Adam, he would have no need of my money."

"Whoever he is, perhaps he truly loves you," suggested Laura.

"The longer he is gone missing, the more I believe he never held me in any particular affection. I'm ashamed to admit it, but the lack of love doesn't bother me a great deal," confessed Emma. "I can see now that I made a mistake in marrying in haste. I was doing it for all the wrong reasons. Love did not enter into it, only the need to resolve a difficult situation."

"You should not have allowed Albert to bedevil you enough to force you into an unwanted marriage."

"At the time, I thought having a man in the house would keep Albert from our door. However, all I've done is to complicate my situation." Emma did not want to relive her mistake again. "Where is Charlotte?" she asked, eager to change the subject.

"Walking," answered Laura. "Can you imagine? The girl has walked more since we have been away from home than she ever has before."

"She's bored, and I cannot blame her," said Emma with a sigh. "She misses her home, and she has had little enough entertainment for a girl her age. She should be enjoying a Season in London."

A radiant smile lit Emma's face. "That is exactly what we shall do," she said. "We have lived in seclusion too long, and I have worried enough about a man who doesn't care a whit about me. As soon as I'm convinced I've learned all I can here, we shall travel directly to London. We'll stay through the Little Season in the fall. It's time Charlotte met some eligible young men."

Laura was happy to see Emma filled with enthusiasm. "What a wonderful idea. I admit I look forward to being in Town again. All the sights to see and the shops on Bond Street."

"I should have known you would want to shop," laughed Emma.

"It is a failing of mine," admitted Laura, "but one I thoroughly enjoy. And Charlotte will be in alt over the entertainments available."

"Perhaps she will forget all about Albert," said Emma.

"And if we can hope for the best of all possible worlds," added Laura, "we will find Richard there, and straighten out this bumblebroth of a marriage which is ruining your life."

Emma thought Laura was being overly optimistic, but did not contradict her. "I will do as you suggested earlier and contact my man of business to make inquiries about Richard. Perhaps he will better know how to go about it than I do."

"That is a sensible idea, to be sure," agreed Laura.

"Then it's settled. I shall also write letters to a few of our acquaintances and let them know we will be arriving shortly. They will be happy to introduce us into society. Oh, Laura!" said Emma, giving her a quick hug, "I am in better spirits already."

Chapter Four

"What is all the excitement about?" asked Charlotte as she came through the door, bringing the scent of sunshine and outdoors with her.

"We are going to London," announced Emma.

"I thought we were staying here awhile," said Charlotte, stopping suddenly and staring at Emma.

"We won't be leaving right away," explained Emma. "Laura needs to rest a little longer, and I want to straighten out the mystery surrounding the locket. I don't know how long that will take, but when we resume our journey, we will travel to Town."

Charlotte threw herself into the nearest chair and glared at Emma.

"I thought you would be pleased," said Emma, puzzled at her sister's attitude. "Remember how you would beg Papa to take us to London? And I promise, you'll like it much better now that you're grown."

"You're doing this just to keep me away from home, aren't you?" accused Charlotte.

"Your sister had hoped spending time in London would make you happy, Charlotte. I know I'm looking forward to it with a great deal of anticipation," said Laura.

"You always take her side," complained Charlotte. "No one ever cares about me."

"That isn't true," denied Emma. "I care a great deal about you. I thought this trip would be exactly what you would like."

"What I would like is to go home. How many times must I say it before you listen to me?" demanded Charlotte.

The responsibility of the estate since her father's death, the advent of Albert soon thereafter, and all that had happened since had nearly exhausted Emma's patience.

"You have said it too many times already," snapped Emma. "It is not homesickness that makes you continue your demands to return. You want to go home only to be near Albert," accused Emma.

"And what if I do? Is there anything wrong with that? Albert has been all that is good to me. *He* doesn't think I'm too young to know my own mind."

"And you show you're nothing but a green girl by believing him. You don't know the difference between his flattery and sincerity. Believe me, Albert would tell you anything to bend you to his will."

"Emma . . . Charlotte . . ." said Laura, attempting to bring an end to the argument, but neither sister would listen.

"You only say that because he likes me better than you," charged Charlotte. "You can't bear to see me happy," she yelled, turning and running out of the room.

Laura and Emma listened until her footsteps died at the slamming of a door.

"She'll have a good cry and everything will be fine by supper," predicted Laura.

"I'm not certain anything will ever be the same again," Emma said glumly.

Emma was shocked at Charlotte's reaction to her news. She had expected her sister to be overjoyed with the prospect of a wealth of new clothes, and nights and days of all kinds of events to keep a young woman entertained. Not to mention the countless gentlemen who, no doubt, would form an admiring circle of gallants.

But it seemed that Emma had misjudged Albert's impact on

Charlotte. She could not believe that her own sister would hold
a blackguard in such high esteem. She reminded herself again
of Charlotte's youth and inexperience; however, she wondered
what had happened to her good sense.

Emma sighed and straightened her shoulders. It would do
no good to begin doubting her decisions at this late date, she
thought. She must continue the course she had set and pray
that the outcome would be agreeable.

Emma attempted to remain in good spirits as she went down
for supper that evening. While Charlotte kept to her room after
their argument, Emma and Laura had revealed their plans to
Lady Melbourne over tea earlier in the afternoon. The countess
had expressed regret at their departure, but had understood their
desire to spend some time in London.

Emma assured herself that once they were in Town, Charlotte
would change her mind. She was saddened to see her sister so
unhappy, but had no answer to her dilemma. She could not
hide from Albert indefinitely, but she hoped to divert Charlotte
from being obsessed with him before returning home.

Emma entered the drawing room, where they usually gathered before going in to supper. She was the last to arrive, and
was happy to see that Charlotte, who had decided to join them,
was deep in conversation with Lord Melbourne. She studied
the earl as he listened attentively to her sister's conversation.

Lord Melbourne was dressed in his usual impeccable manner.
A dark blue jacket stretched across his broad shoulders and,
when he turned to greet her, Emma saw that it intensified his
blue eyes, which needed no help at all in holding her attention.

"I'm sorry I'm late," said Emma.

"We have only just arrived ourselves," answered Lady Melbourne.

"And cook has not summoned us yet," added Lord Melbourne. "So you're safe from her wrath."

"I'm glad," replied Emma, "for I would hate to be served
burnt porridge at every meal."

"Pour Miss Randolph a sherry," directed Lady Melbourne before she went back to her conversation with Laura.

"Thank you, my lord, but I don't care for anything at the moment," said Emma, as the earl reached for the bottle on a nearby table.

"My mother tells me you're leaving. I thought we had settled that you were going to remain a little longer."

"We're not rushing off right away, my lord, but will be staying the few additional days we discussed. Laura should be completely rested by then, and perhaps we shall have found out more about your brother and the locket. If not, I must assume that I can learn no more here, and we will continue our journey. We will enjoy a taste of Town life, and perhaps I shall find out something about my husband while we're there."

"You will certainly find entertainment enough in London, but I hope you do not feel compelled to rush off."

"Not at all. You extended your hospitality to strangers, when I know that you were not overly eager to do so. No, do not deny it," she said, when he opened his mouth to object. "I do not blame you; I would have felt the same had our positions been reversed. And I don't bring it up to embarrass you, but to tell you how much I appreciate your patience."

"Yet you are leaving?"

"We must, my lord. I cannot linger here forever in hopes that your brother might return and prove to be my missing husband, or have knowledge of him. I have a home of my own that I long to see, and I intend to return there as soon as we quit London."

Lord Melbourne decided to say nothing more about her staying longer at Melbourne Park. She sounded set on her plan, and it would do no good arguing with her while she was in her present state. He would wait and try again later.

"Since you will be with us a few more days, we'll ignore your departure until it is upon us."

"Thank you, my lord. If you will excuse me, I must speak with Lady Melbourne."

The earl studied Miss Randolph closely as she moved across the room to join the rest of the group. Her gown was of azure blue, with a round neckline and small sleeves. It clung to her soft curves, giving proof positive that a man would find much to admire about Miss Randolph, or Mrs. Tremayne, or whatever she chose to call herself.

Which brought him to her married state. Her husband, whoever he might be, must have had good cause to leave a bride as desirable as Miss Randolph. What could it have been?

And what did she expect to gain by claiming that Adam might be her husband? Was she an opportunist who had learned that Adam was missing and presumed dead, and planned on taking advantage of the fact by claiming to be his wife? If so, she had taken a strange path to that end. It would have been much more convincing to have professed she had met and married Adam in France, rather than spin such a bumblebroth of nonsense as a disappearing husband.

There was still much to be learned about Miss Randolph, Lord Melbourne decided. It would be to his benefit to remember that whenever he felt the urge to pressure her into telling him her secrets. She was a woman after all, and flattery would get him much further than force. He would make an opportunity to persuade her to extend her departure date beyond the few days to which she had agreed. And with that decision taken, his musing was interrupted by the announcement that supper was ready.

The earl was already in the stableyard when Emma reached it the next morning.

"Why, Miss Randolph, what a delightful surprise. I didn't know you were riding this morning."

Emma doubted it was coincidence that brought her and Lord Melbourne to the stable at the same time, but did not voice her skepticism.

"Good morning, my lord. I usually ride every morning when I have the opportunity. I hope you don't mind if I take advantage of your stable?"

"Of course not. The animals get too little exercise as it is. Would you mind if I join you, or would you rather enjoy the solitude?'' he asked, referring to her comment the morning before.

Emma could not bring herself to refuse his request. "You're welcome to accompany me if you like," she said as their horses were led out.

"You like Devil's Lady then?" he asked, as the black mare pranced out of the stable.

"She's wonderful," replied Emma enthusiastically. "I assume her sire was named Devil."

Lord Melbourne laughed. "Far from it; it's Galahad, and here he is now," he said, nodding toward a large dark bay stallion. "You can blame Adam for the names; he has always been fanciful."

The earl tossed her into the saddle, then mounted Galahad. "Do you have anywhere particular you'd like to ride?"

"None at all," she said. "As long as there's an opportunity for a gallop."

"Then follow me." Lord Melbourne turned east across the open space of the park, setting a good pace.

The horses were fresh and invigorated by the morning air. Giving them their head, they left the park and raced across a meadow. A small stream appeared before them, but Emma did not slacken her pace, and the earl followed, admiring her riding ability.

Devil's Lady was an excellent jumper and cleared the stream without a pause in her stride, but as her hooves touched ground on the other side, Lord Melbourne heard Emma give a small cry of surprise. The mare galloped on, while Emma lay in a small heap on the ground, her saddle nearby.

Lord Melbourne cursed and pulled his mount to a halt; leaping down he ran to Emma's side. She was curled into a ball, and he could hear her painful efforts to fill her lungs with air. Struggling out of his coat, he put it under her head.

"Try to relax, Emma. You have had the wind knocked out of you. It will be better in a few moments." He brushed her hair back from her face, and willed her eyes to open. She was pale, but that was to be expected. He only hoped she had not broken any bones.

Her gasps eased as air made its way back into her lungs, and finally her eyelids flickered open.

"Don't try to talk just yet," he advised, relieved that she did not seem to be in any great pain. He stroked her forehead and cheeks, murmuring comforting nonsense until she was able to speak.

"I'm all right," she finally said. "I think I can get up now."

"No, rest a little longer while we make sure you are all one piece."

He smiled at her, and Emma decided she would lie there forever if it would keep him looking at her in such an approving manner.

"Can you move your arms and legs?" he asked.

"Yes," she said, and demonstrated for his benefit.

"Do you have any pain?"

"I feel a bit sore in spots, but nothing more."

"Good, it would appear your bones are intact. Try to sit up," he instructed, putting his arm around her and holding her within its circle.

Emma leaned against him, enjoying the warmth of his body.

Anger was asserting itself, now that Lord Melbourne knew she was unharmed. "Dammit!" he said. "I will find the groom responsible for this oversight and see he never works again."

"Please, my lord," said Emma rousing herself. "No harm has been done except to my consequence. It was an accident, nothing more."

"My people are paid well to see that an accident such as this doesn't happen. The girth had to be worn nearly through for it to give so easily." The earl could see that she was upset and did not press the matter. But once he got her home, he would pay a visit to the stables that no one would soon forget.

"Can you stand?" he asked.

"I'm certain I can," she answered. With his help, she rose unsteadily to her feet. She stood for a moment regaining her balance. "There, you see, I'm fine."

Lord Melbourne kept his arm about her. "We will need to ride double on Galahad."

"It isn't necessary. I'll wait here while you ride back and send a groom with an extra horse for me."

He looked astonished that she would suggest such a thing. "I will not leave you here alone."

"I assure you, my lord, I will come to no harm until a groom returns for me."

"The matter is not up for discussion. Now, let me help you up on Galahad. I'll try not to cause you further injury."

With his assistance, Emma was soon sitting in front of Lord Melbourne on his mount, his arms pressing her firmly to him. She blushed, and attempted to pull herself erect; but he felt her shift and merely held her tighter.

"I know this isn't the most comfortable way to travel," he apologized, "but it will only be for a short distance."

Without further resistance, she yielded to fate and relaxed in his arms, resting against the firmness of his body and enjoying the contact far more than she should.

Several grooms were saddling mounts as Emma and the earl reached the stables.

"My lord, we were coming to look for you," said George. "When the mare came back without Miss Randolph we didn't know what to think."

"There was an accident, George. The girth on Miss Randolph's saddle broke just as we were jumping the stream. I want you to send someone to bring it back, and I want to see it—and you—as soon as you have it."

George's face paled at the earl's severe tone and angry features. "Yes, your lordship. I'll send someone right away." He strode over and spoke to one of the grooms who immediately mounted and rode out of the stableyard.

"We must get you to the house and attended to," Lord Melbourne said, sliding to the ground and reaching up for Emma. "Can you walk?" he asked, once her feet were on the ground.

"I'm perfectly all right," she insisted.

"You'll be bruised and sore by this time tomorrow, so don't be so eager to claim nothing is wrong. Come, at least take my arm until we reach the house."

Emma did not hesitate to do as he suggested. She was becoming all too willing to take advantage of any opportunity to be close to the earl. She had never felt this way with her husband, and was more convinced than ever that she had made a huge mistake in marrying him.

At Laura's insistence, Emma soaked in a hot bath, was rubbed with a lotion until she felt she might slide out of bed, and lay down to rest. It was late afternoon when she awoke, feeling absolutely decadent at being abed in the middle of the day.

But her body protested when she attempted to get up. Lord Melbourne had been wrong. She had not needed to wait until the next day to feel her bruises; she was already sore from head to toe. Shifting into the most comfortable position she could find, Emma decided to rest just a little longer.

The next time she opened her eyes she awoke to candlelight. "I can't believe I slept so long," she said to Laura, who was sitting by the beside reading.

"You needed the rest. You've been overdoing it for weeks now, worrying about Richard, watching over me, and keeping an eye on Charlotte. The fall finally forced you to stop. Are you hungry?"

"Starved."

"That's a good sign," said Laura, smiling and closing her book. "I'll ring for your supper."

"Have you eaten yet?" asked Emma, grimacing as she pulled herself up to a sitting position.

Laura hurried to her side and placed several pillows behind her back. "Some time ago. Charlotte and Lady Melbourne were here earlier, but they wouldn't disturb you. Lord Melbourne has been asking after you all day. I assured him you were merely catching up on some well deserved rest."

Emma was pleased that the earl had been inquiring as to her health. Then she remembered she was no longer free, nor eager, to seek the attentions of a gentleman, particularly if her husband turned out to be the earl's brother. Not that Lord Melbourne's interest was any more than he would show to any other guest who had suffered an accident at his home. But even if it were, and he were not her brother-in-law, she was already searching for a man who had betrayed her, and had no interest in becoming involved with another no matter how spellbinding his eyes could be.

Emma had finished supper, when a light knock sounded at the door. Laura answered, and murmured a few words before closing and returning to her side.

"Lord Melbourne is asking about you again. I think if you saw him and assured him you were uninjured, it would ease his mind. It might not be strictly proper, but I will be here and no one else will know except the three of us."

"But, Laura, I must look a mess," exclaimed Emma, her hand going to her hair.

Laura's eyebrows rose at her concern. "You look perfectly fine."

"Then I suppose I must, if he is that concerned."

Laura returned to the door, and opened it for the earl to enter.

Lord Melbourne stepped inside, his eyes going immediately to the bed. His relief was obvious when he saw Emma sitting propped up against several pillows. She wore a modest white gown, edged in ribbons and lace. Her hair was loose and trailed over her shoulders. He had been entertained by seductive women since his youth, but he had never been more affected than he was now. Perhaps it was her innocent appearance that roused his jaded senses but, at this moment, she tempted him more than any practiced courtesan he had known.

Suspicion of Emma's involvement in a scheme to prove she was Adam's wife never entered his mind as he approached the bed and stood looking down at her. "I've been worried about you," he said, his voice thick and husky.

"There was no need, my lord. I have taken falls before. But I shall have an even stiffer neck if I must stare up at you so," she said.

He smiled and took the chair Laura had recently vacated. "I will not be responsible for another injury."

"I hope you do not feel accountable for what happened, my lord, for it was an accident, pure and simple."

"I would like to believe so, but I have good reason to think otherwise."

"What do you mean?" she asked, her voice a mere whisper.

"George had sworn to me the saddles were checked regularly for any weakness, so I examined the saddle myself when it was brought back to the stables. The girth had been sliced nearly clear through, ensuring it would give completely with the effort of any strenuous movement. The jump over the stream was enough to cause it to break."

Emma stared numbly at Lord Melbourne.

"I can't imagine who would do such a thing," he continued. "George stands behind the grooms in my employ, and I'm compelled to agree with him. They could not find a position equal to what they have to risk losing it. I must put it down to a prank by one of the lads in the neighborhood, or perhaps by someone who holds a grudge of which I have no knowledge. Although why anyone would choose this type of revenge is beyond my thinking. Everyone is aware I do not ride sidesaddle," he said, hoping to draw a smile from Emma.

But Emma did not respond as he had hoped. She blinked, then opened her mouth to speak, but no sound issued forth. She pressed her lips together tightly, swallowed several times, and tried again.

But it was not to Lord Melbourne that she spoke. Looking to Laura, who had taken a chair near the door, she said, "Laura, begin packing. We must be gone as early in the morning as possible."

"What are you saying?" asked the earl, taken aback at her reaction. "You're in no condition to travel."

She acted as if he had never spoken. "Go to Charlotte and tell her to be ready," she instructed Laura. "And advise the coachman we will leave at first light."

"Emma," said Laura, a concerned expression on her face, "surely a few more days of recuperation won't make a great deal of difference."

"I am perfectly well," she replied shortly. "But if you are

so set against it, I will tell Charlotte myself." Emma began to get out of bed, having entirely forgotten the earl in her determination to set her plan in action.

"Madam, you will not move," roared Lord Melbourne, gaining her attention again.

"My lord, I must ask you to leave, I have things to do."

"Then you will wait until you are better able to do them. Now, tell me why this sudden change of heart compels you to go rushing off so quickly," he demanded.

"We had never expected to stay as long as we have," she said reasonably.

"But you had not planned on leaving tomorrow; not until I mentioned the cut girth," he mused, staring at her.

"That has nothing to do with it," she responded swiftly. Too swiftly it seemed, for the earl's gaze narrowed and appeared to pierce her very soul.

"I believe it has everything to do with it. What are you afraid of, Emma?"

"I'm not afraid of anything," she replied, ignoring his familiar address.

"Then stay until you are better able to travel," he argued.

Emma sank back against the pillows, her mind spinning. He had found them, she thought. Somehow Albert had found them, and she must get them safely away.

She had planned the trip to Paris in order to leave him behind. She had done all she could to keep their identities unknown while Laura was recuperating. She had even married, hoping the presence of a man in their household would deter him. But all of it had been for nothing.

She was convinced that Albert was here and had cut the saddle girth. He knew how she loved riding, and chanced she would break her neck in a fall. That he would put the other ladies in the household at risk would mean nothing to him. There was also no doubt in her mind that he already knew his scheme had failed, and was devising yet another way to get rid of her.

What was she to do now? Perhaps she should take time to think out her next move. Fleeing in fear might be exactly what he was counting on, Emma decided; she would not fall into his trap so easily.

"Emma," said Laura, "listen to his lordship. Rest at least another day."

Emma sighed and sank back into the pillows. "All right," she conceded. "I will wait until tomorrow to determine our departure."

"You've made the right decision," said the earl.

Emma nodded, but kept her eyes lowered.

He settled back into his chair, studying her features in the candlelight. She was the most contradictory woman he had met. The panic she had exhibited a moment ago was gone, replaced by an expression of calm compliance.

"Now, will you explain what set you off?" he asked, hoping she would tell him the complete truth this time.

"It was nothing, my lord. The fall must have affected me more than I thought. I merely felt the urge to get on with our journey."

"There's more to it than that. Tell me what is wrong," he said, taking her hand between his two large ones. "I feel responsible for your distress."

Emma almost gave in to his plea. He sounded so sincere in his concern. The same way her husband had sounded when he had said his vows. The memory strengthened her resolve; she would trust no man's words.

"I am tired, my lord, perhaps we could continue our discussion tomorrow."

Lord Melbourne could not force her to tell him what had alarmed her, at least not now. She looked small in the large expanse of the bed, and he wished for a moment he could join her and hold her tight the rest of the night. Instead, he bid her good night and left her in Laura's care.

Chapter Five

The next morning Lord Melbourne inquired after Miss Randolph's health. Laura informed him that after giving Emma a small quantity of laudanum, she had spent a restful night.

Feeling relieved, the earl searched out David Whitney, who had returned the night before from his uncle's estate. The two men rode out to inspect a drainage ditch that was being dug in the fields on the south side of the estate.

Lord Melbourne returned near luncheon to find Emma ensconced in a chaise longue on the terrace.

Since he had seen her at her most vulnerable, he had been unable to rekindle the suspicions he had of her. It wasn't that he had forgotten them, he assured himself; it was merely that he did not think it honorable to take advantage of an injured woman, no matter how untruthful she was being with him. Until she recovered he would put aside his misgivings concerning her honesty.

"You look as if you are shamelessly taking advantage of your accident," he teased, leaning against the parapet surrounding the terrace.

"Laura insisted that I sit here and allow the warmth of sun to ease my aches and pains," said Emma.

"And is it working?"

"I haven't felt any noticeable difference yet, but it is pleasant to simply enjoy the day without allowing any other problems to intrude."

A footman came through the door with a tray. "You haven't had luncheon yet?"

"No, and I wouldn't be having it now, but Laura insisted. She threatened to call the doctor if I didn't eat."

A frown creased the earl's forehead. "Are you too ill to eat?"

"No, it's nothing like that. I think it's worrying about my husband, wondering where he could be, that is finally taking its toll. That, and perhaps a bit of homesickness, too. It's been months since we've been home, and although our steward has been with us since I was a child, I still feel a responsibility to oversee the estate."

"All that should make it more important that you keep up your strength. Since our acquaintance, you have never once struck me as being missish; now is not the time to begin."

Since Emma did not know whether to be grateful for his concern or irritated at his interference, she kept silent.

"Would you mind if I joined you for luncheon?" he asked as the footman deposited the tray on a nearby table.

"Of course not, my lord. I've been alone all morning, and would welcome your company."

"Bring another tray," directed Lord Melbourne to the footman. "Now, tell me the truth," he said, once the man had disappeared through the door. "Are you suffering much from your fall?"

"I have some lovely purple bruises, and I am a bit sore," acknowledged Emma. "But I must admit I don't remember a fall hurting this much when I was younger."

The earl laughed at her observation. "I've noticed the same thing the past few years. Hopefully neither one of us will put it to the test again anytime soon."

Once they were seated at the table, Emma searched for a topic that would lead them away from her personal predicament. "Did you spend the Season in Town this year?" she asked.

"Not the entire time. I enjoy seeing my friends and some of the entertainments, but I find it begins to pall after a while. When every soirée begins to seem the same, I know it's time to return home for a short visit. I also feel the same as you; I trust David Whitney as much as any man, but I like to see the planting and determine improvements on the estate myself. Fortunately, we're near enough to London that I can travel back and forth whenever I please."

Emma was surprised that Lord Melbourne chose to closely oversee his property. His rakish looks belied the responsibility he felt toward the land and his tenants.

"And you, Miss Randolph, did you enjoy the Season?"

Emma laughed. "I have only been once. I enjoyed the theatre, and bookstores, and exhibitions." Her eyes glittered at the memory. "But the constant round of balls was extremely wearing. I suppose if I could have been more selective in the entertainments I attended it would have been more enjoyable, but at my come-out I was expected to attend every event the Season had to offer."

"Is that the reason you didn't return?"

"My father's health began declining soon thereafter, and I was needed at home."

"I'm sorry."

"Thank you," she said simply. "But Charlotte is nearly ready to take her bow, and I know that she will enjoy London far more than I did."

"You mentioned being in Town for the Little Season this fall. Will you stay there for the Season next spring?" Lord Melbourne's question was not merely idle conversation. He could no longer deny that he was attracted to Miss Randolph.

He intended to prove to her that Adam was not her husband and remove that impediment. If she was what she claimed—an innocent taken in by a scoundrel—then there was no reason he could not pursue his interest in her. Surely by next Season she would have the dilemma of her marriage solved, and they could get to know one another better if they desired.

The thought of an alliance with Miss Randolph made him study her more closely, and he discovered that each time he did so, he found more to admire. Perhaps he had been in the country too long, but to him she was more enticing than any diamond of the first water that London had to offer.

"We shall probably spend the winter at home, but I hope to return for the Season next year. However, it depends on so many things." Emma put down her fork, abandoning the pretense of eating. "First of all, I will need to straighten out the state of my marriage."

Although Lord Melbourne was certain that Adam was not Miss Randolph's husband, there was a small part of him that wondered what he would do if it did prove to be true. Now that he had admitted he was interested in her, could he watch Emma and his brother disappear into their bedroom without a qualm? Could he stand by while she bore Adam's children? It might be possible, but not overly enjoyable. The only solution would be to give Adam an estate as far from Melbourne Park as possible, so that contact would be at a minimum.

The earl had never been one to run from problems, but he found he did not even want to consider the possibility that Miss Randolph was, in reality, Mrs. Adam Tremayne.

"Perhaps I can be of some help," he suggested.

"Have you remembered something?" she asked, looking up eagerly.

"No, nothing like that. I only meant that I could help you search. I have a man of affairs in London who has always served me well. I could give him the particulars of your story, and see what he can come up with. I could also have him check with the Bow Street Runners. I don't mean to dishearten you, but your husband could be known to them."

"I have imagined everything possible, so nothing you say could make me feel worse," Emma replied. "But we may not remain long enough to hear from your man. We have already overstayed our welcome."

"Nonsense. Your company is proving of great benefit to my mother. I have not seen her as lively since Adam left. You must at least postpone your departure until we determine whether . . . whether Adam is your husband." The words stuck in Lord Melbourne's throat, and he had to force them through his lips.

His feelings toward Emma were in such disarray that he needed time to collect them in some sort of order. While he doubted her story and her reasons behind showing up on his doorstep with such an improbable tale, he could not keep her from his mind. He desired her, and no matter what he thought of her character, it did not seem to signify. His only solace was to reassure himself that it was merely a physical need that would soon burn itself out.

"Then, if it will help me straighten out this bumblebroth sooner, I should be glad to have your help," said Emma.

"Good, I shall write Lawrence today, and have him begin his inquiries immediately. With luck, he should have some news for us within a sennight."

"Thank you, my lord."

"There's no need for thanks; I've done nothing yet." She made such a delightful picture, Lord Melbourne did not want to leave her, but he had no choice. "I hope you will excuse me, Miss Randolph. I promised Whitney I would return to the south field this afternoon."

"I understand completely," said Emma, and he knew that she did.

Lord Melbourne was returning from his ride the next morning. He had made no plans for the day, hoping to spend a great part of it with Emma. She had not come down to supper the night before and, since she was in no danger, he had no reason to insist upon seeing her as he had the night of her fall.

He had reached the edge of the park when he saw a woman walking along the edge of the woods stopping now and then to pick a wildflower. He smiled, thanking fortune for shining on him, for if he wasn't mistaken the woman was Emma. He had turned his horse in her direction when a man stepped out of a small copse of trees into her path.

Lord Melbourne was ready to spur his horse into action when he noticed that Emma did not seem disconcerted by the man's sudden appearance. He guided the animal into the shade of a nearby tree, and watched as they stood conversing.

* * *

Emma had kept to her room for the rest of the day after she had luncheon with Lord Melbourne. She was confused by her reaction to the man. No matter how often she reminded herself that she was a married woman, her heart beat a little faster whenever he was near.

He did nothing to hide his skepticism concerning her story about marrying Richard Tremayne, nor about how she came to possess his mother's locket, and she was certain he thought she had some nefarious plot in mind. Yet there were other times, such as at luncheon, that he seemed genuinely concerned with her well-being, and even appeared to be flirting with her. It was nonsense, of course; he was a titled gentleman of more than average good looks, and could have any woman he desired.

And if she happened to be Adam Tremayne's wife or widow, there was no future for them at all, since both law and society would be against them.

But all of her logical conclusions could not do away with the inescapable fact that she was attracted to him. No matter that she had sworn she wanted only to nullify her marriage and never have another man in her life; no matter that she had not been unduly impressed with Lord Melbourne when they first met; her emotions were turning traitor on her. She found herself dreaming about him at night, watching for him during the day, and nearly tongue-tied in his presence.

So she stayed in her room for the remainder of the day and took her supper there, claiming she was still too sore to be comfortable at the table. He did not knock at her door that night, and although there was no reason for him to do so, Emma felt neglected.

She had breakfast in her room the next morning, and waited until she was certain he was away from the house before venturing outside. She decided to take a walk to work out the remaining soreness from her fall, and to have some time to herself to consider her quickly changing opinion of the earl.

She wandered aimlessly for a time, enjoying the light breeze that kept the day from becoming overly hot. Wildflowers were in bloom, and she stooped to gather a few blooms to take back to her room. She was completely lost in her thoughts and the beauty of the day when a man stepped out of the trees to block her way.

Emma gasped, but her fright soon turned to disgust when she saw the man was her cousin. She now realized that she had panicked too quickly the night of her fall. She would not allow him to make a cowering weakling out of her.

"What are you doing here, Albert?" she demanded.

"Why, I've come to take you home," he replied evenly, as if they had parted the best of friends only the day before.

"Then you've made a trip for nothing. Even if we were ready to return, which we're not, I would not allow you to escort us."

"You've been away so long, I can't believe you're not pining for home. It is early enough yet, we can still get away today."

"Albert, listen to me carefully. We are not going home now. When we do go home, you are not invited to come with us." She spoke each word clearly and distinctly, hoping he would take them to heart.

He tipped his head to one side and studied her between narrowed eyes. "Is it Lord Melbourne then? Do you expect to legshackle him? I saw the two of you on the terrace yesterday, and it certainly looked like a cozy tête-à-tête."

"You were spying on me?" said Emma, outraged at the idea.

"Let's just say I happened by at an opportune moment," replied Albert.

Emma was seething with anger. Was there nothing she could say that would discourage Albert?

"And what is this?" he asked, reaching out to touch a small bruise on her face.

She jerked away. "You should know what it is. It was your doing that caused it."

"Why, cousin, I can't imagine what you mean."

"Don't act the innocent with me, Albert. It won't wash. I'm certain you're disappointed that I came away from your latest attempt on my life with only a few bruises."

"Someone has tried to harm you?" he said, failing in his attempt to sound surprised.

"And I suppose you know nothing about it."

"Of course not," he objected. "If you had been with me this would never have happened."

"If I had been with you, I would probably be dead," she hissed. "I don't mean to argue with you any longer, Albert; just go away and leave us alone." She turned and started walking away.

"Oh, cousin?"

Emma did not stop, nor turn, nor give any indication she had heard him.

"I shall see you again soon," he said, the comment sounding more like a threat than a casual remark.

Although the chuckle that accompanied his promise sent a prickle of fear through Emma, she did not slow her stride.

Lord Melbourne watched the rendezvous between Emma and the unknown man. A knot of disgust formed in his chest, whether for himself for letting his guard down, or for Miss Randolph's ability to weaken his conviction, he did not know.

She nearly had him believing every word she had said. He had offered to help her find her husband so that he might have a chance with her. And to what end? She was probably meeting with her husband right now, laughing at what an easy mark he was. Planning whatever it was they hoped to gain by their scheme.

At that moment, the man reached out and touched Emma's cheek. The earl could watch no more. He turned his horse, urging him back the way he had come, not seeing Emma jerk away from the man, then walk angrily toward the house.

Emma was disappointed when Lord Melbourne did not show up for luncheon that day. She could have used his steadiness to support her after her encounter with Albert. She wondered how he had found them. She had been as careful as possible to draw no undue attention while they traveled, but it apparently had not worked. He would be hard to lose again, and she was certain he would not leave as she requested.

Now she had the worry of keeping Charlotte from meeting Albert while he was in the neighborhood. Her brief respite of peace was at an end, and she was thrust into the maelstrom of conflict once again.

That evening, Lord Melbourne arrived just as they were going into supper.

"We had almost given you up, Richard," said Lady Melbourne.

"I'm sorry to be so late," he apologized to the company at large. "It was unavoidable."

After their luncheon on the terrace the day before, Emma expected a congenial supper companion, but she was disappointed. After greeting her, Lord Melbourne turned toward Laura and conversed as long as courtesy allowed.

When he could no longer ignore Emma, he turned and allowed an icy gaze to fall on her. "Are you feeling more the thing, Miss Randolph?"

Emma did not know what had happened since they had last met, but he was no longer the charming host he had been at luncheon yesterday. "Except for some lingering bruises, I am completely recovered, my lord."

Silence fell between them until Emma felt uncomfortable. "And did you get the drainage in the south field completed?"

"Yes," he answered shortly. No matter how the earl tried, he had not been able to wipe the memory of Miss Randolph's meeting with the unknown gentleman from his mind. He resented her ability to disrupt his state of mind, and was determined not to fall victim to her again.

Emma did not know what had caused the earl's change of demeanor toward her in the short time they had been apart, but she was vastly relieved when the meal was over and the ladies could withdraw, leaving Lord Melbourne and David Whitney to their port.

As she sat in the drawing room, pretending to be interested in the conversation going on around her, she pondered the earl's strange behavior. He had been so warm toward her the day before, urging her to stay, offering to have his man of business find out what he could about her husband. What could have altered his attitude toward her so drastically?

Emma watched the men as they entered the drawing room. She wondered whether it was obvious to anyone else that Lord Melbourne studiously avoided all contact with her.

"You aren't going to smoke that horrid thing in here?" said Lady Melbourne to Richard as he rolled a cigar between his fingers.

"I wouldn't dare," he said, offering her a winsome grin. "If you'll excuse me, I'll step out on the terrace."

"You should have smoked it when you had your port, instead of leaving your company," she grumbled good-naturedly.

"I'll wager my absence will not detract from the conversation whatsoever," he replied, strolling toward the French doors.

Emma waited until everyone's attention was focused on Charlotte, who was playing the pianoforte, then followed Lord Melbourne onto the terrace. It was not the thing to do, but she must know what had caused such a change in his conduct toward her.

She cautiously approached the dark figure at the edge of the terrace. "My lord, I hope I'm not unduly disturbing you."

"And if I said you were, Miss Randolph?"

She was taken aback by the bluntness of his reply. This was not the same man who had spoken to her so warmly only yesterday. "Well, then I suppose I would apologize and ask for a few minutes of your time."

He gave a harsh laugh. "Since you're determined to stay no matter what my answer, let's get on with it. What is it you wish to say, madam?"

Emma rebelled against his intentional rudeness. "I see I've chosen the wrong time to approach you, my lord. I'll leave you to enjoy your solitude."

"Oh, no," he said, reaching out to capture her wrist in his

strong grip. "I find myself immensely interested in what brought you here."

His voice had an edge of hardness that had never been there before, and Emma wished she could see his expression. "It is only . . . you've avoided me all evening, and I wondered if I had offended you in any way."

Lord Melbourne gave another harsh laugh. "Madam, your very presence here offends me."

Emma jerked back as if she had been slapped. The rudeness of his comment had caught her unawares, and she was speechless for a moment. How could he say such a thing to her, when she knew of nothing she had done to warrant it?

"Then I shall not force myself on you any further. We shall be gone within the hour."

"In the middle of the night?" he scoffed. "You need not be so melodramatic."

"I will not spend another night under your roof." She tugged at her arm to free herself from his grip, but he only tightened his hold.

"You will spend as long as I say," he commanded sharply.

"You cannot force me."

"Perhaps not, but I can bring charges against you for theft," he warned.

"I've taken nothing from you," she protested.

"Then how did you come to possess my mother's locket?"

"I've told you."

"Ah, yes, some mysterious man whose name just happens to be the same as mine gave it to you as a betrothal gift. The two of you married and he disappeared, leaving you with the locket and nothing else. Now, you've insinuated yourself into my home by suggesting your missing husband is my brother. I'm sure the local magistrate would find nothing suspect in that explanation."

When he said it in that manner, Emma realized how preposterous it all sounded. "Why have you waited until now to question me this harshly?"

"You've known all along that I've always doubted your

story,'' he said. ''Let's just say my eyes have finally been opened as to how truly treacherous you can be.''

Emma was totally confused by his demeanor and his threats. She could think of nothing she had said to him that would cause him to react with such ruthlessness. ''I don't understand,'' she said.

''The only thing you need to comprehend is that I have no intention of allowing you to leave until I am good and ready for you to do so. If you do, I will have you brought back and charged with stealing the locket.''

''But you have it back,'' she objected.

''That doesn't negate the fact that it was stolen.''

''You can't prove that,'' Emma argued. ''You said yourself that your brother could have lost it before he left England.''

''I may not have solid evidence, but you also have no proof that the locket was given to you. It will come down to your word against mine. Would you care to wager whose carries the most weight here?''

He was right, thought Emma. He could make a good case for the theft of the locket. But if he disliked her so intensely, why keep her here? He had the locket back, and there was nothing more she could tell him about Adam. It would be more likely that he would never want to see her again.

''Well, what's it to be?'' he asked, giving her a small shake.

''I . . . I will wait until tomorrow. Perhaps we can discuss this more rationally then.''

''I doubt I will feel any differently tomorrow than I do tonight,'' he said, releasing her arm.

''I don't understand you,'' she said.

''It isn't necessary that you do. And, Emma,'' he said as she began to turn away. ''Don't try to slip out during the night. Believe me, you won't be successful.''

Emma shivered as his words reached her. He was not a man to make idle threats. She stared out into the darkness and wondered how many eyes were watching her at this moment.

* * *

Lord Melbourne was having a solitary breakfast the next morning when he was advised there was a gentleman asking for Miss Randolph. Emma had not yet made an appearance, and the earl could only assume that after their confrontation last night, she was avoiding him for as long as possible.

So much the better, he thought. No doubt the arrival of this man was another part of whatever scheme she was up to. Lord Melbourne could not wait to see what was coming next. He did not stop to determine why he nursed such an enormous sense of anger over the scene he had happened upon the day before; he knew only that he would gain a great deal of satisfaction in meting out his own brand of punishment to the miscreants.

Lord Melbourne stepped into the hall, scrutinizing the visitor as he crossed the floor toward him. He was a man of medium height and build, with reddish brown hair and dark brown eyes. His clothes were respectable if not the first stare of fashion. And, if the earl was not mistaken, he was the same man who had met Emma in the park the day before.

"I am Melbourne," he said, thinking he was finally going to meet Miss Randolph's husband.

"My lord," the man acknowledged with a slight bow.

"I understand you're inquiring about Miss Randolph."

"I am," the man agreed. "I'm Albert Nestor, cousin to Miss Randolph and Miss Charlotte."

Lord Melbourne took a moment to mull over this unforeseen circumstance. Nothing should surprise him, but he wondered how a cousin fit into Miss Randolph's plan.

"Shall we go into the library where we may be more private," said Lord Melbourne, leading the way.

"Would you care for some refreshment, Mr. Nestor?" asked the earl, once the door was closed behind him.

"No, thank you, my lord. I just finished a substantial breakfast at the inn. Although their accommodations are barely adequate, I cannot complain about their food." He gave a strained smile, but the effort did not reach his eyes. "I have come to see my cousins. If you will advise them I'm here, I'll not bother you further," he promised, toying with his watch fobs.

There was a furtive manner about Nestor that Lord Melbourne did not like. He wondered whether he could find out more about the man before he sent word to Emma.

"I don't know whether Miss Randolph will feel up to seeing you. She suffered a fall from a horse the day before yesterday, and has been recovering since."

"I hope she wasn't seriously injured," said Nestor, without any hint of urgency in his voice.

Even if the earl had not seen him talking with Emma the previous day, he would have questioned the lack of concern in the man's voice. If keeping their meeting secret was part of their plan, Emma should have chosen a better actor than Nestor.

"Fortunately, she suffered only bruises and soreness, but she needs to rest," Lord Melbourne said, not revealing he was aware that Nestor had already seen Emma since her fall.

"I knew something would happen. I attempted to convince my cousins to allow me to watch over them, but Emma is a stubborn chit. She insisted they could get by on their own."

Lord Melbourne was puzzled. He wondered if belittling Emma was part of the plan. "A fall from a horse is not a sign of incompetence. I've had my share of spills, as I'm sure you have."

A dark flush stained Nestor's face. He was a man who did not like to be crossed. "It is not just a tumble from a horse, my lord. Since their father died, I have continuously offered my services to the family, but Emma has rejected my every overture. I feel responsible for their safety, but am kept at arm's length."

"I will agree that Miss Randolph has an independent spirit, but she seems well able to determine her future on her own," responded the earl, hoping to draw him out.

"Well, she has not shown good sense in my estimation," contended Nestor. "She and Charlotte disappeared from their home one night with no more protection than an ex-governess. The servants were no use in telling me where she was going, and I have been searching for them since. I am going to insist, if they continue their travels, that I accompany them."

Nestor's acting was improving. If Lord Melbourne did not

know better he would be nearly convinced that Albert Nestor was exactly what he seemed to be: an overbearing man who thought himself better able to direct his cousins' lives than they were.

But not only had he seen the two together; he had watched as Nestor reached out to caress Emma's face. The earl suppressed his distaste at the thought. Emma evidently didn't share his aversion for Nestor, so it was no business of his what happened between them.

"Make yourself comfortable, Mr. Nestor. I'll send a maid to determine whether Miss Randolph feels up to seeing you this morning."

Lord Melbourne left the room determined to put off his other business and remain nearby until Albert Nestor had left the house.

Chapter Six

Emma was furious when she heard Albert was waiting below. Her last argument with Charlotte was still fresh in her mind, and she resented that a man such as Albert had come between her and her sister. In addition, she had warned him to keep his distance, yet he had the gall to invade Melbourne Park to see her.

Emma's temporary weakness from the fall was gone. She was much stronger today, and filled with resolve not to let the odious man get the better of her.

Calling Laura, she asked her to keep Charlotte occupied until she sent Albert packing, and he was far enough away that her sister would not encounter him. Emma then descended the stairs ready to do battle.

"I said all there was to say yesterday," she spat out as soon as she stepped into the room.

Albert flipped open the lid of a small snuff box and helped himself to a pinch. He sneezed, then addressed her in a bored voice. "And I advised you that I'm here to escort you home, cousin."

"Even if I were ready to leave—which I'm not—I would not go anywhere with you. I thought I had made that clear enough."

"You're going to cause a scandal, Emma," he warned, his voice rising. "Sneaking out of the house in the dark of night, keeping your destination secret, and traveling all over England without a proper chaperone."

Albert was becoming caught up in his rhetoric with all the fiery enthusiasm of a zealot. Emma would not have been surprised if he had begun pounding on the table with the fist he held clenched by his side.

"People will begin to wonder what you have to hide. You may not care about your reputation, but think of Charlotte; she could be ruined," he concluded, nearly bellowing with rage.

Emma was furious with Albert, but she vowed to hold her temper. "Albert, listen to me carefully. You are in no way responsible for me or for the decisions I make," she said, maintaining an even, bland tone. "I owe you no explanation as to when or where I might travel, or my departure or arrival times."

Albert made a move to speak, but Emma held up her hand. "Allow me to finish," she said sharply. "Charlotte is my sister, and her future was left in my hands by our father. He knew that I was completely capable of providing for her. As for our reputations, Laura has been with us since we were children; I'm certain her presence is enough to lend propriety no matter where we are."

Emma considered telling Albert that she was now a married woman, but if she did so, he would demand to meet her husband. When it came out that he had deserted her, it would be additional proof she was incapable of handling her own affairs. So for the time being, she would keep her tongue between her teeth.

"I had hoped you had come to your senses, Emma. Why not ask Charlotte what she desires? I'll wager she would want to return home. How can you mistreat her so?"

"Albert, I will tell you again. You are not involved in our lives and, particularly, Charlotte is no concern of yours."

But Albert did not give up easily. "If you care so much for your sister, perhaps you should ask her how she feels about me, my dear cousin."

Emma was tired of arguing, and decided to put an end to

the conversation. "In this instance, her feelings do not matter. While you may be able to fool a green girl such as Charlotte, I am fully aware of your true nature. You did not succeed in deceiving me, and I will not allow you access to Charlotte, no matter how much she believes in you."

"We shall see," he said, drawing on his gloves. "I am staying at the village inn. Humble lodgings at best, but I don't suppose I can expect an invitation to stay here, can I?" When Emma didn't respond, he went on. "I didn't think so. Well, I shall just make do with what I have. See what I'm willing to endure to watch over my dear cousins' safety? And, Emma, do not try to slip away again; I will be on guard this time." He gave her a small bow and an insolent smile before sauntering through the door into the hall.

Emma waited until she heard the heavy front door close behind him, then buried her face in her hands. For the second time in the last twelve hours, a man had warned her not to try and run away. She was undecided whether to laugh or cry.

"What is it, Emma?"

Lord Melbourne had approached so softly that Emma had not even known he was there until his large hands gripped her shoulders, turning her toward him.

The earl's behavior of the night before was too fresh in her mind to allow him even the smallest liberty. "I cannot say, my lord," she replied stiffly, moving away from his touch.

"You mean you will not," he accused in a hard voice. "A falling out among thieves, is it?"

"You think I would tolerate Albert in order to steal a locket?" she said in disbelief.

"No, I think the stakes are much higher. The locket is just a beginning. What if you knew Adam was dead? You could present yourself here claiming to be his wife, and demanding a settlement."

"Do you truly believe that I am despicable enough to prey on your mother's tragedy?"

"I do not know what you are capable of, Miss Randolph, for I cannot believe anything that flows between those lovely lips," he snarled.

"Then believe this: I came to possess the locket in exactly the way I related. I do not know whether your brother is dead or alive, nor whether he is or is not my missing husband."

Emma's temper boiled, and she did nothing to restrain it. "If you think Albert is part of a plan to steal from your family, you are mistaken. It is Albert who has driven us from our home, and caused us to travel the countryside like a band of gypsies. I would no more conspire with someone of his ilk than I would the devil."

"Bravo, Miss Randolph," said the earl, clapping his hands together. "A splendid performance. I congratulate you."

Emma hesitated a moment. There was no guarantee that if she told him her story that he would believe a word she said. Yet, she could not allow him to think so poorly of her without putting up some sort of defense.

She would sound far too melodramatic if she accused Albert of attempting to take her life, but she could tell part of the story; perhaps that would be enough to allay the earl's suspicions.

"It's true that Albert doesn't have a feather to fly with, but that doesn't mean we are in league to steal from you. To the contrary, Albert is attempting to prey upon me."

"Please, sit down, Miss Randolph," invited Lord Melbourne. "I would like to be seated myself so I may enjoy your performance."

"I am not telling you this for your entertainment, my lord. I am attempting to explain how I come to be in this situation."

"Then, pray, continue."

"When my father died, Albert saw it as an opportunity to insure his future. He showed up on our doorstep, saying he had come to take care of us." Even now the idea seemed ludicrous, and Emma gave a short laugh at the thought.

"I assume you're going to tell me you didn't take kindly to his generous offer," said the earl wryly.

"I certainly didn't. My father had trained me well, and part of that was to insure that I could recognize a fortune hunter when I saw one. Besides, even though we didn't see Albert often, his rakehell ways were well known to us.

"The whole situation would have been laughable, if Albert

hadn't been so desperate. I learned he was being hounded by creditors, who finally left him alone only because he told them he was marrying and would soon come into money. Then he set about convincing me that my salvation was to be found in becoming his bride.''

''And, of course, you declined.''

''In no uncertain words,'' she assured him.

''And you had no relatives you could turn to?'' he probed.

''No one close, and I probably would not have called on them in any event. My father had left me in charge and I felt I could not fail him.''

''He must have had a great deal of faith in you,'' remarked the earl, curbing his sarcasm. It would be to his advantage to find out all he could about Miss Randolph. Even though he might not be able to rely on everything she said, a small part of it might be true.

''He did,'' agreed Emma, blinking to keep back the tears that came to her eyes at his memory. ''And, for a short time, I thought I had lived up to his expectations. I believed I had finally convinced Albert that I would never marry him, and that I had seen the last of him.''

''Evidently that wasn't the case.''

''No, it wasn't. Albert's creditors had become even more demanding, and he was desperate to remedy his situation.''

''And I imagine your trip to Paris was an attempt to get away from Albert.''

Emma hesitated. She wanted to keep Charlotte's part in the story as private as possible. Her sister would suffer enough hurt when she realized Albert's true nature. She did not need the further embarrassment of others knowing of her folly. Holding back the fact that Albert had turned his attention to Charlotte, Emma continued her story.

''Yes. I knew he couldn't afford passage or the expense of living in Paris, so I thought we could stay until he grew tired of waiting and had turned to other sources to remedy his problems. Instead, we were trapped when Laura became ill.

''I expected to have him knock on our door every day, but he didn't find us. I'm ashamed to admit it, but when I met

Richard, I considered him the answer to my dilemma. I was convinced if I married, Albert would no longer bother us. I am not proud of it, but that was the reason behind my hasty wedding," she admitted.

"When Richard disappeared, I found myself in more of a muddle than before. I was bound to a ghost of a husband, and we were no safer from Albert than we had been before. Now that he has found us again, I fear we shall never be free of him."

"A very touching story, Miss Randolph, and I might believe you had I not seen something altogether different with my own eyes."

She looked at him, a puzzled expression on her face. His eyes were cold yet seemed to burn a hole right through her.

"You did not at all look as if you wanted to be free of Nestor yesterday," Lord Melbourne said softly.

"What . . . what do you mean?"

"Only that I saw you walking in the park yesterday, and thought to join you, but Nestor beat me to it. Your rendezvous seemed too intimate to interrupt so I left the two of you alone."

Emma's heart plummeted. She had made a mistake by not telling Lord Melbourne about seeing Albert yesterday. "That was the first I knew that he had found us," she confessed. "We argued as usual. He demanded that we return home with his escort; I attempted to make it plain that we were not going anywhere with him."

"Was that before or after he caressed you?" Lord Melbourne asked bitterly.

"What do you mean?"

"You cannot deny it; I saw him reach out to you."

"And did you spy on me long enough to see me jerk away?" she asked, her temper beginning to get the best of her. "Did you see me turn my back on Albert and walk away?"

Lord Melbourne's silence was answer enough for Emma.

"How many times have you reached out to touch a woman without her permission? Countless, I imagine. Of course, all of them would have been responsive to you, wouldn't they, my lord? How could anyone say no to the Earl of Melbourne? How could any woman not yearn for your touch?

"Let me advise you of a surprising fact, my lord. Not all women crave the touch of every man who stands before her, no matter how highly placed he is. Many will accept it because it is what their parents want, some because they are desperate and need the support of a man. I fall into neither category, Lord Melbourne.

"I neither sought nor welcomed Albert's touch. In fact, the mere thought sickens me; that is why I avoided him and walked away. If you had stayed a moment longer, you would have seen for yourself my aversion for my cousin. But, instead, you chose to judge me on a few seconds of observation."

The earl was weary of their argument. "Even if everything happened as you say, it still does not explain the locket, nor your claim on Adam."

"I am sick to death of explaining to you how I came to possess that locket. Thinking that Adam might be Richard is a logical step. In any event, you have the locket, and I'm willing to leave without knowing whether Adam is my husband."

"But I am not willing to allow you to go," he replied.

Emma laughed humorlessly. "You and Albert have something in common, my lord. Both of you are you are determined to control me. Perhaps you could fight a duel to see who will be my jailer."

She rose and made her way to the door. Once there, she turned to face him. "Do not press me too far, my lord." Her voice was as soft as a lover's sigh. "I will do as you say, for I am fond of your mother and do not want to cause her any further upset. However, I will not remain a prisoner indefinitely. Investigate and make your determinations quickly, for one day you will find me gone no matter what your threats."

She had almost convinced him of her story, Lord Melbourne thought, once he was alone. He even found himself wondering about the women he had known. Had they accepted his touch without complaint only because of his title and fortune? He had never thought to ask that question before; never considered that a woman might not welcome his attention. Dash it! Miss

Randolph became more of a burden every day; now she even had him doubting himself.

Lord Melbourne and David Whitney had been closeted in the library for most of the day, and Emma found herself relieved that she had escaped his watchful eye for a few hours. However, when evening arrived, she could do nothing more than take her place by his side at supper. She wondered whether the others would notice the constraint between them.

Lord Melbourne occupied one end of the mahogany dining table, with Emma on his right hand and Laura on his left. Lady Melbourne was seated at the opposite end, flanked by Charlotte on her left and David Whitney on her right.

At present, David was regaling the countess with an account of the more humorous moments of his endeavors to bring her late brother-in-law's estate into order.

Emma had attempted to coax Charlotte into conversation, but her sister made only the most rudimentary replies to her overtures. Emma wondered whether their relationship would ever be as close as it had been before Albert had come into their lives.

Resigned to a silent dinner, Emma unabashedly listened in on the conversation between the earl and Laura. She smiled when she realized he was catering to Laura's interest, recounting the fabulous shops he had seen on his travels, and the incredible treasures they held. Laura's eyes were bright, and she looked better than she had since her illness had struck.

Then David Whitney drew Laura's attention, and Lord Melbourne turned to Emma. "I hope you did not find the day too tiresome, Miss Randolph."

She looked at him with disbelief. "Because you were meeting with Mr. Whitney, was I supposed to fall into a decline?" Emma was surprised when he chuckled at her barb.

"I did not mean that at all," he replied, relaxing a bit. "I merely thought you might be finding the country tedious since you have a penchant for intrigue."

Emma chose to ignore his comment. "It isn't necessary that you converse with me, my lord."

"It will be easier for both of us if we appear to be getting along, Miss Randolph," he replied. "If anyone perceives a problem between us there will be questions to be answered, and I do not relish exposing you in front of everyone's eyes."

"I should think that would be exactly what you would want," accused Emma.

Lord Melbourne accepted a slice of beef and waited until the footman had moved on before answering. "No matter what you believe, I do not enjoy our current situation. I would much rather be carrying on my business as usual, instead of wondering what you're up to, and whether you had anything to do with Adam's disappearance."

This was the first time he had suggested she had a hand in his brother's fate, and Emma was speechless for a moment. She sipped her wine attempting to recover from the shock. It took her some minutes before she was able to speak without calling attention to herself, and she felt Lord Melbourne's eyes boring into her the entire time.

"I know you do not think well of me, my lord, but surely you don't believe me capable of harming your brother."

"I don't know what you're capable of, Miss Randolph; that is why I asked you to stay at Melbourne Park a few more days."

"Asked? You did not ask," hissed Emma. "You gave me no choice but to stay until you decide I'm free to leave." She looked down the table to see if anyone had noticed her agitation, but the others were engaged in a lively conversation and paid them no heed.

"You can leave anytime you wish," said Lord Melbourne.

"And be charged with theft? It is truly a wondrous choice you have given me, my lord."

"You do have another alternative."

"And what is that?"

"Merely tell me the truth."

His gaze bored into her and she met it squarely. She had done nothing to this man and his family except to ask for information. She had been as forthright as she could; what she had left out would not help him in the least.

"I have told you all that I can, Lord Melbourne. If you don't believe me, then there is nothing I can do." She was relieved that Laura chose that moment to ask her a question, allowing her to turn her attention away from the earl.

Lord Melbourne determined to harden himself against the appeal of her hazel eyes. She was probably no more than a bit of baggage who thought to move up in the world by claiming she was his sister-in-law. He thought of Adam and what might have happened to him, and every scrap of compassion he felt for Miss Randolph's situation quickly disappeared.

The men were easily persuaded by Lady Melbourne to forgo taking their port in solitude and join the ladies in the drawing room after supper.

"The evening is a fine one for a stroll in the garden," suggested David Whitney, as he stood at the open French doors leading to the terrace.

"I'm afraid I find the comfort of my chair more desirable," said the countess. "But the rest of you go ahead; I have a book to keep me company."

"I shall stay and read to you, my lady," offered Charlotte.

"I should like that, my dear," said Lady Melbourne.

"And I shall stay and listen," added Emma.

"I'm sure you would rather join the others," said the countess. "Don't let me keep you indoors on such a delightful evening."

"Yes, Miss Randolph, please join us," said the earl, no doubt enjoying her discomfort.

Any further objections would attract too much attention, so Emma rose and prepared for an uncomfortable walk in the garden.

"Then it seems to be the four of us," said David Whitney. "Miss Seger, may I escort you?" he asked, offering his arm.

"Thank you, Mr. Whitney," said Laura, rising and strolling through the door without a backward glance.

The earl offered his arm to Emma, but she ignored it and preceded him onto the terrace.

Lord Melbourne was unaccustomed to having a woman slight him. Although he understood Miss Randolph's aversion for his company, he felt compelled to carry on as usual in case they were being observed. "They have taken a liking for one another's company," he said, nodding toward the couple just ahead of them.

"It's much too early to judge," replied Emma, as she descended the shallow steps into the garden.

"Whitney's a good man; we were friends before he came to work for me."

"It seems an unusual situation, my lord."

"Perhaps, but it's worked out well. He comes from a well-respected family, but is the youngest son. His father gave him a good education, hoping he would find an occupation to his liking. However, the love of the land was too strong in his blood.

"I had not known him long when my old steward fell ill, and was unable to return to his position. David learned of it and asked me for the job. I admit I was skeptical at first, but I've never regretted taking him on. I know it's not done in the best of circles, but we've remained friends. I rely upon him for many things, and I'm lucky to have him working for me," said the earl, more to himself than to Emma.

"He seems to be respectable," she admitted grudgingly.

Lord Melbourne grinned. "You need not worry about your friend. He is not the bully I am, nor is he inclined to hold women against their will."

The earl glanced down at her dark curls barely rising above his shoulder. He was always surprised at her smallness of stature; her convictions and determination made her seem larger than she was.

"It is not comforting that Mr. Whitney has your recommendation, Lord Melbourne. However, Laura has a good head atop her shoulders and will be able to determine for herself whether he is worthy of her regard."

"Well said," remarked the earl, taking her hand and placing it on his arm.

She attempted to pull away, but he held her firmly.

"We must not look as if we're at daggers drawn," he insisted, keeping his hand over hers.

Emma was angry with his forwardness, but could not make a scene by insisting he release her hand. If Laura saw her struggling with the earl, she would not give up until she had heard the whole story, and Emma did not want anyone to know that he thought so lowly of her.

They walked in silence for a time and, much to Emma's chagrin, she found herself savoring the solid warmth of his touch. She had received little enough comfort since she had shouldered the burden of the estate, which had been much heavier without her father at her side.

She had dealt with Nestor, and thought she had succeeded until he returned to lay siege to Charlotte. The decision to travel had been hers alone, and she blamed herself for Laura's ill health. Then, when she thought everything would come right, her bridegroom had deserted her without a word of explanation. Yes, she definitely deserved some comfort in her life.

Lord Melbourne's hand conveyed a warmth that traveled up her arm and into her body. She moved closer, forgetting the animosity that lay between them. She craved this connection and, for once, would not deny herself.

"And what if they determine they are well suited?" he asked casually.

"Then I suppose they will follow the usual course of events."

"And it will not bother you if Miss Seger marries and leaves you?"

"I shall miss her, of course. But if she will be happy then I will only wish her well. Laura has devoted years to us, and she deserves some happiness of her own."

"A very commendable sentiment, Miss Randolph."

"And you, my lord? What will you do if Mr. Whitney decides to marry?"

"Why, it shouldn't change things at all. David will need a job more than ever if he takes on a family."

"Events seldom change a man's life, do they? It is the woman who must do all the bending."

"You sound bitter, Miss Randolph. Knowing what little I do of you, it would seem you have not had to make any concessions yet."

"And I will not," she declared. "I was lucky enough to have inherited; most women are not, and I feel sorry for their utter dependence on men."

"Do you hate us so?"

"Not at all, my lord. Let's just say my experiences over the past year have not spoken well of the male species."

"We are not all terrible, you know."

"No, many of you are worse."

"I understand why you might hold some animosity toward me."

"Might?" she broke in, staring at him in disbelief.

"You are not suffering, Miss Randolph. You are not locked in your room existing on bread and water."

"Neither am I free, your lordship."

Her tone was hostile and, if he were honest with himself, he could not blame her. But he could not let her make him feel guilty enough to let her go.

"You may leave anytime you wish."

"Only to be stopped and brought back before I reach the next village."

"Miss Randolph, let's stop all this wrangling. I may hear something from my man of business any day now which will free you to continue your travel. Until then, why not enjoy your sojourn here?"

"A prison is a prison, my lord, no matter how fine the silk that lines it." Emma jerked away from him and stalked toward the house, her back stiff with anger.

The women were in the drawing room the next morning when Lord Melbourne entered, followed by David Whitney. The earl's hair was mussed, and a film of dust covered his usually immaculate Hessians.

"Ladies, I hope you will pardon us for coming to you in all our dirt," said the earl, "but we must be off again in all possible haste."

The countess raised her head in alarm. "What has happened, Richard?"

"I'm sorry I startled you," he apologized. "It has nothing to do with Adam. Galahad has disappeared."

"Oh, no!" exclaimed Lady Melbourne. "Do you know where he has gone?" she asked.

"That's what we're attempting to ascertain. None of the grooms saw or heard anything. His stall door was open this morning and he was nowhere to be found. From the tracks we were able to find, it looks as if he was led away. We followed them until we reached the main road where they were already obliterated. We came back to better organize before starting out again."

"I know you're fond of the horse, Richard, but don't do anything foolish."

"I'm taking David along to prevent me from doing just that," replied the earl with a reassuring smile.

"I will do my best, my lady," said David.

"Do you know when you will return?" asked the countess.

"When we have run out of places to look," said Lord Melbourne. "I'm sorry I can't be more definite." He directed his gaze at Emma. "Miss Randolph, may I have a word with you?"

Emma was surprised that he would single her out after their conversation of the night before. "Of course," she said, following him into the next room.

"I'm trusting you will be here when I return," he said.

Emma tipped her head back to look up at him, and he felt a sudden surge of desire rush through him. It seemed his body would not listen to his head when it came to Miss Randolph. He did not trust her out of his sight, yet he was tempted, so tempted, to claim her lips for just one kiss before he left.

It would not do, he told himself, to become involved with her. It would give her just the edge she needed, and he had no doubt she would take it.

Emma could not answer. He stood too close, overwhelming

her with his sheer masculinity so that she could not even utter a proper set-down.

"Promise you'll be here," he said. The earl did not know what made him ask, when he should have demanded; nor why he said it with such gentleness.

Emma was held in thrall by the intentness of his gaze. She forgot everything that was between them, and knew only that she was responding to him as she had no other. She could do nothing else but agree with his request. "I will," she replied.

Chapter Seven

The words were too much like a vow. No matter what he might think of himself later, the earl could resist temptation no longer. He framed her face with his hands, staring deep into her eyes. He barely brushed her lips with his, then returned for a deeper taste. When he began to pull away, she followed him, keeping her lips against his. Lord Melbourne groaned and pulled her completely into his arms, molding her soft curves against the firmness of his muscles. She melted against him and he accepted her surrender by deepening the kiss. His hands found the curves of her body, and began to learn them, until a door closing further down the hall brought him back to his senses.

He pulled his lips from hers and buried his face in the curve of her neck, breathing in the sweet scent of roses. Placing a kiss against her soft skin, he ran his hands down the length of her back, pressing her against him one last time before releasing her and stepping back.

Lord Melbourne thought of what she had said about some women not welcoming his touch. "I'm sorry. I shouldn't have forced myself on you."

In all fairness, Emma could not let him take the entire blame. Her face was flaming with embarrassment at her forwardness.

"It was as much my fault as yours," she admitted, her voice trembling.

He reached out and traced her delicate jawline with one finger, stopping at her chin and nudging it upward until she met his gaze. His thumb rubbed her full bottom lip, and he looked as if he might kiss her again.

"I do not like being at odds with you," he murmured.

"Nor I you."

"Do you think we might cry peace until this muddle is straightened out?"

"I do not know, my lord," said Emma, remembering what had passed between them. "You have made some dreadful accusations against me, and you're still holding the matter of the locket over my head."

Lord Melbourne sighed, dropped his hand, and stepped back. "You're right, of course. No matter what the outcome, there is far too much between us to be forgiven."

Emma had hoped for a moment that he would apologize and say that he had made a terrible mistake in thinking the worst of her, but it did not happen.

"Perhaps I cannot forgive, but I will agree to a truce. To show good faith, I will promise not to attempt to leave while you are gone. When you return, I only hope you will find it in your heart to believe me, and allow me to go free."

"That is more than I had hoped for. I must go," he said, his voice already weary. "The longer I tarry, the colder the trail becomes, and I must find that horse." He hesitated a moment before speaking again. "If you are telling me the truth, then be warned that Nestor is still at the inn. Don't stray too far from the house without taking one of the grooms with you."

She thought he was going to take her in his arms again, but he turned quickly and disappeared through the door without another word.

The room seemed too cool, and Emma wrapped her arms around her body, attempting to hold in the warmth his kiss had brought. She wondered why he had done it; he suspected her of all manner of things, yet that hadn't stopped him. It hadn't stopped her either, she admitted truthfully. He had not forced himself on her; she could have pulled away anytime, but she hadn't. Instead, she had encouraged him.

Her face flamed again at the thought of how she had prolonged the kiss when he would have ended it. And what if he was her brother-in-law? If that proved true, there would be no future for them even if Adam was dead. Both society and law would keep them apart. And if Adam was not her husband, what of her vow to renounce men for the rest of her days once out of the mess in which she had gotten herself?

Emma was disgusted by her actions. At one time she thought herself a woman of her word, but she was no less susceptible to an attractive man than the greenest milk-and-water chit. She must stop this madness before her heart was truly engaged, and wondered whether she had waited too long already. What an irony if she were to fall in love with a man who mistrusted her every word and deed.

She was sorry she had promised to stay until Lord Melbourne returned; it would be her best chance to escape. If she were the person he thought her to be, a promise would mean nothing. However, she had given her word and her conscience would not allow her to be less than honorable. How much easier it would be to leave before she was again forced to face her attraction to him, and his distrust of her.

"You've been very quiet," commented Laura as she took a seat beside Emma at the pianoforte.

The earl had been gone two days and, even though they were at odds, Emma missed him more than she ever thought she would. "I am thinking," she replied. She missed a note in the tune she was playing and grimaced.

"Evidently not about music," remarked Laura with a smile. "About Lord Melbourne?"

"Why should you think that?" Emma asked, resting her hands on the keys.

"Because you have been much more pensive since he left."

"We have not exactly been on good terms lately," responded Emma.

"You have not been on good terms since you met," corrected Laura. "What more could you do to get on his bad side?"

"I saw Albert and did not tell him," confessed Emma.

"That's impossible. Lord Melbourne was the first to meet Albert when he called. I understand he talked with him in the library before he called you down."

"That's true, but I had seen Albert before he called."

Laura was astonished at Emma's admission. "You mean since we've been at Melbourne Park?"

Emma nodded.

"But when?" asked Laura.

"The day before Albert called, I went walking in the park. You remember; I said I wanted to get rid of the soreness from my fall." Emma glanced up at Laura, and saw that she had her full attention.

"I had walked farther than I had intended, but the wildflowers were so lovely near the woods and I wanted to gather a few for my room. Before I knew it Albert had appeared from nowhere and was blocking my way."

"What on earth did he want?" quizzed Laura.

"To tell me he was taking us home; I told him we weren't going anywhere with him."

"He could have hurt you."

"But he didn't. I think he mostly wanted to let me know that he had found us."

"What a disgusting man," declared Laura. "But why should Lord Melbourne be overset because you told Albert to leave us alone."

"There's a little more to it. While I was talking to Albert, Lord Melbourne saw us together. He was too far away to hear what was being said, and since I was attempting to deal calmly with Albert, it probably looked as if we were having a congenial conversation. At one point, Albert asked about the bruise on my the face and reached out to touch it. I jerked away and stormed off, but Lord Melbourne didn't see it all. He saw Albert reach out to touch me, but turned away before he saw me leave."

"So he thinks you were having a lovers' tryst," guessed Laura.

Emma nodded, running her fingers lightly over the keys. "We had a terrible argument about it, but I couldn't convince him otherwise." Emma did not tell Laura about the earl's threat to have her charged with theft.

"Men can be so nonsensical at times," Laura commented.

"It gets even worse," revealed Emma. "After Albert visited Melbourne House, the earl suggested that Albert and I were in league to defraud him."

"What! Does he know who you are? That you have no need of his family's money?"

"I didn't say anything; I don't think it would have done any good. He has it set in his mind that I mean to use the locket to claim I'm his brother's wife. Then, if Adam is dead, I would be set for life at his expense."

"Didn't you even try to explain the situation to him?"

"I told him about Albert's need of money, and his attempt to marry me. I revealed the true reason for our trip to Paris, and even the purpose behind my hasty marriage. I said nothing about Charlotte's *tendre* for Albert, however; I didn't want to cause her any embarrassment."

"A little humiliation might do her some good," Laura commented, thinking of Charlotte's behavior since Albert had forced his way into their life. "But didn't your explanation to Lord Melbourne prove to him that he was wrong?" she asked, getting back to the main topic of their conversation.

Emma gave a bitter laugh. "It only seemed to make things worse."

"But he spoke with you before he left," said Laura. "I thought everything was fine between you."

Emma turned away from Laura, not wanting her to see the confusion she felt whenever she thought of Lord Melbourne's leave taking.

"He asked that we cry peace until the matters of the locket and his brother are straightened out."

"But that is a good omen," said Laura.

"I suppose," Emma agreed reluctantly. "He also asked that we not leave until he returns."

"That isn't an unreasonable request under the circumstances," said Laura. "You're as anxious as he is to find out the truth, aren't you?"

"Of course, I just do not like being held captive until we resolve the problem."

"How could you feel that way?" said Laura laughing. "Why, even Charlotte is enjoying our stay here. She walks in the park every day, and is in better spirits than I've seen since we left home."

"And are you happy?" asked Emma.

"How could I not be? The house is well run and beautifully kept, the grounds are lovely, and the cooking is excellent. A few more weeks, and my clothes will fit me again without any alterations."

"And there is David Whitney to keep you entertained."

A faint flush rose to Laura's cheeks. "Mr. Whitney has been very kind to me, and we have a great deal in common. While we were not close neighbors, we came from the same part of the country."

"Ah, and that is all there is? Merely a similarity of geography?" said Emma, with a mischievous smile.

"Oh, shush," said Laura. "and play us a tune."

Emma did as she was told, attempting to drown the memory of Lord Melbourne's kiss in a concentrated effort on the music.

Much to Emma's disappointment, Lord Melbourne had not returned by the next morning. She had hoped he would easily find the missing stallion. Perhaps then he would be more disposed toward forgetting about the locket, and allow them to leave. Instead, more long hours stretched before her.

After breakfast, Emma found she could not tolerate the confinement a moment longer, and decided to enjoy a ride in the park. She would take a groom with her, and would not wander far from the house; that should be enough precaution to avoid Albert.

Emma had reached the woods at the edge of the park, and glanced back to see that the groom was still trailing behind, when a shot rang out. Her mare bolted at the sudden noise, and it was all she could do to hang on until she regained her seat again.

Emma was greatly relieved to find the mare was headed for the stables. She heard someone thundering along behind her and hoped it was the groom, but did not chance a look back to see whether she was right.

One name reverberated in her mind, keeping time with the pounding of the mare's hooves as she fairly flew across the park. *Albert. Albert. Albert.* Leaning over the mare's neck, she urged her on until they reached the drive leading to the stableyard.

The groom pulled up beside her reaching for her reins, but Emma waved him away. The mare was tiring, and beginning to slow as she reached the safety of the stables. They galloped into the yard, bringing the stableboys and George running.

"Miss Randolph, what happened? Are you hurt?" asked George, helping her down.

"I don't think so," she said, holding onto the stirrup until she gathered her strength. "I don't know about my horse."

George took Emma's arm and guided her to the mounting block so she could sit for a moment.

He motioned a stableboy toward the mare, who stood with her head drooping, and sides heaving with the effort of her run. "Unsaddle her, and walk her a bit," he ordered.

"Now, what happened?" he asked, turning back to Emma.

"We were near the woods, when there was a shot. It was so close I thought I heard it hit somewhere nearby. It startled Lady, and she bolted. Since she was headed back to the stables, I let her have her head."

"Did you see anybody?"

"No. It all happened too fast."

"And did you?" he asked, turning toward the groom who had accompanied her.

"Thought I caught a movement in that grove of oaks, but it could've been anything."

"Take four men with you and go back to the spot. See what you can find. Work your way toward the main road. I'll send some others to search the rest of the park."

"Yes, sir," said the groom, hurrying off to saddle a fresh horse.

A few minutes later, the group of men galloped out of the stableyard, retracing the path Emma had taken earlier.

"Is the mare all right?" asked Emma, now that she had gotten her breath.

"Just winded, that's all," said George. "No sign of a bullet wound anywhere."

"I'm so thankful," said Emma. "I would hate to face Lord Melbourne if any harm had come to her."

"And I would hate to face him if any harm came to you," said George.

"You were not at fault, George. I'm sure it was a poacher who is probably more scared than I am."

In truth, there was no doubt in Emma's mind who was responsible for the shot, and it was not a poacher. This was all Albert's doing. He had cut the girth on the saddle knowing she could not resist riding. Now, he had hidden himself in the woods like the coward he was to make another attempt on her life.

"Do you feel up to going to the house, ma'am?"

Emma put her thoughts aside and smiled at George. "I feel perfectly fine," she said. "There is no need for you to worry."

Emma was escorted to the house by George and two other men, all keeping a keen eye out for any sign of movement. Emma smothered a giggle, the stress of the past half hour beginning to catch up with her. She yearned for the quiet safety of her room, where she could stretch out on her comfortable bed and relax for a moment.

Where, oh where, was Lord Melbourne? She never thought she would yearn for him after his accusations, but she needed him desperately. She should be craving her husband's protection and comfort, but found herself able to think of nothing but the earl's strong arms encircling her in safety.

* * *

The earl was not in the best of spirits when he and David Whitney were forced to return to Melbourne Park without Galahad. To be met with the story of Emma's mishap as soon as he reached home was too much for him to stoically accept.

George was surprised, and a little proud, at the length and variety of the earl's curses. There wasn't another gentleman who could match him, he'd wager.

Lord Melbourne questioned the groom who had accompanied Emma, but learned nothing helpful.

"What did the search turn up?" he asked, turning to George again.

"We found a spot where a horse had been tied for some time, my lord. A person would've had a good view of the house and stables. Easiest thing in the world to see who was comin' and goin'."

"What do you think, George? Was this an accident?"

George had had time to think, so it didn't take him long to answer. "Hard to believe a poacher would hide himself nearly in the park. And then to stay there for as long as the signs say he did." George shook his head. "No, I'd have to say it was no poacher, my lord."

In the earl's mind, it was also no accident. Following close upon the incident of the cut girth, he ruled out the idea that it was a prank. It had taken planning and perseverance to wait in the woods until Emma appeared.

There were two possibilities remaining: the miscreant had a grudge against him and did not care whether he hurt an innocent person; or Emma had an enemy who wanted her out of the way.

The first inkling of doubt began to seep into his mind; perhaps he had misjudged Emma after all. If he had, she would never forgive him. However, after further consideration, he realized that it could have been just as easy for Emma and Nestor to have arranged the incident in order to cast doubt on his suspicions.

"Has Miss Randolph been riding since the incident?" he asked.

"No, sir, hasn't gone further than the gardens."

Lord Melbourne, nodded with satisfaction. "Good, I'll get her side of the story now," he said, turning toward the house.

"Begging your pardon, my lord. The ladies went calling earlier in the day."

"Calling!" exclaimed the earl. "While some madman is prowling the woods with a gun?"

"I sent enough men with them to keep them safe," George assured him.

"For your sake, I hope you did," growled Lord Melbourne.

Unable to do anything but pace until the women returned, Lord Melbourne chose to ride out with David to check on work that should have been carried out while they had been absent.

Therefore, it was supper before the earl came face-to-face with Emma. She was the first to arrive in the drawing room, and he went quickly to her side.

"I heard what happened while I was away. Were you harmed?" he asked.

"I am perfectly well, my lord," said Emma, attempting to disguise her relief at seeing him.

"I warned you about straying too far from the house." He watched her expression closely, attempting to determine her innocence or guilt in the matter by her reaction.

"Could we postpone our conversation until after supper?" Emma asked. "Your mother will be here any moment. She was extremely upset when she heard about the incident."

"As well she should be," the earl commented.

"That may be so, but I don't wish to trouble her again with an occurrence that brought me no harm. I have persuaded her it was only a poacher."

"Be warned, I intend to pursue this after supper."

At that moment, the others arrived in a group, delaying the chance for further private conversation.

"You are all looking pleased with yourselves," the earl said.

"We are," answered Lady Melbourne. "We have been to call on a few of our neighbors, and have decided a dance is just the thing to brighten the summer."

"Are you certain you're up to it?" he asked. His mother had not attended any functions since Adam had gone missing, and now she was planning on hostessing a dance.

"Of course. We are not talking about a London ball, Richard," she chided. "Merely a small dance with our neighbors in attendance. It will do me good to see the young people enjoying themselves."

"We will do all we can to relieve the strain on Lady Melbourne," promised Laura.

"Pshaw," said the countess. "I do not need to be cosseted. We shall make a list tomorrow and begin writing out the invitations."

Lord Melbourne did not intend to bring up the disturbing topic of the gunshot when everyone was in such a good mood. Curbing his impatience, he led his mother into the dining room.

The supper conversation was given over to details of the dance, but after they had retired to the drawing room, the earl had his chance to get Emma off to himself.

Lady Melbourne and Charlotte were discussing the novel they were reading, and Laura and David had taken a settee some distance away and were absorbed in conversation.

It did not escape Lord Melbourne's notice that Emma did not attempt to avoid his company. "Do you still think I'm wrong about those two?" he asked, nodding toward the couple.

"They do seem rather engrossed with one another," Emma agreed. "But I wouldn't be too hasty to judge. Laura has always lived a single life."

"All the more reason not to waste time if she's found someone," replied the earl.

Emma considered what life would be without Laura. She was old enough to be guardian to Charlotte and live alone; however, both of them would miss Laura's friendship if she left. Emma was torn between wishing Laura happiness, and the selfish desire to keep their lives undisturbed.

"I suppose we must wait to see what develops," she finally remarked.

"Emma . . . Miss Randolph, the evening is pleasant. Shall we step out onto the terrace?"

Emma knew she could no longer put off their conversation. Besides, he might have decided it was too much trouble keeping her at Melbourne Park, and let her go. "Of course, my lord," she replied and led the way through the French doors.

"Now tell me what happened," he demanded as soon as they were out of the hearing of the others.

"I'm sure George has already told you everything."

"I want to hear it from you. Tell me all you can remember, no matter how insignificant you consider it."

Emma recounted the story with as much detail as she could. She would have liked nothing more than to tell the earl her suspicions concerning Albert, but he would no doubt think she was attempting to shift attention from herself to her cousin.

"It was nothing, my lord," she said at the end of the tale. "Merely a poacher, who was probably more frightened than I when he saw me, and set off his gun by accident."

"George doesn't think so. There was no sign of poaching, only a trampled spot where a horse had stood for some time. Assure me this was not a scheme you and your cousin concocted."

Emma should not have expected a simple kiss to have made any difference in how Lord Melbourne viewed her; but she had held out a faint hope. Now that hope was dead, and in its place was a deep bitterness. She had made such a mess of her life, all by trying to do what was best for everyone.

"If I were at home, I would not need to assure you, my lord. Our family is known as an honorable one, and no one would ever question my word." She held up her hand when he would have spoken.

"I realize you have nothing on which to base your trust, so I will no longer chastise you for not doing so. However, when this is all over and done with, I will expect an apology from you."

"I shall be happy to do so if the situation warrants it, Miss

Randolph.'' The earl could not help but wonder whether he had completely misjudged her, and found himself looking forward to being wrong.

"You should not have ridden until I was here," he admonished her.

"After your accusations, I cannot imagine that you would look forward to spending time in my company. Besides, I needed to get out. I cannot be locked away from everything I enjoy. You must understand that."

"I do, but—"

"And I felt perfectly safe," she said, interrupting him. "I had a groom with me and we were still within the confines of the park."

"Evidently that wasn't enough. Until we find out who's responsible for these incidents, you must stay close to the house."

"I can't live that way," she protested again. "And if these occurrences are aimed at me, I cannot endanger your household any longer. If you will but remove your threat, we shall be on our way."

Lord Melbourne had never held a woman hostage before, and felt a twinge of guilt at doing so. "You, your sister, and Miss Seger will be safer here for the time being."

"I'm sure my safety is your only concern, my lord," she replied bitterly.

"You might not believe me, but I do not want to see you harmed."

"Oh, but I do believe you. How could you prove I'm trying to take advantage of your family, if I'm dead?"

"Miss Randolph, our situation is not one of my choosing—"

"Of course it is. I want to leave, you are forcing me to stay."

"I would be entirely happy if you could leave, but—"

"Then let me," she said hopefully. "I swear to you, I have never harbored intentions to benefit by claiming I'm your brother's wife. I'm willing to leave here and never bother you again. I'll search for the man I know as Richard Tremayne elsewhere, and if I don't find him then I shall give it up."

Lord Melbourne considered her words. "And if Adam doesn't return, I'll never know whether he was your husband. I don't know whether I can be satisfied with no explanation at all." A crooked smile lifted one corner of his mouth. "You see, you have piqued my interest, Miss Randolph, and now you must pay the price."

Emma's patience had worn thin. She had attempted to discuss their problem logically, but had been no more successful than when she had argued with him. "You are a perverse man, my lord. You do not believe that Adam could have married me, yet you will not let me go because you think he might have done so."

"You must understand what my family has been through since Adam's been gone."

"I do. If you will remember, I have a missing husband. I have also not had the comfort of my home and familiar surrounds because of my hateful cousin. But then you suspect that we are in this together, don't you?"

The earl was growing tired of arguing with her. "You forget my mother is having a dance for your entertainment. Surely you would not want to leave before then."

"Does that mean you will let us go after the dance?" she asked cautiously.

"We will discuss it again then," he answered. "I only know that I haven't seen my mother this lively since before Adam left for war."

Emma felt a stab of guilt. No matter how she felt about Lord Melbourne, she must not spoil the event for her ladyship; she was innocent of the earl's actions.

"I shall not argue about staying until then," she conceded. "Charlotte is looking forward to it."

Lord Melbourne was pleased she had volunteered to stay without further coercion. He did not like being at odds with Emma, especially with the memory of their kiss lingering in his mind. He studied her graceful neck as she stood beside him, attempting to locate the exact spot his lips had pressed against that silken skin.

Chapter Eight

"Are you certain this is necessary?" asked Laura, two days later.

"It is the safest idea I can come up with," answered Emma. Perhaps she was reading more into the earl's words than she should, but she was resting her hopes on leaving Melbourne Park immediately after the dance. "If we depart by coach, either night or day, Albert will be certain to see us. I intend to convince Lord Melbourne to arrange for a coach to be waiting in the next town when we are ready to depart. We will leave by horseback after dark, and ride cross-country until we reach it. At the same time, I shall send our coach off in the opposite direction. I'm certain Albert will follow it thinking we are attempting another midnight escape. We will be in London before Albert realizes we are gone."

"And when he does find out?"

"I have received a letter from Lady Ambrose inviting us to stay with her for the duration of our visit to London. We will be safe while we are living in her house."

Laura sighed. She was tired of traveling, and growing more skeptical that this was the way to get rid of Albert Nestor.

"Perhaps Lord Melbourne could help convince Albert to leave us alone."

"I do not want to draw him further into it. Father was confident that I could run our lives, and I intend to live up to his expectations," Emma said stubbornly.

"Everyone needs help sometimes," pressed Laura. "There is no shame in asking."

Emma's small chin lifted. "If you don't wish to go with us, I'll understand," she said stiffly. "Our coach can take you home. You'll be safe there, for I'm certain that Albert will continue to search for us."

"You know I cannot leave you and Charlotte," said Laura. "I've been with you too long to desert you. If you feel going to London is the thing to do, then we shall do it—together."

"Thank you, Laura," said Emma, relief all too apparent in her voice. "I know I sound like a stubborn child, but it will be best for us, I'm certain." Emma sounded more confident than she felt. There was no assurance that Albert would be fooled by her diversion for long, but she could think of nothing better.

Emma watched from her bedroom window as the earl approached the house. He and his horse were covered with dust and one looked as dispirited as another. He had ridden out early that morning chasing another lead as to where Galahad might be. If looks told the tale, then this clue was as false as all the others he had followed during the past days.

Emma wondered at the intensity of his determination to find the stallion. He was showing more concern about this horse than he did about his brother, she thought uncharitably. A moment later she considered that she was being too harsh on him. No matter how he had treated her, she could not see into his mind to discover the amount of distress he was suffering because of Adam's absence.

* * *

"Lord Melbourne," she said after supper that evening, "may I speak with you?"

"Of course," he agreed instantly.

Emma wondered if he would be so eager knowing what she was about to ask. "It is about our leaving . . ."

"I thought we had settled this."

"We did, and I do not mean to debate the issue any longer, but . . ." She hesitated, wondering if she could continue with his fierce blue gaze focused on her. What had happened to her backbone? She had never let anyone stand in her way before.

"But . . ." he urged.

"But if you do agree to let us leave after the dance, I need to have a plan in place."

When Emma had first appeared at his home, Lord Melbourne would have been more than happy to help speed her departure. Now he was reluctant to see her go. Not only because of the unanswered questions about the locket and Adam, but because of the feelings toward her that he had been unable to suppress. Surely a stolen kiss could not have made the difference, he mused. He had kissed many ladies over the years, but most were forgotten as soon as they were over.

The earl observed the determined light in Miss Randolph's hazel eyes, and decided he would not refuse her again until he had come to a decision.

"If I should decide you are free to go, Miss Randolph, I'll do what I can to speed you on your way."

Emma breathed a sigh of relief that she need not endure another bout of arguing. Her strength to resist him continued to weaken, and she did not know how hard she would fight to defy him if he was determined she stay.

"I wonder if you can arrange a coach to meet us in the next village when we are ready to embark on our journey?"

A frown creased Lord Melbourne's brow. "I'm afraid I don't understand," he said.

"I believe we should leave here with all possible stealth, my lord, so that my cousin cannot follow us. I will arrange for our coach to leave late one evening. I'm certain Albert is on the lookout for something like that, since that is how we escaped him the last time. He will think we are again attempting to elude him and will follow. It will probably be daylight before he will be able to determine we are not in the coach. Soon after the coach leaves, the three of us will ride cross-country to the next village. All it needs is for you to arrange a coach to be ready to travel to London. Will you do it?''

She was certainly doing all she could to convince him she wanted to avoid her cousin. "Do you really believe all this is necessary?" he asked, the frown still in place.

"Yes, I do. I know Albert, and he will not give up easily. If we are in London, already settled into Lady Ambrose's household, it will be nigh impossible for him to contact us if we don't desire it."

There was no reason to ask again; he could tell by the set of her chin that she was determined to carry through on her idea, with or without his help.

"You realize all this rests on whether my doubts about the locket and your intentions are erased."

She met his gaze squarely. "I do, my lord, and I think I have found a solution."

"And what would that be, Miss Randolph."

"I have a man of business in London. You may write him for a recommendation of my character."

"And why should I trust him?"

"I have never seen a more suspicious man," she complained irritably.

"You have given me reason to be."

She was clearly exasperated when she answered. "Then have your man of business investigate mine. I'm certain he'll tell you he is a perfectly reputable person. My father dealt with him for years, and I have continued using his services."

"I'll do that, and if it all proves out, I'll be pleased to help you plan your escape."

Emma breathed a sigh of relief. A few more days and perhaps it would all be over, and she need never see Lord Melbourne again. She wondered why she was not as happy as she should be.

* * *

The next morning, a coach drew up before the house. It was a hired conveyance, covered in dust, and drawn by horses that were nowhere near the quality Lord Melbourne owned.

"Is someone coming to stay for the ball?" asked Charlotte, peering unladylike through the window.

"No one of whom I'm aware," replied the countess. "But Richard's friends tend to show up unannounced. I wouldn't be surprised to see them now that the Season is over."

Charlotte looked again. "The coach is not nearly as dashing as I would expect if they are Lord Melbourne's friends," she judged.

"Charlotte! Not everyone can afford the best," admonished Emma. "And stop gaping through the window like a hoyden."

Lady Melbourne only laughed. "After a Season in London many of them return with pockets to let," she replied.

"Oh," said Charlotte. "If it is a friend of Lord Melbourne's, he's injured. Maybe he was wounded in a duel!" she cried excitedly.

"You've been reading too many of my novels," remarked the countess, still amused at the young girl's reaction. "Most likely the scoundrel took a fall while exiting his club late at night."

"They are helping him in," said Charlotte, scampering back to her chair and settling into it as if she had been there all afternoon.

The women heard a flurry of activity in the entrance hall. The butler appeared in the doorway, his face a mask of astonishment. "My . . . my lady," he stammered.

"Out of my way, Roland," said a voice from behind him. "I am capable of announcing myself."

Emma heard Lady Melbourne gasp as she turned toward the door. A young blond-haired man, supported by two footmen, pushed past the butler. Accepting a pair of crutches from one of the footmen, he balanced himself precariously without their help, and glanced around the room.

"Aren't you going to welcome me home?" he asked, his eyes lighting on the countess.

Lady Melbourne sat speechless, tears streaming down her face. "Adam? Adam, is it really you?" She arose from the chair and rushed across the room to stand staring at him a moment before throwing her arms around him.

"It's me, Mama," Adam murmured, as he hugged her as tightly as his crutches would allow.

"Oh, Adam, I cannot believe it," said Lady Melbourne, holding him away from her and studying his face again. "I have hoped and prayed that you would be all right."

"Then it must have been your prayers that pulled me through," he said, kissing her cheek.

Lady Melbourne clasped him to her again, looking as if she would never let him go.

Laura motioned Emma and Charlotte from the room, leaving the countess to reunite privately with her son.

"Do you think Mr. Tremayne will be down for supper?" asked Charlotte, as they gathered in the drawing room before the meal.

"I wouldn't think he would feel up to it," said Laura. "I imagine the trip was hard on him; he was quite pale."

"He is exceedingly handsome, don't you think?" questioned Charlotte, peering into a mirror hanging on the wall, and twitching a curl in place.

"Exceedingly," agreed Laura, hiding her smile.

"I shouldn't be surprised if we dined alone tonight," speculated Emma. "After all, Lord and Lady Melbourne will want to spend time with Mr. Tremayne."

At that moment, Lord Melbourne appeared in the doorway, proving her prediction at least in part wrong. "I apologize for my tardiness; I assume you know that Adam has returned." The lines of worry were gone from his face, and his step seemed lighter as he entered the room.

"We were with her ladyship when he arrived," said Emma.

"I've never seen such a joyous reunion," added Laura.

Even Charlotte had been touched, for her eyes were suspiciously bright when she said, "It was just like a novel."

"The hero returning; Adam would like that," said the earl laughing good-naturedly. "My mother won't be joining us this evening. She will be having dinner with Adam in his room."

"And how is he?" asked David Whitney, arriving in time to hear the last of Lord Melbourne's words.

"Tired, but otherwise his spirits are high. However, it will still take some weeks before he regains his entire strength."

"We are all delighted for you, my lord," said Emma.

"Thank you. David, would you pour the sherry?" asked Lord Melbourne.

"I'd be happy to," said Mr. Whitney, going to the small table that held the bottles and glasses.

Lord Melbourne looked closely at Emma. "Miss Randolph, may I speak with you a moment?

"Of course, my lord," said Emma, puzzled at his need for privacy as he drew her aside.

"I take it you were here when Adam returned," he said, leading her to the far end of the room.

"Yes, I was. It was wonderful. I hope your mother won't wear herself out tending to your brother."

"At present, I can't move her from his room. She is sitting by his bedside watching him sleep at the moment, but she won't fall into a decline now that Adam is back. She'll stay strong for him."

"I can only imagine how she feels," replied Emma.

Now that Adam was safe, Lord Melbourne was anxious to determine whether he was connected to Miss Randolph. Lady Melbourne had forbidden him to question Adam until he was better rested, so the earl had no recourse other than to inquire of the very person he trusted least.

"Now that you've seen Adam," he said slowly, watching her expression closely, "is he your husband?"

Emma had planned on discussing the subject with Lord Melbourne immediately after supper, for she was as eager as he was to have the situation resolved. But evidently his need to know was too great to wait.

"I have never seen your brother before," she admitted. She found she was not as disappointed as she thought she would have been. When she had first come to Melbourne Park, she felt as if Adam would be the answer to her prayers if he proved to be her missing husband, but that was before Lord Melbourne had kissed her. That one moment had changed everything for Emma.

The earl breathed a great sigh of relief. If Adam was not married to Miss Randolph, then he could put aside the guilt he had felt since he had kissed her. There was nothing he could do about the desire that continued to plague him each time he was near her, but he assumed that would pass once she was out of his life. And, unless Miss Randolph had changed her mind, that would be as soon as the dance was over.

Until then he must remember that even though she had been forced to admit she was not wed to his brother, it did not clear her of the intent to dupe his family. "I hope you are not too disheartened," he said, wanting her reaction now that she could no longer insist Adam might be her husband.

"Not at all," she assured him. "I'm only discouraged that I'm no closer to determining the whereabouts of Richard. Perhaps if your brother could tell us what happened to the locket, it would help. He might have given it to my husband for safekeeping," she suggested hopefully.

"It's possible," said the earl, "but we will need to wait until tomorrow at the very earliest to find out."

"Oh, I did not mean to question him tonight, my lord. We must wait until he is stronger. Once I find out whether he can help me, we shall be on our way and you can enjoy reuniting with your brother."

Now that the way had been cleared for her to vanish from his life, Lord Melbourne was unexpectedly reluctant to allow it to happen. Her eyes were more green than gold at the moment, and as he stared into them his mind seemed to detach from his body and become tangled up in her gaze. It was an uncomfortable feeling, this loss of self, and he jerked away, looking across the room until he was once more in control of his faculties.

"Adam is looking forward to meeting all of you when he's feeling more the thing," Lord Melbourne answered, after a slight pause. "He likes nothing better than lovely ladies gathered round him, and I wouldn't be at all surprised that your presence will have him downstairs within a day or two."

"We should not be invading your privacy," insisted Emma. "This is a time you should be sharing with your family without strangers interfering."

"Adam will be bored to blazes within a sennight at most. You would be doing us a favor by staying to help entertain him," replied Lord Melbourne, guiding her toward the three people seated at the other end of the room.

"I'm still convinced it would be best if we left."

"But what about the dance?" asked Charlotte, before the earl could answer.

"Charlotte, Lord and Lady Melbourne cannot be worried about dancing when Mr. Tremayne has so recently returned," chided Laura.

"On the contrary, Adam is looking forward to the dance," remarked Lord Melbourne. "He considers it a welcome home party, and we will probably have quite a crush before all's said and done. I'm sure he would think the whole evening sadly flat if you weren't here. Say you'll stay."

"Please, Emma," pleaded Charlotte.

"I see no harm in it," volunteered Laura, glancing at Mr. Whitney, who nodded his agreement.

Emma could not refuse them. "Oh, all right. You've convinced me. We'll stay until after the dance."

"Good. Now that we have that settled, shall we go in to supper?" suggested Lord Melbourne.

"Has your brother been able to tell you of his experiences?" asked Emma, once they were seated around the table.

"Not in any detail as yet," replied the earl. "As we were told, he was wounded in the battle at Orthez. Two shots struck him: one in the leg, the other his upper arm. The last thing he remembers is his horse going down beneath him. He awoke in what served as a field hospital. He could remember nothing, and there were no personal belongings to identify him.''

''How distressing for him,'' sympathized Laura.

''He was evidently quite ill for a time with fever and complications from his injuries,'' continued Lord Melbourne. ''He regained his memory only recently, but was too weak to travel until a few weeks ago.''

''He's very fortunate,'' said David Whitney.

''That he is,'' replied the earl.

Emma was disappointed that she had no answer to the puzzle that continued to complicate her life, but perhaps Adam would be able to shed some light on how he became separated from the locket. It might tell her something.

''Have you had any luck in finding your stallion?'' asked Laura.

''None,'' said Lord Melbourne impatiently. ''We've followed every lead we've received. I've had the grooms scouring the nearby countryside, but we haven't found a trace. Whoever took Galahad must have done so in the dead of night, for no one saw him being led away.''

''Galahad must be an important animal to warrant such a dedicated search,'' said Charlotte.

''Adam raised him from a foal,'' explained Lord Melbourne. ''I promised I would keep the horse safe until he returned.''

Emma's opinion of the earl greatly improved. She was wrong about his valuing the horse more than his brother; it was only because of a promise to Adam that Lord Melbourne had been searching so assiduously while his brother's fate was still in question.

''My frustration has been high since Adam's disappearance,'' the earl admitted. ''I couldn't travel to the Continent to search for him myself because I have no heir. If anything had happened to me, and if Adam had truly been lost, then the estate would go to a cousin. I couldn't chance having my mother turned out of her home.''

Emma was pleased that her poor thoughts of the earl concerning his brother were unwarranted; however, she did not know if it was enough to overcome her anger at how he had treated her. "So you've poured your energies into searching for Gala-had," she said.

"Without much success," he replied. "But at least Adam is home; perhaps he will forgive me for losing Galahad."

"Galahad was stolen, not lost," Emma reminded him. "I'm sure your brother will not blame you for that. And there is a good chance you may still find him, my lord."

"I'm not ready to give up on recovering him just yet. I haven't told Adam that he's missing. I hope to find Galahad before he thinks to ask."

Emma would have liked to see him find the horse before she left, but since they were planning to leave immediately after the dance, it seemed unlikely.

Lord Melbourne assumed he made the appropriate replies during the remainder of supper, even though his thoughts were on the woman by his side. She had readily admitted that Adam was not her husband, but she could do no less. Would Emma have continued to insist she was wed to his brother if Adam had not returned? Then there was Albert Nestor. Had she truly avoided his touch as she claimed? Or had her show of outrage been for his benefit?

He wondered if he would ever know the answers. And, if he did, whether it would change his thoughts of Emma.

Lord Melbourne's prediction proved right about Adam. Two days later he was in the drawing room, his leg propped up on a stool with a cushion beneath it.

The countess was still fussing about him when Emma, Charlotte, and Laura entered the room, and did not immediately see them.

"Come in," invited Adam, as they hesitated at the doorway.

"We would not like to intrude," said Emma.

"You could never be an intrusion," replied Adam, shameless in his flattery.

"Oh, my, what dreadful manners you must think we have," said the countess. "I have ignored you these past two days and now to leave you standing at the door."

"Don't give it a thought. We're too happy that your son is back to stand on ceremony," said Emma.

"Adam, this is Miss Emma Randolph, her sister, Miss Charlotte Randolph, and their companion, Miss Laura Seger," said the countess. "They are visiting with us for a time."

Adam Tremayne was a more angelic version of Lord Melbourne, and Emma suspected he shamelessly used it to his advantage. His hair was a very pale blond with a slight curl to it. Light blue eyes were filled with devilment, and were nowhere near as intense as his brother's gaze. He had a gaunt look about him, no doubt due to his sickness, but a few weeks of cook's meals would take care of that.

Adam looked pleased at his situation. "Ah. How much luckier can a man be than to return from war and have such lovely ladies staying beneath his own roof."

"Adam," reprimanded the countess. "You have not yet learned to govern your tongue, I see."

"Forgive me," said Adam. "I meant no disrespect. I have not been in the company of ladies of quality for months, and my manners have gone begging."

"There is no need to apologize," said Emma. "We accept your compliments in the spirit they were given."

"Sit with me awhile," invited Adam.

"Yes, please do," added the countess. "I'm certain Adam is ready for some fresh conversation and faces."

"You know I never get tired of you or Richard," said Adam, reaching out to squeeze her hand.

Lady Melbourne looked happier than Emma thought possible. During the time they had spent with the countess, Emma had grown quite fond of her, and she rejoiced in her son's return. However, she couldn't help but wonder why luck had not elected to return her husband as well.

"My mother told me about the locket," said Adam. "I want to thank you for its return. It was the one thing I regretted losing most."

"I was glad to return it to its rightful owner," replied Emma. "I never would have taken it had I known it was not Richard's to give. I still do not know how he came to possess it."

"I lost it in battle," revealed Adam. "I had been shot and was unconscious for some time. I lay on the battlefield overnight and was fortunate to be found the next day. I remember coming to at one point to find someone searching my pockets. Whoever it was must have taken the locket and everything else of value I carried."

"How terrible," exclaimed Charlotte.

"But common," replied Adam. "After every battle you can see the human vultures stealing from the dead and wounded. I'm not accusing your husband of stealing from me," Adam said to Emma. "But the people who *do* dispose of whatever they pilfer to anyone willing to buy or trade. If it's of good enough quality, a shop owner will take it off their hands for the right price."

"I'm afraid that doesn't help you much, my dear," said the countess.

"At least I know that he probably bought it on one of his trips to France," answered Emma. "And it makes it all the more clear that my husband is not who he said he was."

"I'm sorry," said Laura, reaching over to give her a quick comforting touch on the hand.

"There is no need for you to be sorry. I'm the one who allowed myself to be taken in by Richard—or whoever he is. I only hope I come face-to-face with him once again," she said, clenching her fists in her lap.

"But he seemed so nice," remarked Charlotte, a puzzled frown marring her forehead.

"People are not always what they seem to be," said Lady Melbourne. "You must be wary in your acquaintances," she warned.

"But I still do not know how Richard knew so much about the Tremayne family," puzzled Emma. "Could he be someone you know? Perhaps someone you served with in the war?"

"We didn't have too much time to trade histories," said Adam. "We fought, and marched, and when we stopped we were too exhausted to do anything but eat and sleep. Oh, we talked a bit to be sure, but nothing as detailed as I'm told your husband knew about us."

Emma was sorry she had allowed her hopes to be raised; she was all the more disappointed now that Adam had put paid to them.

"I understand my mother thought for a time that I might have married you," commented Adam. "I can tell you if I were fortunate enough to win such a beautiful lady's hand, I would not use my brother's name, nor would I desert her," he teased.

"Gammon," responded Emma, knowing he was speaking nonsense, but finding her spirit reviving under his lighthearted bantering.

"Not in the least," he insisted. "Once you know me better, you'll see I never sink to flummery, particularly with enchanting women."

Emma laughed out loud at his absurd compliments.

Adam placed a hand over his heart and attempted to look injured by her levity. "I can see I haven't convinced you of my sincerity; you must stay longer to allow me to do so."

"We have already overstayed our visit. Our original intent was to rest a day or two at Lady Melbourne's kind invitation," said Emma.

"Nonsense, I am enjoying the company," responded the countess.

"There, that should diminish your fears," Adam declared. "My mother never says what she doesn't mean. I understand we are to have a dance; at least say you will stay until then."

"Lord Melbourne has already extracted my promise to do so, but I will honor it only if I am certain we are not intruding on your homecoming."

"You could never do that. As I mentioned, I haven't had the company of so many lovely ladies for months, and I'm loath to allow you to escape so easily."

"I do hope you will stay," said the countess, adding her plea to Adam's.

"All right," agreed Emma. "I shall keep my agreement with Lord Melbourne. We shall stay until after the dance."

"Good, I'm glad that's settled," said the countess.

Adam allowed his gaze to rest on Charlotte, who was looking

lovely in a morning gown of white French muslin figured with pink flowers.

"Miss Charlotte, do you find Melbourne Park too dull for your liking?"

"Not at all," said Charlotte, blushing at his attention. "I have spent a great deal of time walking in the park and reading to your mother. I've enjoyed it immensely."

Emma could not believe her ears. Charlotte had done nothing but complain since they had left home. Perhaps Laura was right; Charlotte might need only the company of an attractive young man to keep her mind from Albert. She prayed that would be the case.

"When I am better I will show you around the estate myself," promised Adam. "I know all the loveliest spots."

"It will be some time before you can ride," said Lady Melbourne.

"Not so long," answered Adam. "And there is the curricle. I will take Miss Charlotte for a drive in that if I cannot ride."

"We cannot remain much longer," warned Emma, sorry to remind him when he and Charlotte were looking so pleased with themselves.

"You have promised to stay until after the dance," he reminded her. "We shall discuss it again then."

One thing she had to give them, thought Emma; the Tremayne men were a stubborn lot.

"Was the battle so terrible?" Charlotte asked, her expression full of sympathy.

"Charlotte! You should not ask such a personal question," said Laura. "It is sure to bring back dreadful memories that are better left forgotten."

"There's no harm done," said Adam. "It may sound odd, but I find it helps to talk about what happened."

"Would you tell me about it?" said Charlotte with more compassion in her expression than Emma had ever seen her exhibit.

Adam looked to Emma, who nodded her permission.

Chapter Nine

"It happened at Orthez," he began. "A town on the Gave du Pau River in France. It's said there were thirty-six thousand men concentrated there to keep us from crossing; I had no opportunity to count." He shifted in his seat. Lady Melbourne began to rise, but he motioned her back into her chair, and settled his foot more comfortably on the pillow.

"We were but seven thousand strong, but Wellington did not hesitate to act. He divided our force and sent two divisions to cross the river above Orthez. The remainder was sent to the west of the town. When the first assault failed, we renewed it elsewhere, and the fighting became fierce.

"The crowning blow was dealt by the 1st Battalion of the 52nd Light Infantry. They were deployed at a critical moment and, supported by sharpshooters, drove up a hill in a storm of bullets with review precision. I believe it was the most majestic advance I have ever seen," said Adam, his eyes focused on a battle none of them could see. "We fought for six hours and I have never been more proud of my countrymen.

"The French suffered at least four thousand casualties, and we took over thirteen hundred prisoners." He grinned. "It's said they lost as many more from desertion."

"When . . . when were you wounded?" asked Charlotte.

"Charlotte, that is enough," said Emma.

Adam looked offended. "You mean you would stand in the way of allowing me to be a hero, Miss Randolph?"

"I don't think anyone could do that," said Lord Melbourne, strolling into the room to join them.

"Ah, I knew my brother would arrive in time to put a damper on my story."

"Not at all. I only want to see that you do not set yourself above Wellington."

"To answer your question, Miss Charlotte," he said, ignoring his brother's teasing, "it was during the last charge. Bullets were thick, and I was unfortunate enough to get in the way of two of them. One struck my upper arm and did little damage; the other hit my leg."

Charlotte's dark brown eyes were riveted on Adam, her hands clasped tightly in her lap.

"I think I could have still made it back to safety, but my horse was shot out from under me. I received a blow on the head—I don't know how—and that's all I remember until after the battle was over."

"And that's when the locket was stolen," said Lord Melbourne.

"Right. It was almost dark when I finally regained consciousness. Someone was going through my pockets, but I was too weak to object."

"And a good thing too," said Lord Melbourne. "He might have finished what the French soldiers began."

"He wouldn't have," gasped Charlotte.

"Yes, he would," said Adam. "You have no idea what war does to men."

"And women and children," added Lady Melbourne.

Adam nodded in agreement. "No one escapes the horror. But this man had no thought for anything but his own good. After he had emptied my pockets, the scoundrel even stole my Hessians," he grumbled.

Lord Melbourne laughed. "Leave it to my brother to have

been shot twice, hit on the head, and left for dead, only to worry about his boots being stolen.''

Adam grinned in return. "At the time, it was the final insult."

"Lord Melbourne said you were exceedingly ill after being wounded," said Charlotte, her face filled with sympathy.

"That is so," Adam agreed. "I ran a fever, and woke up unable to remember who I was. The doctor said it wasn't an uncommon result, and not to worry. But it was disconcerting not to be able to even recall my own name."

"But what did you do?" asked Charlotte.

"There was nothing I could do," replied Adam, "except to be patient."

"And he has never been any good at that," added Lord Melbourne.

"And I'm afraid I wasn't this time either, particularly after I began to recover physically. Then, bit by bit, pieces of my memory began returning. It was a happy day, indeed, when I recalled my name."

"If you had only written us then," said Lady Melbourne.

"I would probably have gotten here before my letter," replied Adam. "My only thought was to get home as soon as possible."

"Well, I think you were exceedingly brave," said Charlotte.

"I can see you're a most intelligent young lady," remarked Adam, bringing a blush to her face.

"Don't let Adam tease you so," said Lord Melbourne.

"I meant every word," objected Adam. "Pay him no heed, Miss Charlotte."

"You have been ill, Mr. Tremayne, perhaps you're rambling again," Charlotte replied mischievously.

"Miss Charlotte," he said, pretending to be offended, "I will have you know, even at the height of my fever, I never rambled. I am told I quoted Shakespeare, shared my insightful views on politics and the state of the economy, but I always had my wits about me."

"You're doing it up a bit too brown for the ladies to believe," said Lord Melbourne, laughing at his younger brother's exaggerations.

Adam looked hurt. "You see what I must deal with," he said, appealing to Charlotte. "Every word I say is the truth, yet my own brother doubts it."

Charlotte put a hand to her mouth, but was unable to hide her smile.

Adam looked pleased that he had amused her. "I understand you and my mother have been sharing novels."

"It is something we both enjoy above all things," Charlotte admitted.

"Then perhaps you will read to me some day."

"I should be happy to," agreed Charlotte, the blush still lingering on her cheeks.

"Tomorrow will be soon enough to begin," said Lady Melbourne studying her son's face. "Adam, don't you think you should rest for a while?"

"I am sick to death of resting," replied Adam with a grimace. "I haven't been up and around for months."

"And you shouldn't be now by the looks of you," said the countess.

"Perhaps I am a bit tired," he admitted.

Lady Melbourne motioned to Roland, and two footmen appeared to help Adam to his room.

"Ladies, I look forward to seeing you later," said Adam as he struggled to his feet. "And may I ask a favor of you all?"

"Anything," replied Emma.

"Could we dispense with formality? I would much prefer to be called Adam."

"Do not be too forward," warned Lord Melbourne.

"It's quite all right," said Emma. She was in sympathy with Adam, and his request was not an outrageous one considering the circumstances. "I think we would feel comfortable being on a first-name basis with Mr. Tremayne—I mean, Adam." She looked toward Laura and Charlotte, and they nodded their approval.

"Good. It is settled then." He looked very pleased with himself as he turned to go through the door.

Lady Melbourne's gaze followed her son as he was helped from the room. "I shall never doubt miracles," she said, settling into a chair. "I don't know whether I'll ever let him out of my sight again."

"I'm so happy for you," said Emma.

"Thank you, my dear. I hope your dilemma will have the fortunate outcome that mine has had."

Emma smiled, but doubted that she would be as happy as the countess. Lord Melbourne would soon be out of her life no matter whether she found her husband, or whether he went missing forever.

"Come along, Adam," pleaded Lady Melbourne. "I have gone to a great deal of trouble to get a Bath chair for you. At the very least, try it out.

Adam maneuvered the front steps with the help of his brother, and settled himself in the chair. "I have no need for such a thing as a chair with wheels," he grumbled. "I'll soon be up and able to get around on my own."

"I'm sure you will, dear," the countess agreed, "but until then this will be just the thing to allow you to get around a little easier. John will push you down the drive and you'll see that it's very comfortable indeed."

Adam grinned roguishly at the company gathered on the front steps to watch his first ride in the chair. "I will not go alone."

"Then we shall all accompany you," said Charlotte, skipping down the steps.

"Not until you have your bonnet," said Laura.

It took a few minutes for the ladies to fetch their bonnets and parasols, but they were soon on their way. They made quite a procession that afternoon. Adam led the way with the footman pushing his chair. Charlotte and Laura were on either side, teasing him about riding in comfort while they walked, and Emma and the earl followed along behind.

Lord Melbourne had offered her his arm and, after a moment's hesitation, Emma placed her hand on it. While it was true that his suspicion of her had lessened considerably after Adam came home and he found she was neither married to him, nor had stolen the locket, Emma was certain he continued to harbor doubts about her.

"Are you still determined to leave after the dance?" asked Lord Melbourne, looking at Emma. Her face was partly obscured by a straw bonnet, tied beneath her chin with a green ribbon, but he could see the pert tilt to her nose, the fullness of her lips, and the determined angle of her chin. He remembered how soft her lips had felt, how her body had fit itself to his, and the desire to repeat that pleasurable experience made him want to stop in the middle of the drive and pull her into his arms.

He wondered again about her husband. She had not mentioned love when she had talked of him, only the convenience his protection would offer. Did she yearn for him, or did she want to find him merely to sever the connection? The chance of her being able to do so was slim indeed, but if he had learned nothing more, he knew how stubborn Emma could be.

Then there was her cousin, Albert Nestor. Lord Melbourne did not like to remember the man reaching out for Emma, but he could not ignore the fact that he had done so. The earl only had Emma's word that she had avoided his touch.

Yes, despite Adam's return, there was much to be explained. How, for example, had Emma's phantom husband come to possess the locket, and how did he know so much about the Tremayne family? Was Emma's story of her marriage the truth, or was she involved in a scheme to somehow defraud him?

He had not questioned either Laura or Charlotte. They could be innocent of Emma's intent. Charlotte did not seem to have a serious thought in her head, and would probably follow Emma's lead without question. Laura had been gone for several years, and might not be mindful of the changes time had wrought in her former charges.

Lord Melbourne had asked his man of business to find out what he could about the man who called himself Richard Tremayne, and the woman who vowed she came from such an honorable family. He hoped the report he received would verify her claims. Until then he would keep his doubts to himself and attempt to delay her until he knew more.

"I cannot linger any longer," said Emma. "My husband's trail grows colder by the minute, and I've not yet found any indication of his direction." Emma's frustration was mirrored in her voice.

He laid a detaining hand on her arm, and turned her to face him. "Miss Randolph . . . Emma," he said. "You realize it's possible you may never see your husband again."

Emma met his eyes with a troubled green gaze. "My lord, I cannot allow myself to think that."

"You indicated you did not marry for love," he said softly, wondering if he had assumed something that wasn't true.

A flush appeared along the ridge of Emma's cheekbones, and she dropped her gaze from his. "It's true, ours was not a love match," she agreed, "but we are nonetheless wed."

"Are you certain of that?" he asked, willing her to look at him again.

"You did not consummate the marriage, did you?"

The flush on Emma's face increased. "My lord!" she said, shocked that he would ask her such a personal question.

"If you didn't," he continued, as if they were discussing the weather, "then there is a chance for an annulment. And if that is not enough, what if his name is not Richard Tremayne? What then? I think there would be enough to question the legality of your union."

A mixture of alarm and hope filled Emma. Would an unconsummated marriage or a false name be enough to invalidate the ceremony? Could her problem be solved that easily? But, in an instant, hopelessness overcame her again. If she could not find the man, how could she prove what his name was or wasn't? It seemed as if she were traveling in an endless circle with no hope of escape.

"I will know nothing until I locate him," she replied dispiritedly, pulling from his grasp and beginning to walk down the drive again. "That is why I must leave here and continue my search."

"And you think to find him in London?"

"It's as good a place as any to begin. Earlier you had mentioned the Bow Street Runners. I'm considering hiring them to investigate; perhaps they can succeed where I have failed.''

Lord Melbourne still could not like her plan of leaving in the dead of night. ''Then let me escort you,'' he suggested. ''We will take as many outriders as you need to feel safe. I promise you'll arrive in London without so much as a glimpse of your cousin.''

''And what then, my lord? Will you stay and guard us?'' she asked. ''I think not. You have your own life to live. I must learn to deal with Albert. You may regard it cowardly for me to run from him, but for the time being, I consider it is the best for us.''

Emma had not confided Albert's pursuit of her sister, nor her other suspicions of him to the earl. So she could not explain that she hoped to keep Charlotte away from Albert until her attraction to him vanished, and they could safely return home.

''I don't think you a coward at all,'' protested Lord Melbourne. ''You have accepted full responsibility for yourself, your sister, and your property; that is not an easy feat.''

Emma could not help but be pleased with his praise. ''Thank you. But I would still not feel comfortable taking you away from your own family, particularly since your brother has returned.''

''Adam would be the first to demand I assist you if possible.'' Lord Melbourne could not explain why he was so reluctant to let Emma go. It was true, their kiss had unsettled him, had left something unfinished between them, but nothing more could come of it since Emma considered herself a married woman who, the earl believed, took her vows seriously. Perhaps it was mere curiosity on his part as to what had happened to her husband, and whether she was truly innocent of any planned wrongdoing against him.

''I can believe that,'' she said, smiling fondly at the group walking ahead of them. ''He is an extraordinary young man to have come through such an experience with the positive outlook he holds.''

''He seems to be nearly the same as when he left,'' disclosed Lord Melbourne. ''Yet sometimes I see a look in his eyes that has never been there before. I think it impossible to experience the horrors of war and be unchanged. However, he hides whatever doubts he has about man now that he has seen him at his worst, and presents a normal appearance.''

"It is for his mother's benefit," judged Emma.

"Yes, she would be devastated if she learned the truth of his ordeal. He has told me some, but has made me promise never to repeat it in her presence.''

"It would do no good to tell her now," said Emma.

"Only ruin her happiness," agreed the earl. "And neither Adam nor I want that. She suffered enough while he was missing.''

They walked on in silence for a short time, each occupied with their individual reflections; neither knowing that they were consumed by thoughts of one another.

Lord Melbourne finally realized they had not spoken for some time. Normally, he would have felt compelled to converse nonstop with a woman, and she with him. However, he was entirely comfortable walking in silence with Emma, enjoying the afternoon outdoors.

She looked the essence of summer in a white muslin dress embroidered with yellow flowers and trimmed with green ribbons.

"We've become far too solemn, Miss Randolph.''

"And that would never do, would it, my lord?" she answered, giving him the full benefit of her smile.

"No, it would not," he agreed, suddenly unable to take his eyes from her. His thoughts were in a jumble, and he wondered whether he was suffering some sort of seizure. But through all his confusion, one concept remained clear. He wanted this woman more than any other he had met in his lifetime. He knew she was married, and that she was most likely running a rig on him, but it didn't seem to matter to his mind, or his heart, or to whatever part of his body was directing his emotions at the moment.

"I'm sorry," he said, realizing that Emma was staring at him, a puzzled look in her eyes. "I'm afraid you caught me wool-gathering," he apologized.

"A sorry indication of my ability at scintillating conversation."

Lord Melbourne struggled to recover his senses lest he appear the veriest fledgling in the throes of his first *tendre*. "Not at all, Miss Randolph. I was merely taking advantage of the moment to admire what a lovely picture you make in the afternoon light." He spoke the compliment lightly, but meant every word.

"You are doing it up a bit too brown," laughed Emma. "We have been at odds too often for me to believe such fustian."

The earl was relieved she did not take him seriously. If she knew how vulnerable he was to her charms at that moment, she would no doubt press her advantage if she had set her sights to do so.

If he were foolish enough to pursue Miss Randolph, he was certain the alliance would not be a simple one. First, there was the matter of her husband, who could be waiting for him to be drawn into her net before he arrived, enraged at Lord Melbourne for ruining his wife. Of course, he would probably be willing to forget his anger for enough money.

Second was his current reaction to Emma. He could no longer deny that she appealed to him on every level, and until that attraction wore off, he would do well to hold her at arm's length. If he did not contain his feelings, he might find himself doing whatever it took to have her. He was less concerned that his pockets would be the lighter for it than the condition his heart would be in once they were finished.

No, best to stay with a mistress who knew her place, and expected nothing more from him than a visit now and then. She could be sent on her way with an appropriate parting gift when boredom set in, and there would be no unfavorable repercussions afterwards.

"You are silent too long again, my lord. I must indeed be sadly lacking in conversation skills. Laura will be appalled that she did not teach me better."

"Miss Seger has nothing for which to apologize. The fault lies with me," he admitted.

"You have no need to use flattery," said Emma. "I know what is bothering you."

Lord Melbourne had always believed he could conceal his interest in a woman if he so desired, but then he had never wanted a woman as much as he did Emma. He would be in an extremely susceptible position if Miss Randolph could read his thoughts.

"You do?" Rhetoric failed him except for the rudimentary return.

"Yes, I do, and you have no need to hide your emotions, particularly when we are alone."

Dammit! How could she have discovered his feelings so quickly when he had only recognized them moments ago? He did not know whether to deny his desire and spend countless sleepless nights, or admit to his passion, enjoy their time together, and pay the price when it was over.

"I know you're worried about Galahad," said Emma. "But I'm convinced that you'll find him before long. And if you shouldn't, I'm certain Adam will not blame you for his disappearance."

Lord Melbourne had already bowed to his fate and was envisioning long evenings spent in intimate moments with Emma. Her statement jerked him out of his fantasy with a suddenness that again nearly robbed him of speech. "I . . . er . . . I appreciate your confidence in me, Miss Randolph. I hope I'm able to live up to it."

"You will, my lord. You have had a great deal of worry lately, or I'm sure your confidence would not be at such a low ebb."

"You call my brother by his first name. Could you not grant me the same favor?"

"It would be awkward for me to call you Richard," she said.

Lord Melbourne was disappointed that he would not hear his name fall from her lips, but he understood her difficulty. Each time she said his name, she would think of her husband. The earl was not a happy man.

"Now, let us hurry on," said Emma, tugging at his arm. "The others are too far ahead of us."

Lord Melbourne matched his stride to hers, wondering

whether to be amused at the past few minutes or take it as a warning to avoid Miss Randolph at all costs. But he did not have time to come to a decision, for when they came in view of the rest of the group, Albert Nestor was in the middle of the drive, blocking their way.

"We have received a great surprise," said Laura, as Emma and Lord Melbourne joined them. "Mr. Nestor is here."

"Yes, I can see," replied Emma, wondering why Albert had chosen to reappear when she had warned him away. It was most probably his way of proving she could not control his actions.

"You didn't tell us you had spoken to him," charged Charlotte, her color high.

"It slipped my mind," said Emma.

"How could it?" Charlotte asked, as if Albert's appearance ranked along with the Prince Regent's arrival.

"I only remember important events," Emma said in a disdainful tone.

A smile twisted Albert's face at Emma's reply. "I was just inquiring after your well-being, Cousin Emma, but I can see for myself that you've fully recovered from your accident."

"Which accident is that?" she asked sweetly.

"Why, your fall, of course," he answered, beginning to toy with the numerous watch fobs stretched across his waistcoat.

"Then I'm afraid you're somewhat behind on the news." Emma watched closely to see whether she could read anything from his expression.

"You mean something else has befallen you?" he asked.

Albert's acting was just as inadequate as everything else he attempted. In Emma's view, the falseness of his reaction proved beyond all doubt that he was the one who had lain in wait to end her life.

"A poacher's shot came too close," she replied shortly.

"You are surely more prone to mishaps than anyone I know," he declared.

"I'm not convinced it was an accident," growled the earl.

He did not like Nestor's attitude. Whenever he was in the man's presence, he could believe everything Emma had said about him. It took no stretch of the imagination to see Albert waiting in the woods to fire the shot. Emma had evidently not told her cousin she was married; and if he was as desperate as Emma said, he might attempt to frighten her, then offer her protection by suggesting they wed.

Just the thought of Emma with Albert Nestor stirred Lord Melbourne's anger even more, and he exercised considerable will curbing his impulse to pull Nestor from his horse and demand if he knew anything about the deed.

Emma heard Laura's indrawn breath and knew she would have some explaining to do once they were private.

"No," replied Albert in astonishment. "Who could want to cause you harm?" he asked, then went on before she could answer. "You must be more careful."

"I did not expect to be shot at on an ordinary ride," said Emma.

Lord Melbourne placed his hand over Emma's, which still rested in the crook of his arm. The gesture was not lost on Nestor, and the earl was pleased to see a frown settle on his face.

Albert started to dismount, then thought better of it and remained on his mount. "All the more reason to allow me to escort you home. I've told you women shouldn't be traveling alone; it isn't safe."

"You may rest easy on that account," responded Lord Melbourne. "The ladies will be safe under my protection."

"It does not seem so," challenged Nestor.

"I was unaware there was any danger," replied the earl, fixing a steely gaze on the man. "But now that I'm apprised of the situation, I'll be on guard against further mishaps."

"I would hope so," said Nestor. "If anything should happen to Cousin Charlotte I hold you responsible." He allowed his gaze to rest on the young woman until she blushed furiously. "And, of course, Cousin Emma, too," he added.

"Your concern is unneeded," said Emma. "We are perfectly capable of directing our own lives, and intend to continue to do so. I would suggest you leave us to determine our own fate and go on about your business." Anyone else receiving such a sharp set-down would have made haste to depart; however, Nestor was too thick-skinned to be affected.

"Your fate is my business," insisted Nestor, "and I fully intend to see you safely home." He had turned his horse and urged it into a trot before anyone could reply.

"Oh, that man is the . . . the most . . . ." Emma was at loss for an adequate description of Albert that could be uttered in mixed company.

"He is only concerned for us," spoke up Charlotte, a slight flush remaining on her cheeks.

Emma did not intend to discuss their private business in front of Lord Melbourne and Adam, so she kept her thoughts to herself. She would speak to Charlotte later.

Adam had followed the entire exchange with unconcealed interest. His attention had fixed on Charlotte and her reaction to Albert Nestor. "Your cousin seems to be a determined man," he said to her.

"He only wants what is best for us," insisted Charlotte.

"I'm sure he does," said Adam soothingly, continuing to watch her closely. The rest of the party might be blind to what was going on; but if he was any judge, Charlotte felt more than mere cousinly affection for Nestor.

"You've had enough fresh air for today," said Lord Melbourne to Adam. "Perhaps we should start back. It looks as if it's going to rain any minute."

Emma had been so involved with Albert she had been unaware of the gathering clouds. The afternoon, which had begun so sunny, had grown gloomy. The burly footman turned the Bath chair and the small procession began the walk back to the house.

Charlotte followed Emma into her room when they returned from their walk. "Why didn't you tell us you had talked to Albert?" she demanded.

"Charlotte, you must learn to close doors unless you want

the whole world to know your business,'' reprimanded Laura, following her into the room, and shutting the door firmly behind her.

"Albert called on me,'' replied Emma. "We had a private conversation and he left. There was nothing to tell.''

"You told him he couldn't see me, didn't you?''

"He knew that months ago, but it hasn't stopped him from following us.''

"You have no right to treat me like a child.''

"I do as long as you behave like one,'' shot back Emma. She caught a look of disapproval from Laura, and realized she was comporting herself almost as childishly as Charlotte.

"Charlotte, you don't know the real Albert.''

"Yes, I do.''

"You don't,'' Emma insisted gently. "He's hiding behind a facade, and turning you against your own family.''

"Albert is my family, too, and I would much rather be with him. At least he understands that I'm an adult.'' Charlotte ended on a sob as she turned and ran out of the room.

Chapter Ten

"I wonder whether she will ever learn to shut the door behind her," remarked Laura calmly, going to close the offending piece of oak.

"Are you going to ring a peal over me as well?" asked Emma with a sigh.

"Not for keeping Albert's visit a secret from Charlotte. And, if you remember, you never told me the content of your discussion."

"I'm sorry, Laura, it was an unintentional oversight."

"I'm not overset. Conversations between you and your cousin tend to be remarkably similar. It was probably no different from what I've heard numerous times before."

"You're right. It was just another tedious refrain of how he is going to take care of us."

"Did he tell you how he found us?"

"No, but it must have been sheer luck. The steward was the only one I told in case an emergency should arise, but he holds too low of an opinion of Albert to have passed the information along to him."

"Does he know that you're married?"

"No, and I don't intend to tell him. Can you imagine his

reaction if he knew that I had wed and had been deserted by my husband all in a matter of hours? Although it might keep the pompous oaf quiet for a time,'' she reflected, a mischievous grin on her face.

Laura smiled at the idea. ''There is the matter of the shot that I would like to discuss,'' she said, sitting in a pale green upholstered chair.

''Oh, Laura, must we?'' pleaded Emma.

''Yes, we must,'' the older woman responded firmly. ''You should have told me that Lord Melbourne wasn't convinced it was an accident.''

Emma didn't want to worry Laura just when she had nearly recovered from her illness. ''I'm certain it was a poacher's shot gone awry, but you know how men are. They see intrigue behind every little thing.''

''Being shot at is no little thing,'' argued Laura. ''Does the earl know who it might have been?''

''If he does, he didn't tell me. I'm certain there's nothing to worry about,'' Emma assured her.

''Promise you'll take extra precautions and won't go wandering about by yourself.''

''If it will make you rest easier, then I shall promise,'' said Emma, hoping Laura would drop the subject.

''Do you think I should try and talk to Charlotte?'' asked Laura, rising from her chair.

''I doubt anyone could talk any sense into her. She sees Albert as a white knight, and until he shows her his true worth, she will not change her mind.''

''I suppose you're right,'' agreed Laura, opening the door. ''Perhaps I'll just look in on her and see if she's all right.''

The door closed softly behind her, and Emma dropped into a chair, sighing in relief. It had been a demanding day, and it wasn't over yet.

''What is it between Miss Randolph and her cousin?'' asked Adam, while he and the earl were waiting for the rest of the household to assemble before supper.

"What makes you think there's anything but cousinly concern between them?" Lord Melbourne replied.

"I'll admit to being injured in body, but there's nothing wrong with my mind," said Adam. "I would have to be dead in order to miss the sparks flying."

The earl grinned at his younger brother. It was good to hear him sounding like his old self. "I can only tell you what Miss Randolph has revealed to me. To be brief, Nestor thinks it's his place to oversee the Randolphs' life, particularly since there seems to be some money and an estate involved. If you get to know Miss Randolph better, you'll find she does not take kindly to anyone telling her what to do, let alone someone the caliber of Nestor."

Adam gave a low whistle. "I should say not. And Charlotte, does she agree?" he asked. "It seemed to me that she does not hold Nestor in the same contempt her sister does."

Lord Melbourne heard more than disinterested curiosity in Adam's voice. What a coil if they both succumbed to the charms of the Randolph sisters.

"It's possible, I suppose, that a young girl with little experience might hold a *tendre for* an older man," Richard said thoughtfully. "I don't think she's seen him at his worst, and refuses to believe any criticism of him."

"I've known men like him before, and he bears watching," warned Adam.

"I can't trust him myself," agreed the earl. "I hope he has enough sense to keep his distance from the ladies."

"Don't tell me you're taken with Emma," remarked Adam. "She's a married woman, no matter that she insists upon being called Miss Randolph."

"I remembered, I only wondered whether you did. Unless you intend to give her a slip of the shoulder," said Adam, watching as his brother moved restlessly to the window.

"In my own house, in front of my mother?" asked the earl, still staring out onto the park.

"A man in love will stoop to desperate measures."

"I'm not in love," barked Lord Melbourne, irritated that Adam was hitting so close to what was bothering him. "And if I was, I'd choose someone other than a married woman of dubious character."

"No need to get on your high ropes with me," said Adam, in an amused voice. "Emma is a dashed attractive woman; couldn't blame you if you took a fancy to her."

"And I suppose you're totally uninterested in Charlotte?" charged the earl.

"Never said I was or wasn't. Must admit though, she's as pretty as her sister, in her own way."

"There's only one problem. It would seem she's enamored of her cousin."

"A childish admiration," replied Adam, waving it aside with a flick of his hand. "Most young girls experience one or two inappropriate attachments before they mature."

"Since when have you become an expert on immature young ladies?" asked the earl, amusement curling his lips.

"I'm not completely without experience. If you find that hard to believe, just look back on what you were doing at my age."

Lord Melbourne took a moment to do just that. "I shudder to think you have followed in my footsteps."

They were still laughing when their mother entered the room. "What are you up to now?" she asked, happy to see her sons together again.

"Merely a brotherly joke," responded the earl, giving his mother a kiss on the cheek.

"You sound just as you used to before you got into trouble," said Lady Melbourne. "I hope you'll behave yourselves while we have guests in the house," she teased.

"You may rest assured we will be the very pattern card of good breeding," promised Adam.

"I don't expect the impossible," said Lady Melbourne smiling at him. "Merely that you conduct yourself in a reasonable manner."

Their conversation was cut short as Emma, Charlotte, Laura, and David Whitney entered the drawing room.

* * *

Lord Melbourne awoke before daylight the next morning. He had spent a restless night doing exactly what he was determined not to do: thinking of Emma.

After realizing, on their walk the previous afternoon, how much he desired her, Lord Melbourne had vowed to keep his distance from Emma until she was safely on her way out of his life. During dinner the night before, he had spent equal time in conversation with Laura and Emma. The subjects were common ones which left no room for personal involvement, and as the men were left to their port, he felt relieved that he had made it through dinner without becoming further involved in the Randolphs' problems.

Later, when he and Adam joined the ladies in the drawing room, he told himself he wasn't disappointed to find that Emma had already retired for the evening. But in the darkness of his own room, he could not avoid the truth: he had missed Emma's presence and—dammit!—he wanted her all the more.

Now, after barely closing his eyes, he was off on another chase after Galahad. He was convinced this one would prove no more successful than all the others, but he could not ignore even a small chance at recovering the horse.

He had finally told Adam what had happened to Galahad and, while his brother had attempted to take it in stride, the earl could see beneath his bravado to the disappointment lurking there.

When George brought him news of another possible sighting of the horse, Lord Melbourne was glad for the diversion. It would take him away from Emma for a moment, and allow him to get his mind in order. Perhaps after he checked out this sighting, he would take a short trip to Town. One of the Fashionably Impures would surely clear his mind of a woman with flashing hazel eyes and an independent nature.

* * *

Emma awoke feeling out of sorts and, for a short time, could not recall why. Then it all came back to her. An absolutely perfect stroll with Lord Melbourne the day before had been interrupted by the appearance of Albert.

He had attempted to be concerned about the shot that had been fired and solicitous of her well-being, but she had seen beneath his feigned anxiety. He wanted her out of the way, so that he could take advantage of Charlotte's attraction to him.

After that the day had gotten worse. While they were walking, Emma had thought she perceived a warming in Lord Melbourne's manner toward her. However, at supper he had treated her too much like a guest for her liking. Her spirits had been so dampened by the day that she had excused herself and retired before the men rejoined them. She could not tolerate any more of his lordship's courteous treatment.

Emma stood at the window watching the faint blush of morning touch the sky. A nearly inaudible sound drew her attention, and a lone rider rode down the drive. The man and the horse made a dark silhouette in the dim morning light, but she needed nothing more to tell her it was Lord Melbourne. She watched until he was out of sight, then turned with a sigh and sat on the side of her bed.

Emma wondered if and when he would return. He had been so cool to her last night that she knew he was having doubts about her again. She considered telling him the entire story the next time she saw him, but just as quickly decided against it. He would probably not believe her; not too many would. And even if he did, she would not feel right about dragging him into the midst of her problems.

She was a married woman, and should be depending upon her husband rather than a stranger. Her anger returned at the man who had promised to protect her, then had left her to confront Albert alone. She yearned to see him just one more time to hear an explanation of his actions if he had one.

"Oh, Papa, what a mess I have made of everything," she whispered. Lying back upon the bed, she curled into a ball seeking comfort that could not be had.

* * *

"Have you heard anything from your man of business about Richard?" Laura and Emma were sitting embroidering the morning after Lord Melbourne had left on his latest search for Galahad.

While Emma might successfully hide her unhappiness behind a normal demeanor from most people, it was difficult to fool Laura. She had been with the Randolphs too long not to know something was bothering Emma. Laura wondered whether she might have received some bad news from Mr. Watterson in London.

"He only wrote me to say he was pursuing the matter, and would let me know as soon as he came across something definite," replied Emma, never taking her eyes from the needle-work she held.

"You must not let yourself lose hope," urged Laura.

"It is so difficult," complained Emma, sorting through a basket of silk thread, holding up several shades of green to compare. "I have tried, Laura, you know I have; but I don't think I can continue with this uncertainty much longer. Yet, what can I do? To think that I may never know what happened to Richard, to know who he really was or why he married me, seems more than I can bear at times. Then I remember Charlotte, and that I must protect her from Albert, and I know I must not weaken."

"It is early days yet. Mr. Watterson may be able to clear everything up for you."

"I hope so," replied Emma with a heavy sigh, selecting a dark green shade and replacing the other silk threads in the basket.

"And you may not need to worry about Albert much longer." Laura nodded toward the window where they could see Adam sitting in the sun on the terrace. Charlotte sat nearby, reading aloud to him.

"I doubt it's her choice of reading material that is holding his attention so completely," judged Laura.

"But would Lord Melbourne approve if they made a match?" mused Emma.

"He would have no choice; Adam is well above his majority. And I understand that he is not dependent upon Lord Melbourne for a living."

"How do you know that?" asked Emma.

"Lady Melbourne mentioned it when we were talking one morning. His grandfather left him well fixed. I also know she wants nothing more than both her sons to settle down and present her with some grandchildren."

"Adam may fulfill her wish," said Emma, "but it looks as if it will be a long wait before the earl fathers an heir for Melbourne Park."

"I'm not so sure," replied Laura, knotting and cutting off a thread, then studying her workmanship. "Lady Melbourne says he was greatly concerned when Adam was missing. He realized that if something happened to him without an heir, Melbourne Park would pass out of their hands. I don't think he will allow the situation to stand as it is for much longer. He's much too responsible for that."

"Did . . . did Lady Melbourne mention a lady?"

"Several," declared Laura. "She says he's quite sought after in London, and I can see why. I imagine any number of mamas have set their sights on him for their daughters."

Emma frowned at the image of the earl being pursued by a bevy of lovely young girls. "He's managed to elude them so far."

"Because he wanted to," Laura agreed. "But if he's in the frame of mind to be married, he will no doubt choose the best of the lot."

"You sound as if he's picking an apple," grumbled Emma, jerking impatiently at her tangled thread.

"In a manner of speaking he is. He will select one of the best stock, with the fewest blemishes. Then he will set about furnishing enough heirs to ensure the Tremayne line for generations to come." Laura seemed very pleased with her pronouncement.

"I'm not at all interested in Lord Melbourne's progeny," Emma said crossly, pulling at the thread that refused to unsnarl.

"Here, let me," offered Laura, taking the embroidery out of Emma's hands. "You must admit, though, that Charlotte switching her affections to Adam would solve a great problem for you."

"Yes, it would, and I find nothing objectionable with Adam. However, I doubt whether Charlotte will give up her interest in Albert so easily. She's not only stubborn, but hates to admit she's wrong. I think she'll continue mooning about after him because she feels committed, and will not admit that I am right."

"Well, I'm going to do all I can to encourage the match. She could not find a better husband, no matter how many seasons she spent in London," said Laura, pulling the last tangle from the thread and handing the embroidery back to Emma.

Nodding her thanks, Emma began plying her needle again. "It would be a great relief," she acknowledged. "Then Albert would have no reason to hang about, and perhaps life would go back to normal."

"I don't remember what 'normal' is," teased Laura, "but I don't think things will ever be as they were."

"Laura," said Emma, after a small pause. "Do you . . . I mean, I've noticed you and Mr. Whitney spend a great deal of time together."

"He's a very interesting man," Laura answered noncommittally.

"How interesting?" pursued Emma, tangling her thread again.

Laura reached out for the embroidery and Emma willingly gave it up. "If you're asking me how I feel about him, I like him better than any gentleman I've met," Laura revealed.

"Has he . . . are you . . . ?"

"Has he offered for me yet? No, he hasn't. But if he did, I would be very tempted to accept."

"And you must do so," insisted Emma. "Don't let any

responsibility toward us keep you from finding happiness,'' she urged.

"I wouldn't leave you to struggle with all your current problems," said Laura. "But I have faith that they'll all work out in a very short time."

"I wish I had your confidence," said Emma, taking her embroidery and immediately snarling the thread for the third time in a very short interval.

"It's time to ring for tea," said Laura, removing the embroidery from Emma's hands and placing it in the basket.

Charlotte looked over the top of her book at Adam sitting in the sun with his eyes closed. "Would you like me to stop?" she asked.

"No, please continue. Listening to your voice is most soothing," said Adam, without opening his eyes.

"I didn't know whether you were attending; you looked as if you were asleep."

Adam's lids lifted, and his gaze immediately settled on her. "I would never be so ill-bred as to fall asleep while you were reading," he said, a lazy smile curving his lips.

Charlotte experienced an odd feeling inside when Adam looked at her. She had never felt it before, but it was a distinctly disturbing sensation. She wanted to reach out and touch him, but knew it would be considered too forward; he might think her fast.

"What is it?"

"Nothing," she answered quickly. "I was merely wondering whether we had been out here too long."

"My mother insists that rest and fresh air is the best medicine. I'm certain she's extremely grateful that you're keeping me company."

Charlotte did not like to be thought of as a mere convenience. "But we are alone," she protested.

Adam laughed. "With all those windows," he said, waving toward the house. "There are more eyes watching us than if we were on the streets of London."

Charlotte was suddenly embarrassed. The women he knew probably didn't give a thought about being alone with a man, particularly in the middle of the day, on a terrace. She felt even more foolish when she remembered he was wounded and could not pursue her even if he had the desire.

She glanced at him again. His light blue eyes looked as if they could see exactly what she was thinking. It had been a mistake to strike up such a close friendship with Adam. Albert would not approve at all.

"I . . . I am tired of this book. I think I shall go search for another." She rose, ready to rush into the house away from his steady gaze.

"Don't go; let's talk for a while."

He smiled, and butterflies took control of her stomach. She settled back into her chair, unable to deny him. "What would you like to talk about?"

"You."

In the normal course of events, Charlotte would have been happy to chatter on about herself, but surprisingly enough she found herself unable to put a coherent thought together.

"I'm sure my life would be much too ordinary for your entertainment."

"I'm not merely looking for a diversion," he said. "I would like to get to know you better. My mother has probably told you everything about me, but I know nothing of your likes and dislikes."

"Oh, is that all you want to know?" said Charlotte, giving him a smile. "Well, let me think a moment . . . I like lively music, and I love to dance. I like my horse, and my dog, both of whom had to be left at home. My favorite color is blue, and I adore the peach tarts our cook makes. You already know that I love to read novels, as does your mother, although I'm willing to read whatever you choose." She paused to grab a quick breath. "Is that enough for you?"

"Not nearly, but it will do as a beginning. You did not mention a beau. Surely you have many admirers."

"There is not an overabundance of gentlemen at home," admitted. "And those who are there do not interest me."

"And in London?"

"We have been in mourning for my father, so I have not had my come-out yet. I expect I will next spring, but I am not looking forward to it. I will be on display, and everyone will be a stranger to me."

"I could be there to help you through it if you like," Adam assured her.

"Oh, would you? It would be wonderful to see a familiar face."

"My face will be much more than familiar by then," he promised. If it was true that Albert Nestor was a contender for Charlotte, then Adam was determined to make certain he would not easily win her.

When Lord Melbourne returned two days later, preparations for the dance had begun. A bevy of servants were cleaning and dusting and shining everything in sight. Lord Melbourne walked directly through the entrance hall for he knew one of them would begin polishing his Hessians if he paused for a fraction of a moment.

He found his mother enjoying a bit of solitude in her small sitting room. "You seem to have everything well in hand," he said, kissing her cheek and taking a seat across from her.

"I've had all the help I could want. Emma and Laura, and even Charlotte, have insisted upon doing practically everything."

"I'm glad it hasn't proven too much for you."

"I'm not the invalid," objected Lady Melbourne. "Adam is, but I don't think that will last for long."

"He would be better if Galahad hadn't gone missing," said Lord Melbourne glumly.

"I take it you weren't successful in finding the horse."

"It was another dead end," he admitted.

"You must stop blaming yourself," said Lady Melbourne. "It was no more your fault than mine that Galahad was stolen."

"Perhaps I wouldn't feel so guilty if I hadn't promised Adam

I would keep him safe. He didn't rail at me when I told him about it, but I would have felt better had he done so.''

"Adam may be unhappy about losing the horse, but I can't believe he blames you any more than I do.''

"At any rate, I may have to learn to live with my guilt, for it doesn't seem as if I'm going to be successful in finding Galahad.'' Lord Melbourne leaned his head back against the chair and closed his eyes.

"You look tired,'' said Lady Melbourne. "Why don't you try to rest before dinner?''

"I just might do that,'' he said, opening his eyes and sitting up straight. "I'll admit I haven't gotten much rest since I left.''

"And Richard,'' she said as he was beginning to rise. "I hope you'll spare some attention for Emma tonight.''

"Why? What's wrong with her,'' he asked sharply.

"She's been very downcast these last few days. She's probably just thinking of her husband again, but she could do with some cheering up.''

"I'll do what I can, but I'm not in too lighthearted a mood myself.''

"Then you can console one another,'' said Lady Melbourne with a smile. "Now go ahead and get some rest; I don't want you falling asleep in your soup.''

Lady Melbourne watched her oldest son walk from the room, head bowed in thought. His reaction when she had mentioned Emma's name had not gone unnoticed. It was as she had thought before he left; he had begun to feel something more than friendship for Emma.

Ordinarily, Lady Melbourne would have been happy to see him take an interest in a woman. She had waited for him to set up his nursery for years to no avail. And while what she knew of Emma's background seemed unexceptionable, and while she liked her well enough, the fact was she was already married.

Even if a divorce were obtained, Lady Melbourne could not imagine that Richard would disgrace the entire family by marrying a divorced woman. An annulment was probably out of the question, and if the man were never found, it would be seven years before Emma would be free to marry.

No, an alliance between Emma and Richard was out of the question, but if he were truly taken with the woman, he must get her out of his system before he could seek a proper wife.

Perhaps she had done the wrong thing in inviting the women to stay with them; perhaps she should have let them travel on no matter how tired they had appeared.

It was really too bad that Emma was married. She seemed to fit in with the family, and would have probably made Richard a good wife. No matter, thought the countess, it couldn't be. The best thing now was to hope that her son would find some fault with the woman which would cool his ardor toward her.

Emma's heart gave a strange thump when she entered the drawing room and saw the earl that evening. The sun had darkened his skin and his blue eyes seemed even more vibrant as they met hers.

She found herself struck silent at the intensity of his gaze. "My lord, it is good to see you again," she at last managed to squeeze out between her lips.

"And it is good to see you also," he replied. Lifting her hand, he pressed his lips to her warm skin, and kept them there just a fraction longer than a casual salute.

"I hope you were successful," she said, fully aware that he still held her hand in his grasp.

"I'm afraid it proved to be another false lead," he admitted, rubbing his thumb over the back of her hand while gazing at her intently.

"Don't lose faith," she said. "I'm sure you'll find Galahad eventually."

"I won't stop looking, but I fear the trail has grown too cold to be very optimistic."

Emma noticed David Whitney approaching and pulled her hand from Lord Melbourne's grasp.

"How was your trip?" asked Whitney.

Emma moved away as the two men began a discussion of

Lord Melbourne's latest quest to find Galahad. Her hand still tingled from the earl's touch, and she wondered if she was all about in the head to be thinking of him when she could not even hold a husband by her side.

She had thought if she was away from him she could keep him from her thoughts, but she had been wrong. The last two days had only proven that he would fill her mind as much when he was not there as when he was.

Emma took a sip of sherry, and wondered whether she would be missed if she took the bottle and retired to her room. Drowning problems by drinking seemed to be a common custom for men, but she doubted whether it would help solve her dilemma.

She was married, yet could not find her husband. Her sister was enamored of a man who could only bring her harm. To further confuse the issue, Emma was falling in love with a man she could not have, and who most assuredly did not want her even if no obstacle stood between them.

Oh, yes, thought Emma, emptying her glass. Everything was just fine.

Chapter Eleven

Lord Melbourne watched Emma move away from him, wishing that David had allowed him a little more time alone with her.

"The journey was uneventful and disappointing," he answered. "The horse looked similar to Galahad, but that was all."

"I'm sorry."

Lord Melbourne shrugged. "It can't be helped. How are things here?"

"Going smoothly. We have had enough rain for the crops to be doing well. It looks as if this year's harvest will be a successful one." Even though he was talking to Lord Melbourne, David's gaze was focused on the other end of the room where the ladies were seated.

"And Miss Seger? How are the two of you getting along?"

David looked at him, startled by his question.

"Don't bother to deny it," said the earl with a grin. "It's all too apparent you admire her."

"Yes, I do," admitted David, "but I doubt anything will come of it."

"Why do you say that?"

"She is devoted to the Randolphs. Not that there's anything wrong with that, but I cannot see her leaving them until they are settled."

"That may be sooner than you expect. Adam seems quite taken with Miss Charlotte, and Miss Randolph is already married."

"But her husband is missing, and that is what will keep Laura with her. If he is never found . . ."

"Then, you fear she will never leave Miss Randolph," said Lord Randolph, finishing his thought.

"It is as bad for you as it is for me," said David, with a wry smile.

"Does everyone know my business?" grumbled the earl.

"I recognize the way you look at her," explained David. "I'm certain I look at Laura the same way."

"But Miss Seger is not married, nor do you suspect she is hiding secrets."

"Surely you don't think Miss Randolph is not the lady she seems to be. I can't believe Laura would be involved with her if she wasn't."

"Perhaps Miss Seger doesn't know."

"It would be difficult for her to hide anything from Laura; she's known Miss Randolph since she was a child."

"But Miss Seger was away from the Randolphs for some time; they could have changed."

"I suppose it's possible," he agreed, "but I hope not, for Laura's sake."

"What will you do if Miss Seger is favorable to your suit?" asked Lord Melbourne.

"I don't know. I would want a proper place for her. I meant to talk with you about it later. My brother has written asking me to come home. He hasn't been successful managing our land and has asked for my help. There's plenty of room for me to build a house and I think Laura would like the area."

"You would be sorely missed," said Lord Melbourne, his mind exploring possibilities.

"If I should be fortunate enough to convince Laura to accept my offer, I would stay until you hired someone to take my place.''

''There is my Uncle Charles' place,'' suggested the earl. ''If it suited you, that is. I intended to install someone there to oversee it, and you've certainly worked hard enough bringing it back to what it should be.''

David's eyes brightened with excitement. ''It has great potential. And I could keep my eye on Melbourne Park until my replacement was trained.''

''It's yours if you want it,'' said the earl.

''I'll take it,'' accepted David, after a moment's consideration. ''Now I must convince Laura to be my wife. Wish me luck.''

''I have faith that you will succeed,'' replied Lord Melbourne, raising his glass to him.

Emma was still in her room the next morning when a knock sounded at the door.

''Where did this come from?'' she asked as she accepted the note the maid carried on a small silver tray.

''A lad brought it, ma'am. That's all I know,'' the girl replied.

Emma shut the door and studied the outside of the letter. It was smudged with dirt—most probably from the boy's hands—and her name was written in a script she had come to recognize and abhor. What could Albert be wanting now?

She debated on whether to burn the note or read it, but decided it was better knowing what he was up to. Moving to the window, she unfolded the paper, and quickly read the few sentences inside.

He wanted to meet her in private. Did he think her an idiot? An encounter in a secluded place would be the perfect situation for Albert to successfully do away with her. Then he could marry Charlotte without any opposition. Tearing the paper into shreds, she crumbled it in her hand until it was a small damp ball.

But what if he wanted to tell her he was going to leave them alone? It might be wiser to hear him out than to ignore him completely.

Sitting down at the small rosewood desk in the corner of her room, she quickly penned a note. She would meet him at the village church; surely even Albert would not attempt to harm her there. She folded the paper and rang for the maid.

It was mid-week, and the church stood serenely on its neatly kept plot of land. A shaded cemetery stretched away on one side of the church, looking cool and inviting in the afternoon sun. Emma wandered into it, reading the inscriptions on the stones, wondering about the people who lay below them.

"Cousin."

Emma could not help but start at Albert's greeting. He had approached her without the slightest sound, and Emma questioned her safety. When she turned to face him she also began to have misgivings about her decision to meet him. Albert's demeanor was not a pleasant one, and she sensed she would not like what he had to say.

"What do you want?" she asked bluntly.

Albert glared at her, his eyes narrowed. "What you will not give me," he snarled.

"I will not marry you," said Emma. "And I will not allow Charlotte to waste her life on you no matter how much duplicity you practice on her."

"I have more urgent matters to attend to," said Albert. "I need money. I thought you might be willing to part with a bit of blunt to keep me away from Charlotte."

"That is blackmail!"

He glowered at her. "It will also keep your sister safe from me, and that's what you want, isn't it?"

"How do I know you'll keep your word? If I'm to judge by your actions, you don't know the meaning of honor."

"I've wasted too much time on the two of you already. My creditors are getting nasty, and I don't even have enough to pay my bill at the inn. I need money to get away from here, and since it would be to your benefit . . .'' He allowed his words to trail off, but kept his hostile gaze focused on her face.

Emma turned away from him and took a few steps, her arms wrapped around her upper body to ward off the chill that ran through her. She did not trust him at all to keep his word, but if his position was truly as uncomfortable as he described, there was a small chance he might take the money and run. It was worth the gamble, she finally decided.

She turned back to Albert. "Meet me here tomorrow at the same time. I'll give you enough to pay your bill here, and a draft for additional funds."

"It had better be adequate or the deal's off," warned Albert.

"You are in no position to demand anything of me. I'm being generous as it is. If you cross me I shall turn to more drastic measures, rest assured of that. I am through with running, and allowing you to beleaguer me any longer. I will give you your money, and expect never to see you again."

Albert executed a mocking bow as she swept by him.

Emma shivered with distaste as she approached the church the next day. It was against her better judgment to give money to Albert, but if it offered the smallest chance of getting rid him, she could not ignore it.

Albert was pacing back and forth in the cemetery when Emma arrived. Without a word, she pulled the money and a draft from her reticule and held it out to him.

An offensive smile crossed his face. "What? No words of good luck, dear cousin?"

"The only good luck I'm concerned with is my own," Emma replied. "And that is my wish to never see you again."

Albert took the money from her hand. "I promise this will be the last time I approach you."

"Your promise is worth nothing, but I'm hoping you'll find better game elsewhere."

"But none so beautiful," Albert replied, his gaze gliding over her.

By a concentrated strength of will, Emma kept from shivering beneath his regard. "You have what you came for. Now, keep your part of the bargain; stay away from Charlotte and me." Emma turned and forced herself to keep a steady pace on her return to the carriage.

Lord Melbourne sat his horse not far from the church. When he hadn't been able to discover Emma's whereabouts on his own, he had asked Roland, who had advised him that Miss Randolph had gone to the village. The butler had understood she wanted to look through the few shops that were there and to visit the church, which was known for its stained glass windows donated by an earlier Earl of Melbourne.

The current earl could think of nothing more enjoyable than conducting a personal tour of the church with Emma. He had ridden to the village thinking of the cool, dim interior of the church; wondering whether he could entice Emma into forgetting her married state long enough to enjoy another kiss. Surely she did not intend to spend the rest of her life as a married spinster, if there was such a thing.

But once he had arrived all thoughts of lovemaking left his mind, for there was Emma in close conversation with her cousin. He watched as she reached into her reticule and handed something to Nestor which he put into his pocket. A few more words passed between them, then Emma left Nestor standing in the churchyard staring after her.

Lord Melbourne turned and rode away; he had seen enough. He had finally convinced himself to believe Emma's story of pulling away from Nestor's touch the day he had seen them in the park, but he could not be fooled a second time. He had watched the entire proceedings of their meeting, and Emma had not seemed in any hurry to leave her cousin.

The countess explained that Lord Melbourne had some unavoidable business to attend to that evening and would not be dining with them.

With Adam at the table, the company was lively, but Emma

was continually aware of the empty chair beside her. Even though they were often at odds, she always felt safer when Lord Melbourne was around, and after her encounter with Albert she was in sore need of comfort.

Emma recalled her meeting with Albert that afternoon with disgust. His face had never lost its sneer and his manner had been rude, but he had been quick enough to snatch the money from her hand when she offered it to him. She had given him one final warning, and hoped she would never need to gaze upon his face again.

Now she looked down at the untouched food on her plate. She could not help but feel her trouble with Albert was far from over.

Laura and David Whitney strolled through the garden after supper. It had become a habit with them; one they both looked forward to.

"Lord Melbourne has made me a generous offer," said David, hoping they would not be interrupted before he spoke his piece.

Laura looked at him curiously, waiting for him to continue.

"He's turning over his late uncle's estate to my care."

"David, how wonderful!" said Laura, her eyes sparkling.

"I will live there as if it were mine, which it well might be if I make a success of it, and the earl agrees to sell."

"I'm so happy for you. I have no doubt that the estate will thrive under your direction. You are going to accept, aren't you?"

"It depends," he said, hesitating.

"What could possibly keep you from agreeing?"

"The house is too large for one man. I would come home to have dinner by myself and to spend the evenings alone. I don't know whether I care to lead such a solitary life."

"You will have your neighbors, and the village is nearby," Laura reminded him.

"I am at an age where I desire more than conversation with

my neighbor. I want a wife by my side." He stopped and turned her to face him. "I would like that to be you, Laura."

Her eyes were wide and her mouth opened in astonishment. "I . . . I . . ." she stuttered. "I did not expect this at all."

"You should have, for I know I've been unable to hide my regard for you. I love you, Laura, and I want you to marry me as soon as possible. We've both wasted enough time in finding one another. I want us to have children; I hope you do too."

"Oh, yes," she breathed.

"Does that mean you accept?"

"I don't know, David. I have Emma and Charlotte to think of."

"Miss Randolph is a married woman herself, well able to take care of her sister. I can't imagine she would stand in the way of your happiness."

"But I have been with them so long."

"Too long," he insisted. "Say yes, Laura, please."

"I want to," she whispered, placing a hand on either side of his face and staring into his eyes. "But I must know that Emma and Charlotte have no need of me any longer. Please, David, understand. They are the closest thing to family that I have, and I could not rest easy if I thought I had failed them. You know a little of their problems with Albert Nestor; let me see them safe from him."

"Then will you marry me?"

"Yes," she answered, her eyes glowing with happiness. "When everything is settled, I shall be honored to be your wife."

"Then you must tell me if there is anything I can do to help, for I cannot wait to be your husband." He took her in his arms, relishing their closeness. He had never felt this way about any other woman, and was surprised at the magnitude of tenderness that filled his heart.

"I will cherish you forever," he murmured in her ear, and felt the wetness of her tears as they coursed down her cheek. "Don't cry, my love, I never meant to cause you tears."

"These are tears of happiness," replied Laura, turning until her lips met his, and conversation was needless.

* * *

The night of the dance had finally arrived and excitement pervaded the house.

Charlotte burst into Emma's room. She wore a white dress which set off her dark hair and eyes to perfection. Emma had allowed her to wear their mother's pearls and they glowed against her skin. She was a lovely young lady, and Emma was relieved to know she would not be wasted on a man such as Albert Nestor.

"You look beautiful," she said, meaning every word.

"And you aren't even dressed yet," accused Charlotte, whirling in a circle to show off her gown. There was no sight of the moody girl Charlotte had become of late.

Emma laughed, caught up in her gaiety. "I will be soon. Is Laura ready?"

"She's still fussing over her hair. I've never seen her in such a taking. I think it's because of Mr. Whitney," she confided in a whisper. "She won't admit it, but I'm certain she likes him."

"Don't plague her, Charlotte. She's old enough to know her own mind, and will tell us anything of importance when she's ready."

"What would we do if she left us?" asked Charlotte, suddenly sober.

"We would be lonely, but we would get along fine," assured Emma. "And we could visit often."

"Yes, we could, couldn't we?" Charlotte's spirits revived and she waltzed around the room, humming a tune.

"Besides, you will probably be married soon yourself," said Emma, thinking of Charlotte's come-out.

Charlotte stopped her dancing and stood considering her sister's remark. "I think I would like to be a married woman, presiding over my own house," she remarked in a queenly manner.

"And I shall visit in order to spoil my nieces and nephews," teased Emma.

"But you will have your own children by then," remarked Charlotte.

"It does not seem likely without a husband," Emma contended.

"Oh, Richard will return," Charlotte said with all the confidence of a young woman with eighteen years to her credit.

Emma did not argue the point. "Why don't you hurry Laura along," she suggested. "We should be going down in a few minutes."

After her sister left the room, Emma stared at her reflection in the mirror. She had no doubt taken as much time as Laura in getting ready for the evening. She had even been brave enough to admit it was all for Lord Melbourne.

Her hair was pulled back into a mass of curls, with gold silk roses tucked in among them. A gold and green gown was spread across her bed waiting to be slipped over her head, and gold satin slippers rested on the floor beside it.

She fastened a topaz and diamond necklace around her throat and added matching earrings to complete the look. They had been a gift from her father at her coming of age, and she felt the warmth of his love each time she wore them.

Emma rose and nodded to the abigail waiting patiently near the door. The woman helped her into the gown without disturbing her hair, and settled it around her, straightening the skirt.

"You do look a picture, ma'am," she said as Emma stood in front of the mirror staring at her reflection.

"Thank you, Betsy." Emma pulled on long gloves and accepted an ivory fan worked in gold from the maid. Taking one last look, she opened the door, prepared to face what might be the best and the worst night of her life.

"You look lovely," said Laura, when they met in the hall.

"Thank you," said Emma, studying her ex-governess.

Laura wore a blue dress that deepened the blue of her eyes. Her return to health had brought the sheen back to her blond hair which was threaded through with blue ribbons.

"You are in looks tonight also," complimented Emma. "Mr. Whitney will be quite overcome by your appearance."

A faint flush came to Laura's cheeks.

"I'm not telling you anything new when I say he is taken by you," continued Emma. "His regard is obvious whenever you're together. And, Laura, I urge you again to accept if he should offer, and if you return his regard. Charlotte and I would miss you terribly, but we shall get by on our own. You must take your happiness when you can."

"I don't think your trouble with Albert is over with yet," objected Laura.

"It doesn't matter. I'm determined to keep him away if it means I must take some sort of action against him. I will no longer allow him to bully us, nor to drive us from one place to another. Albert is only one man, and a despicable one at that; he will no longer control our lives."

Emma's voice was uncompromising. Laura firmly believed that she had come to the end of her patience with Albert, and was relieved they were finally to be rid of him. She would reveal David's offer of marriage in the morning.

"I hope the earl is back," said Laura as they strolled down the hall toward the stairs. "He has been absent quite a bit these past few days."

"He attributes it to business," Emma replied.

"From what Lady Melbourne says, the family does have vast holdings. It can't be easy looking after them all."

Emma nodded her agreement. Lord Melbourne had made only brief, sporadic appearances since he had returned from his last search for Galahad. He had missed almost every meal, and when he did show up his manner was extremely reserved.

She thought she had convinced him she had not sought Albert's touch, but he could have reversed his opinion and again decided she and Albert were in league against him. If so, he was welcome to his opinion. She would not attempt to persuade him any differently. She had had her fill of men and their strange starts to last a lifetime.

"Where is Charlotte?" Emma asked.

"She had forgotten her fan and went to retrieve it."

Charlotte came out of her room, and the three women linked arms and continued down the hall, giggling like young girls at their first dance.

"Oh, isn't it beautiful?" breathed Charlotte as they stood at the ballroom door.

The room was indeed lovely. Lit by hundreds of candles and decorated with arrangements of flowers that filled the room with their heady scent, it rivaled any ballroom in London.

"You will have enough time later to admire it. Come along now," Emma said, taking Charlotte by the hand. "Lady Melbourne insists that we join the receiving line."

Lord Melbourne had waited until he heard the first coach rolling down the drive to join the others in the entrance hall. He had successfully avoided spending time with Emma since he had seen her and Albert Nestor at the church, and intended to continue evading her until she left.

He no longer cared whether she had come to Melbourne Park with the intention of running a rig on him. She had not been successful, and now he only wanted her, and Nestor, out of his life.

However, he could not help but search her out when he entered the hall, and was immediately sorry he had. If he could forget what he knew about her and could follow his inclinations, he would take her in his arms right there in front of everyone. But he must remember that her beauty was completely deceptive, and not allow himself to be fooled by her innocent protestations again. His hands clenched as the memory of Emma's and Nestor's clandestine meeting flashed before his eyes, as it had done time and time again since he had seen them.

It was odd that all along he had been hoping she would forget her marriage vows to have a liaison with him, but when her attentions turned to another man, he deemed it a most despicable action.

Emma was glancing at him oddly, and he knew he should

attempt to greet her in a normal manner. However, he did not know whether his tenuous hold on his composure would be strong enough to withstand a close encounter with her.

Fortunately, Lady Melbourne arrived and positioned them in the receiving line mere seconds before the sound of the first coach could be heard arriving outside the door. They were far enough away from one another that he was spared the decision.

"We have been standing here forever," whispered Charlotte in Emma's ear. "Do you think we will be finished soon?"

"I don't see anyone else arriving," answered Emma. "Be patient a few more minutes and I believe you will be free." Emma smiled at Charlotte's enthusiasm. She had thought that her sister might choose to sit in the corner and play the tragic heroine since Albert had not been invited. She was more than happy to be proven wrong.

"I think we may join our guests now," said Lady Melbourne.

The sisters looked at one another and smiled. "You were right," said Charlotte.

"Of course, I'm your older sister, I'm always right," replied Emma. She watched Charlotte turn eagerly toward the ballroom, and a bit more weight dropped from her shoulders. But she had spent too much time reflecting, for when she turned she was alone with Lord Melbourne.

The earl was disgusted with himself; he had stood watching Emma until he had been caught alone with her. There was nothing to do but to appear as normal as possible.

"You look pleased with yourself," he said as he joined her.

It was the first he had spoken to her that evening, and she was happier than she had any right to be that he had noticed her. His black evening clothes made him appear even more dangerous than usual, and she thought that no man had the right to be so handsome.

"I'm relieved that Charlotte seems more her old self this evening," answered Emma.

"A dance will do that for a young lady," the earl replied, offering her his arm to escort her into the ballroom.

Lord Melbourne could not give Emma the cut direct in front of his family and guests; it would arouse too many questions he was unwilling to answer. He would play out the charade this evening, then return to avoiding her company. Perhaps he would even take that trip to London he had considered a fortnight earlier. She would surely be gone by the time he returned.

Emma hesitated for only a moment before she took his arm. They would be gone in a day or two, so she would enjoy herself tonight.

The countess beckoned them to her side as soon as they came through the door. "Richard, you and Emma should take the floor first. I believe David and Laura will join you."

"And what of Miss Charlotte?" he asked.

"She has been besieged by offers, but has decided to sit out a few dances with Adam. His conceit has grown enormously because such a lovely young lady has given up dancing for him."

"I would not count on her sitting out every dance," said Emma. "There's nothing Charlotte loves more."

"Which makes her sacrifice all the more meaningful to Adam," said Lady Melbourne. "Now, go ahead. The musicians are ready to begin."

"Miss Randolph, will you do me the honor?" Lord Melbourne asked.

"I would be delighted, my lord," she answered, laying her hand lightly on his arm and following him onto the floor.

The first dance was a lively one, but the touching of hands, the parting, then the coming together again, caused a tension to build between Emma and the earl that seemed at odds with the sprightly music.

There was no time to discuss what lay between them, even if they had been inclined to do so, for as soon as the first dance ended, Emma was stolen away by Mr. Hathaway, a neighboring widower with three children. It was well known he was searching far and wide for a suitable mother for his family, and evidently thought Emma might be the answer to his prayers.

But Mr. Hathaway had no chance to press his suit, for Emma stood up with a different gentleman for every dance. Each one looked entirely enchanted by the green and gold-clad woman who gave him her entire attention until being swept off by the next gentleman.

Emma had not given Lord Melbourne a backward glance when they had parted, and even though he had sworn to avoid her again after tonight, he found he did not like the slight at all. The longer he observed her move from man to man, the less he liked it.

Emma was aware of the earl watching her from the edge of the dance floor. Perhaps glaring would be a better description, for she could feel his gaze burn through her. She was still in no mood to attempt to appease him. He had ignored her for days; he could not expect her to fall at his feet the moment he walked through the door.

Emma glanced over to where Charlotte sat next to Adam, smiling at everyone who stopped to welcome him home. Her sister seemed happier than she had ever been, and she began to have a faint hope that Adam had replaced Albert in Charlotte's regard.

Chapter Twelve

"You do not need to sit out every dance with me," said Adam to Charlotte, as she turned down another invitation to join the next set.

"I'm entirely content," she replied, plying her fan, and giving him a glance from beneath her dark lashes.

"Quite a few gentlemen have been anxious to make your acquaintance. You should not be so hard-hearted."

Charlotte folded her fan and turned toward Adam, a serious light in her eyes. "I would much prefer to stay here with you, but perhaps you're growing bored. If you would like for me to dance, then I shall accept the next person who asks," she said earnestly.

Adam took her hand and raised it to his lips, unmindful of anyone who was watching. "I would keep you by my side forever if I could," he replied, his eyes holding her captive with his blue gaze.

Charlotte shivered, then grew warm beneath his steady regard. Perhaps she had made a mistake after all, she thought, and felt a pang of regret, for she was too involved to turn back.

* * *

"You have been standing here looking like a thundercloud all evening," said David, taking a place by Lord Melbourne's side, and watching the colorful swirl of the ladies' gowns against the more somber hues of the mens' evening clothes.

"I have a great deal on my mind," Lord Melbourne said gruffly.

"And she's about shoulder-high, with hazel eyes and wearing gold silk roses in her hair."

"No, he stands about seventeen hands high, with brown eyes, wears a saddle on his back, and has been missing for the last fortnight," replied the earl.

David's eyebrows rose in disbelief. "You're surrounded by the most beautiful ladies in the county and are consumed by thoughts of a horse?"

"It's a failing of mine," said Lord Melbourne, parting with a faint smile. "But not of yours, I've noticed."

David smiled broadly. "You're looking at a happy man, my lord. Laura has accepted my offer. We must keep it secret for the time, but I wanted you to know."

"Congratulations. Miss Seger is a fine lady and will keep you content. I wish all the best for you."

"Thank you. And how goes it with you and Miss Randolph?"

"There is nothing between us and never will be. You seem to forget she's a married woman."

"Admit it—so do you."

"At times; then I regain my good sense." Lord Melbourne watched Emma smile up at her dance partner. "I cannot deny I'm attracted to her, but nothing can ever come of it."

"Your cause is not yet lost. I had given up all hope that I would find someone like Laura to share my life, but it happened when I least expected it."

"Your situation is entirely different. Miss Seger does not have a husband to stand in your way, as does Miss Randolph," the earl pointed out.

"Laura's told me the story. The whole thing sounds like devilish queer business to me, and if the man isn't using his real name, I question whether the marriage is binding."

"If Miss Randolph can't find this other Richard Tremayne,

she may never know. Besides, there are too many other things standing in our way; I don't know whether they could ever be explained to my satisfaction."

David did not press the issue. The earl had been more forthcoming than usual about his personal feelings, perhaps demonstrating the extent of his turmoil concerning Miss Randolph. The two men looked on in silence as Emma changed partners once again.

The evening was more successful than anyone could imagine. Adam's safe return seemed to imbue the gathering with an additional element of gaiety. The music seemed particularly well rendered, and the floor was full at every set.

Protesting her need to rest, Emma came off the dance floor with Squire Windom, plying her fan industriously.

"You look in need of some fresh air," said Lady Melbourne, as she returned to their group.

"The squire is a most enthusiastic dancer," gasped Emma, still short of breath from the country dance.

"That is a courteous way to describe him," replied the countess, chuckling.

"We are going outside for a few minutes," said David. "Why don't you and Miss Randolph join us?" he said to the earl.

Lord Melbourne thought he detected a glint of amusement in David's eye before he turned away, and vowed to take him to task when they were private.

"It would be my pleasure," replied the earl.

He held out his arm and Emma was forced to take it. Not to do so would invite questions from those around them. They followed Laura and David through the French doors, out onto the terrace, and down the shallow steps into the garden. Lanterns dotted the paths, shedding a dim glow in the darkness of the soft summer night.

Although he would never admit it to anyone, Lord Melbourne was irritated with Emma's success. It renewed his anger at seeing her and Albert Nestor together, allowing it to simmer within him. He forgot his avowals at the beginning of the evening, and was again plagued with doubts as to whether anything Emma had told him was the truth.

He vowed to make his trip to London and, while he was there, he would see if his man of business had found anything out about Emma or her husband. In the meantime, she would pay for disturbing his life. Since she consorted with the likes of Albert Nestor, she should be vastly gratified by an earl's attention.

Lord Melbourne slowed their steps, allowing Laura and David to draw ahead of them, their conversation growing fainter until it vanished altogether. Finally, only the elusive sounds of evening and faint strains of music drifting on the night air surrounded Emma and Lord Melbourne.

"It is a perfect evening, is it not?" asked Emma in a hushed voice.

"Not quite yet," replied the earl, stopping and turning her toward him. Lord Melbourne did not know what possessed him; he must be mad. He knew how deceptive Emma was, and had sworn to keep his distance from her. Yet, he could not help himself. His hands trembled like the greenest schoolboy's as he touched the softness of her skin. "This will make it perfect," he murmured, bending until his lips brushed hers, lightly at first, then increasingly more demanding until they were one shadow in the dim light of the garden.

Emma did not struggle against the strength of his arms, but gave a small murmur of protest when his lips left hers.

"Don't worry, my love, I'm not leaving you," he murmured in her ear as he nuzzled the delicate shell.

Emma's gown was a flimsy barrier between them, and she was on fire at Lord Melbourne's touch. She pressed herself closer to him, and followed his lead by placing small kisses on his neck, tasting the warmth of his skin, breathing in the clean scent of his thick, dark hair.

A groan sounded deep in his throat, and to Emma's surprise she felt his teeth gently worry the lobe of her ear. Her knees turned to liquid, and she relied on his strength as he gathered her closer, lifting her from the ground and fitting her curves to his hard muscles.

His lips claimed hers again in a kiss more intimate than Emma had ever experienced. All sense of propriety disappeared from her mind, leaving only a burning desire for something more from the man who held her.

He had slipped the small sleeve of her gown from one shoulder and was pushing the neckline lower when the sound of voices permeated the haze of passion that engulfed them.

"Keep quiet," he warned, lifting her and stepping into the deeper shadows of a tree close by. He held her fast until the couple had passed and they were safe from discovery.

"I . . . I did not even hear them," she stammered, her voice quivering.

"I don't know how I did," he replied, his voice as unsteady as hers.

"I think men are more adapted to situations such as this," she whispered.

"Are you saying I'm proficient at sneaking around?" he asked, amusement filling his voice.

"I think you are much more experienced," she said, attempting to match his teasing tone, despite the fact her voice did not come out as steady as she would have liked.

God, why must it be this way? thought Lord Melbourne, his anger forgotten in his powerful surge of desire for Emma. *Why must I steal away to a dark corner of the garden to snatch a few moments with this woman?* But he knew the answer better than anyone.

It was not just because she was married; David had almost convinced him that was an obstacle they could overcome if both were willing. It was Emma's duplicity that held them apart. She had lied to him over and over again. It was probable that Nestor was her lover, if not her husband, and both were most likely guilty in conspiring to take what they could from his family.

How could it be? his mind continued to argue. Emma's response to him seemed to prove she was inexperienced in the ways of men and women. It did not seem possible that her lovemaking could be the practiced art of a woman hoping to gain by her skills, but more an innocent one. The earl's internal struggle was tearing him apart, and he knew they must return to the house before he lost all control.

"I'm sorry, my lord, I can't believe that I've forgotten I'm married," Emma said weakly, wondering how his merest touch could cause everything to disappear from her mind.

"I haven't," he muttered harshly, straightening the neckline of her gown and pulling the sleeve back onto her shoulder. "Not for one minute since we met have I forgotten you belong to another," he said, taking her in his arms again. "To my shame, it has not kept me away from you." His voice was rough, but he held her gently.

The passion that had swept through him earlier had been replaced by a tenderness previously unknown to him, and he marveled at the simplicity of its nature. It was love, pure and simple, and it made everything he had ever felt for other women pall in comparison.

And what was to be his reward for such a pure and shining love? Nothing. There had never been a chance for the two of them. She had told him from the beginning that she was married, and that should have stopped him, but it hadn't.

Her treachery and conspiracy would have deterred anyone else, but he had allowed himself to be convinced that what he had seen with his own eyes was false. Then, he had seen it for himself a second time. How he could feel anything but contempt for such a woman was beyond his comprehension. Yet here he was in the garden, with Emma in his arms.

"I . . . I suppose we should return," said Emma, hoping he would suggest they tarry a while longer.

But she was to be disappointed, for he only said, "It would probably be best."

Running his fingers through his dark hair, he offered Emma his arm and they stepped out onto the main path of the garden, coming face-to-face with Charlotte and Albert.

Charlotte uttered a gasp and cowered by Albert's side, her eyes wide with apprehension. Emma was speechless as she stared at her sister.

Albert must have contacted Charlotte and arranged the meeting. Perhaps he even planned to go through with an elopement now that he had enough money. How could she have been foolish enough to give him the means to do so?

"Charlotte? How . . . how could you do such a thing? And you, Albert; you vowed not to see her again!"

Lord Melbourne did not know whether Emma was truly shocked at seeing her sister with Nestor or whether her reaction was solely for his benefit; but at the moment, it made no difference. He had wanted to warn Nestor away since he had first seen the man, and he would not miss the opportunity.

"Take your sister into the house," said the earl. "I will talk to Mr. Nestor."

The sound of his words broke the tableau; Charlotte pulled away from Albert, turned, and ran down the path toward the house.

"Go ahead," Lord Melbourne said to Emma, never taking his eyes from Albert Nestor.

Emma hurried after Charlotte. Only after both women had disappeared and they were alone, did the earl speak.

"I don't think I need tell you you're no longer welcome here, Nestor."

"Protecting your interests? It'll do you no good at all. You observed how close Emma and I were at the church, didn't you? Oh, yes, I saw you watching."

"What you do elsewhere is none of my business," Lord Melbourne replied stiffly. "But I need not accept you in my own home. If you want to meet either of the Misses Randolph again, you'll do it elsewhere. Have I made myself clear?"

"Absolutely, my lord," said Albert, giving a bow that mocked the action. "Tell Emma I will talk to her later."

The earl watched the man saunter off toward the front of the house. He had confirmed the earl's belief that he and Emma were conspiring. Perhaps she was jealous of his connection with Charlotte, and that was the reason for her dismay at seeing them together. Well, he was not going to allow himself to be involved or hoodwinked any longer. She and Nestor could settle their problems by themselves and a long way from Melbourne Park. He could not wait to see the last of both of them.

The next morning Emma was again awake at daybreak. She started to go out into the garden, but too much had happened there the night before for it to be soothing for her.

The evening had begun so promisingly. Charlotte was acting more like herself, and Lord Melbourne had invited her for a walk.

Their lovemaking in the garden had been far more than she had expected. She had shared only a few kisses with her husband before he had disappeared, and they were nothing like her experience with Lord Melbourne. The earl made her forget anything or anyone else existed except for the two of them. It was a feeling she yearned to experience again, but her marriage precluded any further experiments with the earl, no matter how pleasant.

She should be glad that he had called a halt before anything more could develop; instead, she was inexplicably disappointed that she would never be in his arms again.

While that had been enough for one evening, there had been more to come. Her shock at seeing Charlotte and Albert together caused her already shattered constitution to crumble further. At that moment, she could do nothing more than follow Charlotte into the house, leaving Lord Melbourne to deal with his uninvited guest.

Emma had been relieved to find Charlotte locked in her room when she arrived in the upper hall, for she had no energy left to confront her; the morning would be soon enough. And now dawn was upon her, and she no more knew what to do than she had the night before.

There was no decision to be made about Lord Melbourne; he was unattainable. No matter how much she yearned for him, she could never agree to become his mistress; and he had not asked it of her, she acknowledged ruefully. That left only the problem of Albert Nestor with which to deal.

It had been sheer wishfulness to think he would take her

money and leave. His deceitfulness made Emma more determined than ever to remove Charlotte from his influence. She decided to change her plans to visit London. Instead, she would revert to her original scheme of traveling to Paris.

She would appeal to Lord Melbourne for his help in sending Albert on a fool's errand. She would ask him to spare three of his maids who would take her coach and start in the direction of London during the early evening hours. It would be light enough to see the forms of three women, but too dark to recognize their features. It was Emma's hope that Albert would think that she, Charlotte, and Laura were attempting to elude him again under the cover of night and escape to London.

After giving the first coach a good start, Emma, Charlotte, and Laura would board the earl's coach and depart for the coast. By the time Albert became aware of the hoax, the women could be far enough ahead of him that he could never catch up before they were aboard a ship in the middle of the English Channel.

While Albert might scrape up enough for passage to France, he would have nothing to live on once he was there. Emma would stay long enough to either ensure his creditors would be onto him, or until he had found another solution to his problems, before she returned.

Emma considered the plan from all angles, and decided it was the safest strategy she could devise. She would speak to Laura and Charlotte as soon as they awoke, then seek out the earl and ask for his cooperation.

After last night, he would no doubt do whatever he could to see the last of her.

"There's something I need to discuss with you," began Emma a few hours later. Since Charlotte had not come down for breakfast, she and Laura had gone to her sister's room.

Charlotte sat in the window seat, her legs drawn up beneath her. "If it's about last night, I don't wish to talk about it," she said, without looking at her sister.

"I had not meant to be drawn into a debate over your behavior of the night before, but now that you mention it, there is one thing I'd like to know. Why have you led Adam to believe there is something more between you than friendship? He's a sincere man who has suffered greatly these past months. He does not deserve to be treated so shabbily."

A contrite look passed across Charlotte's face. "I did not mean any harm. I do care about Adam, but . . ."

"But not enough," said Emma, finishing her sentence. "As I said, I'm not here to chastise you; it's far too late for that. I wanted to tell you about our travel plans."

Emma had already confided her thoughts on their departure to Laura. While the older woman was not convinced it was the right thing to do, she knew that protesting would do no good. Emma had made her decision and would not be swayed. Laura had not mentioned David Whitney's offer of marriage. If Emma knew, she would insist upon Laura's staying; despite her feelings for David, Laura had been with the girls too long to allow them to take on such a trip alone. Her own happiness could be put aside until she knew Emma and Charlotte were safe at home.

Charlotte remained stubbornly silent, staring out the window as if fascinated with the view.

"We will be leaving here as soon as I can make arrangements for our travel," Emma informed her.

Charlotte turned to look at her, but still did not utter a word.

"I've decided we shouldn't travel to London—"

Charlotte did not let her finish her sentence, but jumped from her chair to hug Emma, then danced around the room.

"Oh, Emma, I'm so happy we're going home," she cried.

"But we're not—" began Emma, attempting to interrupt her sister.

"You saw how happy we were last night, didn't you? You could tell we were meant to be together. I knew if you only allowed yourself to forget your prejudice against Albert that you would understand."

"Charlotte," said Laura, thinking she could get the girl's attention long enough to halt her prattling and explain the real situation. But Charlotte could not be stopped.

"I am so happy, I can tell you now. I hated to keep anything from you, but I knew you would forbid me," she chattered on. "I couldn't live without writing Albert to let him know I was all right. I knew he would be worried about me. And before I knew it he had followed us. Doesn't that prove he's sincere?"

"You wrote Albert?" asked Emma, as the significance of Charlotte's words reached her.

"Yes, as soon as we reached Dover. Perhaps I shouldn't have," Charlotte confessed, "but I couldn't help it. And it has proven you wrong because Albert has caused no problems after all. He merely followed us to make sure we were safe. I admit I slipped away to meet him on occasion. That was the reason for my new fondness for walking," she said, glancing mischievously at Laura.

"Albert made me promise I wouldn't breathe a word about my letters or our rendezvous to you, but now that we're going home, I see no harm in telling you everything. We will soon be back, and Albert can call on me as any suitor would. Oh, Emma, I am so happy."

Emma sat, numb from the flood of words pouring over her. Her plan, which had been carried out to keep them safe from the machinations of her cousin, had been an illusion. Albert had known where they were the entire time, and it was her own sister who had betrayed her.

Emma was through making excuses for Charlotte, through allowing her age to absolve her of her selfish childishness. Emma had been learning how to run the estate when she was Charlotte's age, not moping about because she couldn't form an alliance with a man who was totally unsuitable for her.

Certainly part of the blame rested on Emma's shoulders. She had sheltered her sister from every difficult decision, thinking to allow her to grow up without a care. Now she found Charlotte had matured without a sense of responsibility or loyalty toward her family. It was time she faced the truth, and Emma was angry enough to spell it out for her.

"Why do you think I told you to keep our destination a secret?" she asked in a tightly controlled voice.

"To keep me away from Albert," said Charlotte, without hesitation.

"That's true, but the reason behind it was to avoid danger. Do you remember the accidents I suffered at home? The broken carriage wheel, the bridge that gave way beneath me? They were not accidents, Charlotte. They were designed to do away with me for good."

Charlotte turned pale and dropped into a chair. "I don't believe you."

"It's true."

"You didn't tell me," said Laura, as shocked as Charlotte.

"I didn't want to worry you; either of you. I thought I could handle it all by myself. Now I see I should have explained everything; perhaps it would have made a difference. Although Albert would probably have absolved himself in your eyes," she said to Charlotte.

"Albert?" gasped Charlotte. "What does he have to do with it?"

"He is most likely the person attempting to kill me," Emma answered bluntly.

"No! He cannot be," blurted out Charlotte.

"I have no proof, he's too clever for that. But when I took my fall from the horse, Lord Melbourne found the girth had been cut. And the shot that barely missed me was not from a poacher's gun, but from someone waiting for me to appear."

"You should have said something," said Laura.

"It would have done no good," Emma replied. "And you were so ill, I didn't want to worry you further."

"I've totally failed you," said Laura, tears welling in her eyes. "I should have been there when you needed me."

"You've done nothing of the sort. There was nothing either of us could do since Charlotte led the wolf right to our door."

"I don't believe you," cried Charlotte. "Albert would never cause harm to anyone."

"You may believe it," said Emma. "I have ruined my life trying to protect you, and it has been all for nothing. I have weathered at least four attempts on my life, and uprooted us from our home to keep you safe. Laura fell ill and almost lost her life because of my mad scheme to get you away from Albert, but my biggest folly was marrying for your sake."

"What did your marriage have to do with me?" asked Charlotte.

"To begin with, I thought a man in the house would keep Albert away. I also thought that if I had a child, he would see that marrying you would not get what he wanted and direct his attention elsewhere. But after I have seen what he is capable of, I believe he would not have hesitated to kill me and any child of mine to get his way."

"No!" cried Charlotte, placing her hands over her ears. "I will not listen to anymore."

"You must listen, Charlotte, for your own sake. He is deeply in debt and only wants you for your money."

"No! No!" repeated Charlotte, leaping to her feet and running to the door.

"Charlotte, don't leave. I haven't told you everything yet."

Charlotte jerked open the door and ran from the room. Emma listened as her footsteps faded into silence down the hallway.

"There is more?" asked Laura.

"A little," said Emma. "She does not know that Albert attempted to persuade me to marry him first."

Lord Melbourne sat at the breakfast table, staring into a cup of coffee. He had spent another restless night because of Emma. It was beginning to become a habit which he did not relish, but one to which he feared he must become accustomed.

The smell of food offended him, so he pushed back his chair, deciding that a morning gallop might raise his spirits.

His discovery that he truly loved Emma had not brought him the happiness that should have accompanied the moment, he thought, as he accepted his hat, gloves, and riding crop from Roland. He had not declared his feelings to her, nor had he asked if she returned his sentiments, for if her answer was yes, it would haunt him the rest of his days. He would not know whether she was being sincere, or whether it was part of her and Nestor's plan.

The earl made his way down the hall toward the back of the house, pulling on his gloves. His mind was still filled with Emma; unable to relinquish a tiny hope that perhaps she was what she claimed to be. But, even so, her marriage—if there was one—was an impregnable wall between them, one that had no possibility of being breached until the fate of her husband was known. And that did not seem likely since the man appeared to have vanished from the face of the earth.

No. Best to forget any future with Emma and turn his attention to something useful, such as ridding the neighborhood of Albert Nestor. Last night Nestor had left before Lord Melbourne could do more than warn him to stay away from the two sisters. Now he meant to see the innkeeper. Nestor would find there was no room available for him this evening, and he would be forced to find shelter elsewhere. Preferably, a long way from Melbourne Park.

The earl stepped through the door, breathing in a great breath of morning air. Walking down the path to the stables, he glanced toward the garden where last night he had held Emma in his arms. A sudden flash of color caught his eye, and he wondered whether she was reliving their time together. Cursing himself for his weakness, he changed direction, and turned onto the garden path, making his way through the summer blooms.

He heard his quarry before he saw her, but it was not Emma. Great sobs flowed from Charlotte, and Lord Melbourne was tempted to steal away to continue his morning's business. But this was Emma's sister, and he felt a certain responsibility to help her no matter how foolishly the chit comported herself.

Taking a seat beside her, he said, "May I be of help, Miss Charlotte?"

She did not seem at all surprised to see him, but only sobbed all the harder at his question. "There is nothing anyone can do. My life is ruined and there is no need for it to go on," she declared dramatically.

Lord Melbourne wondered why it was his fate to come across the girl. His spirits were sufficiently low as it was, but a few minutes with Charlotte could make the day even worse than he had anticipated.

"Nothing could be that bad," he assured her, slipping a handkerchief into her hand. "Now dry your eyes and tell me what is bothering you."

"It is Emma. She's doing all that she can to ruin my life."

"I'm sure your sister wants only what is best for you," said the earl.

"That may be what she wants you to think, but it isn't true. She told me this morning we were leaving," revealed Charlotte, mopping her eyes with his handkerchief.

Lord Melbourne's interest was piqued. He had wondered what Emma's reaction to last night's confrontation would be and now he knew. "Did she say when you would depart?"

"As soon as she can make the arrangements; but that isn't the worst part of it. We are not going home!" she declared, bursting into a bout of fresh wailing.

Lord Melbourne felt the urge to shake her until she stopped her bawling, but sensed that would only make matters worse with Charlotte. "If you aren't returning home, where are you going?"

"To . . . to Paris. I will never see Albert again," she moaned.

And a good thing that is, said the earl to himself.

"She said the most horrible things about him," Charlotte continued. "She accused him of trying to kill her. There was a broken carriage wheel and a bridge that gave way with Emma at home. She said Albert had caused them both. She even blamed her fall from the horse and the poacher's shot on him."

Emma had never mentioned the broken wheel and bridge to him, but the two incidents at Melbourne Park were certainly not accidents. "And you think she's mistaken?" he asked.

"I know she is; Albert would never do anything like that. He is too . . . too . . . gentle and loving to ever hurt anyone."

Ah. How blind love could make a person, thought Lord Melbourne, remembering his own inability to let go of Emma no matter what she did.

"Emma blames Albert for everything that has happened to us," Charlotte continued, unaware of the earl's inattention. "She says our trip was to save me from him. She insists that Laura would not have come near death if it had not been for our fleeing in such a manner. She even attributes her marriage to Albert's pursuit."

Lord Melbourne frowned. "Did she explain that?" he asked.

"Emma said she thought if there was a man in the house Albert would not be so forward. She also claims that if she were to . . . were to have a child, he would see that there would be little to gain by marriage to me. Then she turned right around and said he would no doubt murder her and any child she had to get what he wanted."

"I don't understand," said Lord Melbourne, completely puzzled by this turn of events. "Why would an innocent child stand in Nestor's way?"

Charlotte mopped at her eyes again, and sat up straighter. Talking had helped calm her and she appeared more rational than she had for the past few minutes.

"It is very easy," said Charlotte. "When Papa died, Emma—being the oldest—inherited. I am well provided for, but unless something happens to Emma, I shall not have the title nor control the estate. And if she had a child, it would inherit."

"What title?" the earl asked, wondering whether it was she or himself who was becoming disoriented.

Chapter Thirteen

"Baroness. My father was Baron Randolph, and the title went to Emma on his death," Charlotte explained impatiently.

Lord Melbourne's head was spinning. It seemed that Emma had been less than forthcoming when explaining her situation.

"That is why Albert has tried to kill her, Emma claims. She insists he is deeply in debt, and wants to do away with her so I will inherit. Then he will marry me and have the entire estate at his disposal. Did you ever hear of anything so preposterous?" asked Charlotte indignantly.

"No, never," agreed the earl, unaware of what he was saying. "Why don't you sit here and try to compose yourself," he suggested. "I'll go talk to your sister and see whether I can make some sense of all this."

"Oh, would you?" said Charlotte happily. "I would be so grateful. I know that if Emma will just listen she will see how wrong she is about Albert."

Lord Melbourne did not attempt to dissuade her from her view of Albert. A young girl in love as much as Charlotte thought herself to be would not listen to anyone but the man of her dreams.

Giving her hand a comforting pat, he rose and made his way

back to the house. Adam was standing beside the door, leaning on his cane.

"Is there no one about this morning?" he complained peevishly.

"By no one, I assume you mean Charlotte," replied the earl.

Adam looked slightly embarrassed. "She would do well enough," he admitted.

"It seems Charlotte has been highly upset this morning. I've been attempting to comfort her, but I'm sure you could do a better job."

"What! What happened? Where is she?" said Adam, firing questions at Lord Melbourne without giving him a chance to answer them.

"I think you'll find her in the garden," the earl said, pointing the way. What was it about the Randolph women that attracted the Tremayne men? he wondered as he watched Adam hurry away.

If Adam was truly enamored of Charlotte, then Lord Melbourne wished him well. As soon as she saw Albert for what he was, the earl was certain Charlotte would turn to Adam for support, and his brother would have the woman he desired.

But his own future did not bode so bright, for everything he learned only pushed Emma further away. He had thought the situation as bad as it could get, but now he found even more she had hidden from him. That she was not compelled to tell him her story at all did not enter his mind as he stalked through the house searching for her.

Adam found Charlotte exactly where his brother had left her. He sat beside her on the bench and reached over to capture her hand.

Lacing his fingers with hers, he squeezed gently. "It's much too early to cry," he said softly.

His sympathy caused fresh tears to trickle down her face. "I don't think I shall ever stop."

"I'm sure that isn't true. Everything will come right," he promised.

"I don't see how it can. Emma and Laura hold me in the highest contempt, and so would you if you knew what I had done."

He reached over and gently turned her face toward him. "There's very little that can't be forgiven," he said, leaning forward and brushing his lips across hers. Charlotte looked surprised, but did not pull away. He released her hand and slid his arm around her waist, pulling her closer.

"What if someone should see us?" she protested feebly.

"It will not matter a whit, my dear." *For you will soon be my wife, no matter what your cousin thinks,* he finished silently. He kissed her then with all the feeling he had been restraining.

She was young and thought herself to be in love with Albert Nestor, but Adam believed he could change her mind. He raised his lips from hers; Charlotte sighed and laid her head against his chest.

"I have made such a mess of everything," she confessed, tentatively putting her arms around him.

Adam smiled in satisfaction; she might not know it yet, but she already loved him. "We shall straighten it out, my love."

"Oh, how I wish I could, but it is far too late. There are things that cannot be undone."

Placing a finger under her chin, he tipped her face up to his. "I will help you," he promised. Her eyes fluttered closed again as his lips sought hers. Lifting her onto his lap, he fitted her closely to his body, kissing her so deeply neither had thoughts for anyone else.

Lord Melbourne reached the front hall just as Laura and Emma were descending the stairs. For a moment he was taken aback at her appearance. He had not seen her since their kiss in the garden, and wasn't prepared for the effect she had on him.

He could not help but stare at her for a moment. She was as lovely in her blue morning gown as she had been in all her finery at the dance. Her hair was worn looser than usual, as if she had not found the energy to confine it in its customary cluster of tight curls, and she looked slightly paler than normal.

"My lord," she greeted him, before she reached the bottom of the stairs.

"Miss Randolph. Miss Seger. I'm happy to see you suffered no detrimental effects from last night's entertainment."

"None at all, my lord. It seems I am completely recovered from my illness," replied Laura.

"And you, Miss Randolph? May I hope you are also in good spirits?"

"I am quite well," lied Emma, wondering at this sudden concern of his about her health. She was not left in doubt for long.

"Then perhaps I could have a word with you in private," Lord Melbourne said.

"Of course, my lord. I also need to speak with you." Emma could not understand what he could want, but she would take the opportunity to arrange for his help with their departure. She was certain he would go along with any scheme she proposed to get rid of such an irritating annoyance as they had proved to be.

Lord Melbourne led her into the library and closed the door behind them after admonishing Roland they were not to be disturbed.

"I have just come from Charlotte. I found her in the garden extremely upset."

A faint flush stained Emma's cheeks. "I'm sorry you've been drawn into our personal affairs, my lord. I assure you it will not happen again, for we plan to leave perhaps as early as this evening."

"Oh, do you?"

"With your help, that is," she qualified. "I know you had agreed to help us get to London, but our plans have changed," she rushed on, not noticing that he did not appear surprised at her announcement.

"I think it would be better if we went to Paris as we had originally planned. If you could spare us your coach for a few days, I believe we could escape without Albert's notice and have the Channel between us before he could catch up with us."

"If that is what you wish, I will arrange it, Baroness Randolph."

"Oh, thank you, my lord. I . . ." Emma's voice trailed off, and she stared at him.

"Charlotte told me," he said in answer to her unasked question. "Why did you keep it from me?"

Emma sank into the nearest chair. "There is nothing sinister in my silence," she said. "I simply wanted to remain as inconspicuous as possible. A baroness living in Dover would have attracted much more notice than a mere Miss Randolph. I thought the less attention I drew to our party, the less chance of Albert finding us. Now I discover it would not have mattered whether I proclaimed myself the Queen of England, he would have found us in either case."

"What do you mean?"

"Charlotte did not tell you?"

When he shook his head, Emma continued.

"This morning, when I began to tell Charlotte we were not going to London, she immediately assumed we were going home. She confessed she had been unable to live without Albert and had written him giving him our direction. He knew our destinations almost as soon as we arrived and followed us," she revealed in disgust. "Her new interest in walking was an excuse to meet him secretly. I can only assume she told him everything we discussed. I was such a fool! I thought we were safe, and all the time he was watching our every move."

"And why couldn't you tell me the whole story?"

"I did not know you well enough at first," she admitted. "Then it didn't seem to matter whether you knew I was a baroness. We would soon be out of your life and forgotten before a fortnight was over."

The earl considered how mistaken she was in her assumption. He doubted whether she would ever completely leave his thoughts.

Emma hesitated, then shrugged. There was no reason to keep silent any longer. Lord Melbourne knew nearly everything already. "Part of it you already know. My father died two years ago," Emma explained. "Our estate is not nearly as vast as this one, but it is productive and well cared for. When it was evident that there would be no son to carry on in his name, my father began training me to take over his responsibilities. I followed in his footsteps for years, and at his death, life continued as usual. At least, for a time.

"Then approximately a year after my father's demise Albert Nestor arrived. He was extremely attentive, particularly toward me. He said he had just returned to England and had rushed to our assistance as soon as he heard of our father's death. I assured him we had no need of his help, and thanked him prettily. I expected him to be on his way the next day, but he insisted upon staying, and helping us through our difficult times, as he put it.

"It was soon apparent that he had set his sight on me. He proposed time and time again, and each time I firmly rejected him. It didn't take a bluestocking to realize his avowals did not include love, but were offered solely in an attempt to gain control of the estate."

Lord Melbourne smiled. He had decided not to be taken in by Emma again. But if what she said was true, and if Albert had been observant, he would have immediately seen that Emma was too strong-minded and dedicated to her responsibilities to give everything over to him.

"I finally rebuffed him in no uncertain terms, and endeavored to send him on his way. And, while he accepted that I would never marry him, he still lingered in the neighborhood. It wasn't long before I found the reason why.

"Albert had begun charming my sister. Charlotte was just out of the schoolroom, and eager to prove she was grown up. She was completely susceptible to the accomplished flirtations of an experienced scoundrel such as Albert.

"At the same time, several accidents nearly took my life. There is a bridge on our estate where I often go to think. A portion of it gave way one day giving me quite a fall. I was lucky to have escaped with scrapes and bruises. I insist everything be kept in good order, but the planks that gave way were old ones, and while I could not prove it, I know the original ones were removed and replaced with the rotten ones.''

"Couldn't your man merely have overlooked the needed repair?'' Lord Melbourne asked.

"He swore to me that was not the case, and I believe him. And if the accidents had stopped there, I might have forgotten about it.''

"There were more?''

"Only one, but it was enough to convince me I was in danger. I have a curricle that I drive,'' she said.

The earl raised a quizzical brow.

"I am quite a hand with the ribbons,'' she said with some pride. "It's well known that no one else uses the curricle but me. I was driving it to the village one day when the wheel gave way. If I had not been quick, I would have been thrown out and most probably severely injured. The spokes on the wheels had been cut nearly completely through.''

"Like the saddle girth,'' he added.

"Just so,'' she agreed.

"Why didn't you tell me about this when you took your fall?''

"I didn't want to involve you any further in our troubles. You and your mother were offering us your hospitality, and I had only caused her worry to increase by showing up with her locket. I couldn't call on you for any more. I merely wanted to get away as soon as possible before anyone here could be harmed.''

She was convincing, and Lord Melbourne decided to go along with her until he discovered the truth. "It would have been better had I known it was Albert rather than wondering who it could be.''

"Yes, I can see that now,'' she admitted, "but I wasn't thinking very clearly. Even before he showed up the next morning, I knew Albert had somehow found us and was up to his old tricks. Now I know how he located us so easily,'' she said, grimly.

"And that was how you knew that the shot wasn't a poacher, but was from Albert.''

"I suspected as much," she confessed. "By that time I was beginning to tire of running. I would have been willing to confront Albert, had it not been for the safety of others."

If she were not telling the truth, he had to admire her acting ability.

"But I did not finish my story," she said.

"You mean there is more you haven't told me?"

"A little," she admitted. "And I want you to hear it all this time.

"One evening, after Albert had switched his attention to Charlotte," she said, picking up her story, "I was attempting to go over the workings of our affairs with her. This was after the carriage incident, and I told her if anything should happen to me she would need to know certain things.

"She was shocked at the thought, but assured me not to worry. Albert had already promised that he would always be by her side to guide her through any difficulties. She blushed and said he had even hinted at marriage.

"I knew then that the accidents would not stop until one proved fatal to me. I had no proof against Albert. If I lodged a complaint, he would probably have claimed I was jealous of his attentions to Charlotte.

"I decided we must get away from Albert until I worked out a solution, or came up with some positive proof of my suspicions. Since Napoleon had abdicated, I concluded a trip to Paris would be just the thing. We could lose ourselves in the hordes of people who were pouring into France. And even if Albert could find out where we were, I doubted he had the money to follow us."

"I assume Charlotte wasn't happy with your suggestion," said Lord Melbourne.

"Not at all," Emma replied. "but I did not give her enough time to even think about it. We packed swiftly and left home late that evening, so that Albert would not know we had gone until it was too late. Unfortunately, by the time we had reached Dover Laura had fallen ill, and we were forced to remain there for months. I'm assuming that's when Charlotte first wrote Albert. The rest, I believe you know."

They were both silent for a moment, then Emma spoke again. "I don't regret anything that I've done," she said, more to herself than to the earl. "Marrying a virtual stranger to save myself and my sister was an extreme measure, but would have been worth it had it worked. I thought if I conceived an heir, then Albert would have no reason to make any further attempts on my life, and I'm certain his interest in Charlotte would have immediately vanished."

Then she smiled; a small, lonely smile, that could not fail to reach any man's heart. "There is only one thing that I regret, and that is not being able to wear my mother's wedding dress. I had dreamed about it all my life, and now that opportunity is past."

Lord Melbourne cleared his throat. The story sounded like a Minerva novel, but he could not help but be moved by Emma's disappointment in her wedding. He wanted to think that she would not lie about something that close to her heart.

Emotions warred against common sense inside of him. Would he ever know the truth about Emma?

While there were many things he didn't know about her, there was one thing he did know for a fact: Emma had met with Nestor of her own free will at least once.

"You say you have done everything possible to avoid Nestor?"

"I have," agreed Emma.

"Then what of your meeting in the churchyard a few days ago?" he asked abruptly.

Emma's breath left her body in a rush.

"Don't bother to deny it. I saw it with my own eyes, and he didn't appear to be holding you against your will."

"I . . . he . . ." Emma stammered to a stop. Taking a breath, she began again. "Albert sent a note. He was desperate for money; he didn't have a feather to fly with. He promised to leave us alone if I paid him enough."

"And I suppose you agreed."

"I met him at the church to give him the money; he said he would leave."

Lord Melbourne gave a bitter laugh of disbelief. If everything she said was true, how could she have trusted Nestor's word?

"I know it was foolish, but I was desperate to get rid of him. You must believe me," she said, her voice pleading for understanding.

"Must I, madam? I'm afraid I cannot. I will, however, help you rid yourself of Nestor if that is truly your wish. If not, you can follow him and join up somewhere far from here."

"I do not wish to ever see him again," she replied, her face even paler than when he had first seen her that morning.

"Then if that is truly your wish, you should be happy to know I plan on making it clear to him that he should be out of the neighborhood by nightfall."

"Then we shall be packed and ready to leave tomorrow, my lord."

"I will have my coach ready for your use."

"There is no need," she said stiffly. "For if you do not believe my story, I will not involve you in the ruse to throw Albert off our trail. And if what you say is true, he should be far enough away by tomorrow to allow us safe passage."

"As you wish," said the earl, a foreboding sensation nagging at the back of his mind. He wondered whether he had allowed jealousy to prejudice his decision and force him to act too swiftly in making a final judgment about Emma.

Lord Melbourne left Emma in the library, deciding to confront Nestor immediately and get it over with. When he reached the stables, he found a boy had just ridden up.

"What is it, George?" Lord Melbourne asked.

George nodded toward the boy who still sat astride his horse. "The lad here has a message from a John Stansbury. Says he has a horse that fits the description of Galahad in his stable. Wants you to come and identify him."

What an inopportune time for this to happen, thought the earl. He was torn between finding Nestor and sending him on his way or leaving immediately to see whether the animal in question was Galahad.

"Is your master certain about the horse?" he asked the boy.

"As much as he can be, my lord. Says you should hurry like, since the man what boarded him might come back any time now."

The decision was made; Lord Melbourne could not risk losing the horse if it was indeed Galahad. His warning the night before would keep Nestor at bay until he returned.

It was nearly dark when the stableboy led the earl and his groom down a well-trod lane past a small cottage. Behind it were several large stables, much better kept than the house. A tall, gaunt man stepped into the stableyard as they came to a halt.

"Yer Lord Melbourne?" he said.

"I am."

"Name's Stansbury, John Stansbury."

Lord Melbourne nodded. "I understand you may be stabling a horse that's gone missing from my estate."

"That I am. Leastwise he looks to be answering the description that's been put about. Would yer like to see 'em?"

"I would," replied the earl firmly. He swung stiffly off his horse and followed Stansbury through the stable door. He was glad to note that the stable was clean and well-kept. If Galahad was here, he was most probably getting adequate care.

"Here he is," said the man, stopping at a stall on the right. "He's a handful all right. Like to tore the place apart before he settled down."

Lord Melbourne paused, and breathed a small prayer that his search would end here and now, before looking into the stall. The horse was standing with his hindquarters toward the door. "Galahad," he called out.

The animal threw up his head and neighed softly. Turning, he thrust his head over the door, butting Lord Melbourne in recognition.

"Must be him," said Stansbury.

"It is," said the earl. He rubbed Galahad's head, ashamed to let Stansbury see that his eyes were moist. He had given up on ever finding the animal, and knew that he would never be free of the guilt no matter how often Adam said it didn't matter. Now he was absolved of all fault. He could take Galahad home, and concentrate on finding a way to be rid of his thoughts of Emma. Then maybe life would return to what it was before she came into his life.

"How did he come to be here?" Lord Melbourne asked.

"The coaching inn's jest down the road," Stansbury said.

The earl nodded; they had passed the inn on their way to Stansbury's stable.

"I raise horses. Keep extra so when the inn runs out, or they don't have the quality some want, they come here. Do a good business," he bragged. "Man come along a while back. Said the innkeeper sent him. Wanted me to keep his horse until he was settled. Didn't know how long it would be, but paid for a month in advance."

"Do you know who he was?"

"Said his name was Tremayne, Richard Tremayne."

Lord Melbourne was not surprised. His name seemed to be meeting with uncommon popularity, and he wondered where it would crop up next. Perhaps, when he returned home, George would have changed his name to Richard Tremayne. He was becoming too fanciful, thought the earl. Best stick to the business at hand.

"And what did this Richard Tremayne look like?" he asked.

"Shorter'n you. Smaller built too. Had sorta reddish-like brown hair, and dark brown eyes. Acted like he was better 'n what he was, if you get what I mean."

"I think I do."

"Wore a buncha fobs and fiddled with 'em all the time we were talking. Made me want to tie his hands up just to keep 'em still," Stansbury added.

While the physical description could match many men, the habit of toying with the fobs clearly condemned Albert Nestor as the culprit who had stolen Galahad. The use of Richard's name was merely a jab meant to make him appear the fool. It seemed he would need to do more than merely chase Nestor away from Melbourne Park after all; the man deserved some punishment for taking Galahad.

"What made you contact me?" asked Lord Melbourne.

"His month run out, but I weren't worried. I knew the horse was worth a fair price. I was at the inn one evenin' and heard 'em talkin' 'bout a horse some earl was lookin' for. Description matched this 'un," he said, motioning toward Galahad. "Thought it wouldn't hurt to look into it."

"I'm happy you did," said Lord Melbourne. "I'll make it worth your while."

"There's the cost of stabling the animal due."

The earl reached into his pocket. "I'll take care of that, too," he said.

"We had best put up at the inn tonight," the earl said to his groom a short time later as they made their way back down the lane leading Galahad.

Lord Melbourne was puzzled. He could think of no good reason for Albert Nestor stealing Galahad unless he had meant to return the horse and gain the earl's gratitude. If so, he had let the matter drag on far too long and, no matter what the earl might think of him, he did not believe Albert was a fool.

Lord Melbourne ate a fairly decent meal at the inn and decided to stay the night and start back to Melbourne Park the next morning. He lay in his bed, a candle left lit, staring up at the rough ceiling, still wondering how Galahad's disappearance would benefit Nestor.

He put aside his distrust of Emma. What if everything she said was true? Emma contended Nestor wanted her out of the way in order for Charlotte to inherit and for him to marry the girl. She claimed he had attempted to kill her twice while she was at home; and the earl could not deny that she had suffered two mysterious incidents, which were certainly not accidents, while at Melbourne Park.

What if she were right? Lord Melbourne's presence would greatly reduce Nestor's chances of success in getting rid of Emma. The best possibility of accomplishing the deed would be to make sure the earl was out of the way. And what better way to do that than steal Galahad? Nestor could have found out from anyone in the village or at the inn about Galahad's worth.

Taking the horse had been easy, for no one had expected it to happen. Then Nestor had waited until Lord Melbourne was off looking for Galahad to attempt to harm Emma. He had undoubtedly planned for the saddle girth to break while the earl was away and Emma was riding on her own. Perhaps he had even been waiting nearby to finish the job if the fall didn't do it. Lord Melbourne flinched at the thought.

When that hadn't accomplished what he wanted, Albert had again waited until the earl was away before taking a shot at Emma. She claimed Nestor was desperate for money, and it must be true or he would have never chanced showing up at the dance. Lord Melbourne had to believe that he was attempting to convince Charlotte to elope with him, but Nestor hadn't even been able to accomplish that because of the earl's intervention. And this, thought Lord Melbourne, was his solution to the problem.

Nestor had only to plant a rumor at the inn near John Stansbury's stable about Lord Melbourne looking for a horse that fit the description of the stallion he was boarding, to put the plan into action.

Anticipating a large reward, Stansbury had reacted in exactly the manner Nestor had foreseen. He had contacted the earl, and here Lord Melbourne was far away from home, giving Nestor an unopposed opportunity to either harm Emma or elope with Charlotte. Or he could do both and accomplish everything he hoped to achieve. Nestor had set the trap and the earl had stepped right into it.

Lord Melbourne could not believe he had been so easily duped. It was true he had doubted everything about Emma, but he should have been able to see the truth. He could only blame his obtuseness on his determination not to succumb to his attraction to her, and where had it gotten him? Too many miles away from the woman he loved to keep her safe.

Nestor could have already taken advantage of his absence

and have harmed Emma. Lord Melbourne's chest tightened and his breathing became labored when he thought of Emma lying still and white, injured and needing help. He leaped from the bed and began throwing on his clothes.

Dammit! Why hadn't he stayed and faced his feelings instead of running off after Galahad? He was too far away to be any help to Emma, and it might be too late before he was able to reach her.

Lord Melbourne raced down the stairs and into the stable. He was not taking any chances of losing Galahad again, and had left the groom to guard him.

"Saddle Galahad," he ordered, shaking the groom.

"What, my lord?" asked his groom, quickly coming awake.

"Saddle Galahad," he repeated. "I'm returning to Melbourne Park immediately. Stay here the rest of the night and start back in the morning. Here's something to get you home," he said, tossing some coins to the groom.

Galahad would be fresh after his long period of inactivity, and they should make good time, thought the earl, pacing in front of the stable while the groom saddled the horse. He only hoped it would be soon enough to save Emma.

Chapter Fourteen

"Shouldn't we wait until Lord Melbourne returns before leaving?" asked Laura for the third time since Emma had announced they would depart as soon as they could pack their trunks.

"There's no reason to do so," Emma replied. "He knows we plan to leave."

"But he expected to help us get away without being observed by Albert."

"I told him it wasn't necessary," said Emma.

"Does that mean you no longer believe Albert is a threat to us?"

"It merely means that we have overstayed our welcome and should be on our way. There's no need to wait for Lord Melbourne. I have contended with Albert for this long and I can continue to do so," Emma said with more confidence than she felt.

"Do you think it's safe to leave in daylight?"

"Lord Melbourne said he was sending Albert on his way. He should be far enough away to be harmless."

"I hope you're right," said Laura.

"Is Charlotte ready?" asked Emma.

"Yes. She said she wanted to take a last walk in the garden and would meet us in the front hall."

Emma gave a final look around the room. She had first entered it angry at a husband who had deserted her. She was leaving it despondent that the man she loved thought her a liar and a schemer, and would never return her feelings. That the men were not one and the same made her question her own integrity.

"Then let's go downstairs," said Emma. "There is nothing more here for me."

"I wish I could convince you to stay until Richard returns," said Lady Melbourne, as they gathered in the front hall a few minutes later.

"I'm afraid it's impossible," said Emma. "Convey to him our appreciation for his hospitality."

"I will, but it would be better coming directly from you."

"I'll add my entreaty to my mother's," said Adam. "Surely another day here would do no harm."

"Our trunks are already on the coach," replied Emma. "We had best be on our way."

"Where is Charlotte?" Adam asked.

"She should be here any moment," said Laura. "She wanted to see the gardens one last time."

"It must be her favorite place," interjected Lady Melbourne. "She has spent a great deal of time there."

"Ah, here she is," said Laura, as Charlotte approached from the back of the house, her cheeks flushed.

"You've been hurrying," judged Emma.

"I didn't realize so much time had passed, and I had to rush so I wouldn't hold up our departure," said Charlotte.

"We have been attempting to convince your sister to stay with us a while longer," said Adam.

Charlotte blushed, and avoided his gaze. "It would be pleasant, I will admit," she said. "But we have planned our trip to Paris for some time now."

"May I hope you'll visit with us again?" asked Adam.

"If we are able," replied Emma, anxious to get away before the farewells became too painful. "And you must feel free to visit us once we are home again."

"I'll hold you to that," Adam replied, still watching Charlotte.

The women climbed into the coach, and waved to Lady Melbourne and Adam as the coachman started the horses down the drive.

Emma glanced across at Charlotte. She was staring out the window with a dreamy expression on her face. She had not seemed depressed that they were going to Paris, and had not once begged to return home since Emma had told her about their new destination. Charlotte's demeanor was unusual, but Emma could not deal with it now. She would have time enough once they were on board the ship leaving the shores of England behind.

"Where is she?" demanded Lord Melbourne as he burst into the drawing room later that morning.

"You nearly frightened me out of my wits," said Lady Melbourne. "And look at the state you're in."

Her usually impeccable son was covered with dust. His jaw had not felt a razor since he had left and was covered in a dark stubble. With his blue eyes flashing, he was a menacing figure, and appeared completely out of place among the delicately wrought furniture and pastel hues of the drawing room.

"Emma! Where is she?" he said repeated.

"What's all the uproar?" asked Adam, coming through the door. "Richard, you're back," he said, catching sight of his brother.

"Dammit! Will someone tell me where Emma is?" the earl bit out between gritted teeth.

"She's gone," said Adam. "We tried to convince her to stay until you returned, but she insisted on leaving. Said to thank you for your hospitality."

"My hospitality?" he said, with a harsh laugh. "When did she leave?"

"Earlier this morning," said Adam.

"What is it, Richard? What is wrong?" asked Lady Melbourne.

"She's in danger," he replied distractedly. "I must go after her immediately."

"That means Charlotte is at risk also," said Adam.

"I doubt that she will be harmed; she's too valuable to Nestor. Roland!" Lord Melbourne shouted. "Have a fresh horse brought around; the best we have in the stables," he ordered when the butler appeared in the door.

"Make that two horses," ordered Adam.

"You cannot mean to go with him," said Lady Melbourne.

"Of course, I do."

"But your leg—"

"Is fine," said Adam.

"Are you certain?" asked the earl.

"Positive. It would be worse sitting here waiting for word."

Lord Melbourne understood Adam's concern and did not argue further; he doubted his brother would listen even if he did. Adam's company would be welcome, for he did not know what he would find when he caught up with Emma.

While they waited for the horses to be brought round, the earl quickly recounted what had happened since he had left the day before, and what he suspected. As soon as they were able, the men mounted and galloped down the drive, leaning low over the animals' necks and urging them on.

At the first posting inn, Lord Melbourne learned that a coach carrying three women had stopped there for luncheon. They could not be far ahead of them. His hopes revived that they would find Emma before Nestor did.

A short time later they rounded a curve and saw in the distance a coach tilted on its side in a ditch beside the road. Lord Melbourne motioned to Adam and they both pulled their horses to a halt. Moving slowly they guided their mounts off the road and approached the scene under cover of the thick woods.

As they grew closer, they could see that the horses had broken loose and were standing a short distance away. The coachman was lying, unmoving, in the road. Laura was propped against the underside of the coach, with Charlotte by her side. But what was most frightening was the pistol that Albert Nestor was pointing at Emma.

Albert had never meant to keep his word to Emma. If he used the money she had given him to pay his debts, he would have nothing to live on. He was still at the inn when the Randolphs' coach passed, and a sly smile lifted the corners of his thin lips.

Emma thought she was leaving him behind, and would be safe in Paris before he found out. What she didn't know was that he had met with Charlotte a short time ago, and the chit had told him of their plan. His horse was saddled; he would ride cross-country and be in front of them before noon. Then he would finally accomplish what he had set out to do so many months before.

Albert finished his ale and went outside to where his horse waited. Mounting, he guided the animal out of the village, more than happy to put the place behind him.

He was relieved that all his problems would soon be at an end. He had grown desperate over the past fortnight. His creditors had become even more demanding since his marriage had not materialized. Emma stood in his way, and his resentment of her had increased until it consumed him. The chit had no concept of family loyalty. He had offered to marry her and take on all the responsibility of the estate, but she had refused.

Albert had felt the Randolph fortune slipping from his grasp, so he had turned to Charlotte as a way to solve his problems. Once they were married, Emma would not allow her younger sister to suffer, and would no doubt be happy to pay off his bills in order to keep the family name respectful.

But Emma had done all she could to keep them apart. She had forced him to sneak around in order to see Charlotte, and his anger had grown. He was determined to make Emma pay for this and for her rejection of him. A little flattery had convinced Charlotte that Emma was merely jealous of his attentions, and that she should keep their meetings a secret.

Emma had thought she had eluded him by sneaking away so that he couldn't follow them, sneered Albert. What she hadn't counted on was Charlotte's loyalty to him. The girl had written as soon as they had settled to tell him where she was. She hadn't wanted him to worry, the silly baggage. As if he cared what happened to her as long as she could say her vows.

Meanwhile he had concocted a plan that would remove Emma from the picture for all time. And, with only one minor problem, his scheme had worked perfectly up until the time Emma had decided to go haring off after her husband.

Albert's satisfaction increased as he thought of how Emma had expected marriage to solve all her problems. His cousin might be able to run her estate without his help, but when it came to plotting he could not be beaten. He must take a little time to tell her what he had done; he would enjoy the look on her face before he killed her.

Albert no longer cared about making Emma's death look like an accident. Time was too short to worry about such niceties. He merely wanted her out of the way so that he could marry Charlotte.

He had removed another potential problem by luring the earl away from home. Albert had arranged for John Stansbury to hear of the large reward Lord Melbourne was offering for the return of a stallion that fit the description of the horse he was boarding. Stansbury had sent a note off to the earl, which had brought Lord Melbourne running, leaving the women virtually unprotected.

Then luck seemed to shine on him. When Charlotte had met him this morning, she told him of their trip to Paris. Albert's mind worked furiously to take advantage of the opportunity which had presented itself. He had urged Charlotte not to worry, and assured her they would be together just as he had promised.

He vowed that before they reached the coast, he would carry her off to Gretna Green. It was as romantic as one of her novels, she had foolishly commented, before returning to the house.

Albert checked his watch. Time had slipped by quickly while he was immersed in thought. He was near the inn where the women would be stopping to rest and have luncheon.

Albert approached The Oak and the Acorn cautiously, searching the yard for the Randolphs' coach. It was nowhere in sight, and he smiled. The first part of his plan had worked; he had beaten them to the posting inn. Now, to find a willing accomplice.

Albert noticed a man idling away his time on a bench near the door. "Would you like to do a job for me?" he asked.

"Depends," the man answered shortly. "Not lookin' for any hard work."

"This will only take a few minutes and you'll be well paid for it," he promised.

The man grinned, showing dark stained teeth. "Sounds like the kind'er work I like."

Albert smiled back. He had always been a good judge of character.

It was an hour or so later that Albert watched the Randolph coach pull away from The Oak and the Acorn. He was behind a thick screen of trees which effectively hid him from view. After the coach had passed, he guided his horse onto the road and followed at a leisurely pace.

A short time later he came upon the coach overturned in a ditch, its wheels still spinning and dust settling around it. Albert looked both ways in the road, and was satisfied when he saw no one approaching. He had taken a chance that he would be the first one to arrive at the coach, and his luck seemed to be holding.

He ignored the driver who was lying unmoving in the road and approached the coach. Albert could hear sounds from inside. He climbed up and pulled open the door.

"Oh, thank God, someone was near," said a voice he recognized as Laura Seger's.

Albert did not relish rescuing her, but it was necessary. He reached for her hand and pulled her through the door, then lowered her to the ground. Blood from a gash on her head ran down her forehead. She seemed groggy and did not indicate that she recognized him. So much the better, he thought.

Charlotte came next, and he put a finger to her lips to keep her quiet. "Miss Seger is injured; take care of her," he said to distract her.

Emma was an altogether different matter. As soon as she saw his face, she jerked her arm back. "Come now, cousin. I know you've taken a dislike to me, but surely you'll allow me to help you out of your predicament."

As much as she disliked it, she had no choice but to do so, decided Emma, reaching up and allowing Albert to pull her out through the door. As soon as she could, she jerked away from his distasteful touch, and looked around to determine the damage.

Laura was leaning against the coach, while Charlotte applied a handkerchief to a cut on her forehead. "How badly are you hurt?" she asked, leaning over to study the gash.

"Not badly at all," replied Laura. "It appears the bleeding has almost stopped."

"I think you're right," agreed Emma. "And you, Charlotte?"

"Except for a few sore spots, I'm all right."

"Good," Emma said, glancing around. "John Coachman looks to have gotten the worst of it." She turned to give aid to the man, when Albert stopped her.

"I wouldn't worry about him, cousin. He isn't going to survive this accident no matter what you do."

"Don't be foolish, Albert. Now get out of the way and let me see to our driver."

"You'll do nothing but stay where I tell you to," he replied, pointing a pistol at her, an evil smile on his face.

"Albert! What are you doing?" cried Charlotte.

"Shut up, you idiot!" he barked. "Stay with your governess and keep your mouth shut until I tell you differently."

Charlotte fell quiet, more from shock that Albert would talk to her so, than from following his instructions, thought Emma. Her sister had never been spoken to so harshly in her entire life. Emma only hoped that it opened her eyes to the kind of man Albert was hiding behind his civilized exterior. The realization might be too late to save Emma, but perhaps Charlotte would not give in so easily to his demands.

"What do you want?" she asked, attempting to keep her voice steady.

"What I've always wanted," he said. "A bride; and since you're not willing, then Charlotte will have to do."

"What do you mean she isn't willing?" asked Charlotte.

"He tried to get me to marry him before he turned to you," Emma explained, hoping to further tarnish Albert in her sister's eyes. "When I turned him down—not once, but several times—he turned his attentions to you. You see, it didn't matter to him which one of us he married. Only that we brought enough money with us to pay his debts."

"Albert, tell me it isn't true," Charlotte pleaded tearfully.

"I've told you to be quiet," Albert said to Charlotte. "I'll teach you soon enough to follow orders."

"Do you think she'll marry you after this?" said Emma, motioning toward the pistol he held.

"It doesn't matter what she wants; she'll do as I say. Most people will do anything to stay alive."

"You won't harm her; you need her too much. Since you know I'll not have anything to do with you, she's your last hope. Unless you have another heiress in mind who's clamoring to be your bride," she said sarcastically.

"Charlotte is more receptive to my advances than you, my dear cousin. She'll be my wife as soon as we can reach Gretna Green. Now, I'm tired of arguing. It's time to get on with this."

Emma knew she needed to keep him talking until someone appeared to help them. "I had expected to see you," she said scornfully, "but not quite so soon."

"You can thank your sister for that," he answered. "You remember her last look at the rose garden? Well, she met me and told me your entire plan. Accommodating little wench, isn't she? I wonder if she'll be as obliging once we are married?"

"I'll never allow that."

"You'll have no choice, once you're dead."

Charlotte uttered a cry.

"What about Laura and the coachman? Surely, you won't make them suffer for something they have no part in."

"You well know I can't leave any witnesses to what's going to happen to you."

"Albert, you cannot mean what you say," said Charlotte. Her eyes were huge in her pale face, and it was apparent she was having a difficult time accepting what was happening. "You've made your point, if that's what you intended to do. I'll convince Emma to allow you to travel with us if you will only finish with this pretense."

Albert's laugh sent chills through Emma. She knew then that there was no avoiding her fate unless someone came by in the next few minutes to interrupt Albert's plan.

"You are more dense than I thought," Albert said to Charlotte. "The pretense was everything that came before: the secret meetings, the flattery, the melancholy from being unable to see you. This is reality, my dear, and it would be best you accept it.

"As for what will happen to you and your companion," he continued, turning to Emma, "you suffered a coaching accident. Then, unfortunately, a band of thieves came upon your coach. They shot and robbed all of you, leaving your bodies in the road. Before I leave, I'll make sure the wheel spokes are too badly smashed to show they were cut."

"At your direction, no doubt," said Emma.

"Exactly," he agreed.

"But what of Charlotte? How will you explain her escape?"

"Why she had eloped with me before you left the inn. You were driving too fast attempting to catch up with us when the wheel gave way. By the time we return from Gretna Green, the story will be accepted."

"Emma, I'm so sorry. I should have listened to you," sobbed Charlotte.

"Shush, Charlotte, it doesn't matter," said Emma, then turned her attention back to Albert. "You'll be caught no matter what you do. I left a letter for Lord Melbourne explaining everything that has happened since you came into our lives.

He will see that you're brought to justice. Let us go now, and we'll say no more about it."

"I've invested too much to give up. If you had only married me, none of this would have been necessary. But you resisted, and that left me with Charlotte. A silly chit, but far more gullible than you."

Emma hoped that Charlotte was not too shocked to absorb what Albert was saying.

"I convinced her you would be jealous of us and persuaded her to keep our meetings secret." He laughed. "She believed every word I said, and from there on it was almost too easy to manipulate her."

"How could you do that to me?" wailed Charlotte.

"Be careful what you say, for we shall be husband and wife in the very near future," he warned her.

"I will never marry you," Charlotte vowed, leaning against Laura and sobbing onto her shoulder.

"Of course you will," Albert said confidently. "And the first thing I'll do as your husband is turn off all your servants. They would do nothing at all to help me find you. That fool of a steward swore you had only left instructions for the running of the estate and nothing more."

Emma vowed that if she lived to get out of this tangle, her staff would receive large bonuses for their loyalty.

"I spent several weeks searching, and more money than I could afford, before I received Charlotte's note."

"This is all my fault," moaned Charlotte.

"That it is, my darling," Albert agreed. "It was then I concocted my plan. I decided if Emma did not fancy me for a husband, I would find someone else to suit her."

"What are we waiting for?" whispered Adam. "Let's move before he harms them."

"I want to hear this," said Lord Melbourne, knowing he was about to have all his questions answered. "He wants to tell them how clever he's been. He won't do anything until he's finished. We'll take him then."

"You'd better be right," warned Adam, giving his brother a withering look.

Emma felt a sudden shifting in her stomach and wondered whether she was going to be sick after all. "What do you mean?" she asked Albert, anticipating his words.

"I'm talking about your husband, Richard Tremayne; he was handpicked by me," revealed Albert. "And I couldn't have done a better job," he bragged.

"You knew Richard?" Emma whispered.

"Knew him? Why, we were the best of companions. We met years ago at a gambling hell in London. Many times we've helped one another over a rough patch. He was the first person I thought of when I saw I needed assistance.

"By the way, you might be interested to know his name is not Richard Tremayne, but Edward Tremayne."

"Edward!" exclaimed Adam, in their hiding place.

"Our missing cousin," said Lord Melbourne, his lips tight with anger. "The scheme would be something he'd jump at, particularly if there was a great deal of money involved."

"Edward Tremayne," repeated Emma. The name sounded familiar but, under the circumstances, she could not bring it to mind.

"Lord Melbourne's cousin," Albert clarified.

She had heard the name only once. That is why she had not remembered it readily. "Then Charles Tremayne was his father, and he did grow up on the estate we first visited."

Albert nodded in the affirmative. "He had drained his father of as much as he possibly could long ago, and hadn't returned in some time. I had seen him not long before in Bath, where he was romancing an elderly widow. I contacted him and explained my situation.

"I told him I needed to get you out of the way, and suggested he court and marry you. After you had returned home, we would arrange for you to have a fatal accident, which would clear the way for me to marry Charlotte.

"He was the one who decided to take the name Richard Tremayne. Thought it a great joke on his cousin. He had run across his aunt's locket while he was in France; said he could put it to good use.''

"I never knew he hated me so much,'' murmured Lord Melbourne, in a low voice.

"Envy is more like it,'' replied Adam, keeping his eye on the group. "He always thought he should have been the earl instead of you.''

"I hope you never get the same idea,'' said the earl with a grim smile.

"I have no desire to be in your shoes. I'll be satisfied with a wife and a home, without the title; and before this is over, I hope to have both.''

"I'll do all I can to accommodate you,'' promised Lord Melbourne, returning his full attention to Albert Nestor and Emma.

"The arrangement was simple,'' continued Albert. "As soon as you were dead, and Charlotte and I were wed, I'd pay Edward off and he'd be on his way, a sad but rich widower.''

"But he left before you had the chance to do away with me,'' said Emma. "He ruined your plan.''

"He did,'' agreed Albert, "but it isn't what you think. He didn't do it for love; he became too greedy. He said he was tired of his tedious manner of living and had decided your marriage would be a real one. Instead of a payment from me, he would have the entire estate and live in comfort for the rest of his days. Unfortunately, his days did not last long after he said his vows.''

Chapter Fifteen

Emma knew the answer before she asked the question, but she had to hear it from Albert's lips. "Do you know what happened to him?" she asked.

"After the service, I sent a message to Edward telling him it was urgent I see him immediately. I asked him to meet me in a grove of oak trees not far from the inn where you were holding your wedding breakfast. When he arrived I questioned whether he had changed his mind. He said he hadn't, so I shot him, and buried him there."

"No! Albert! How could you?" wailed Charlotte completely stunned by his confession.

"It was easy, my dear. When we are wed, you'll find I'm a man not to be crossed. Keep that in mind."

Emma wanted to keep Albert talking, praying someone would come along to rescue them. "Why did you stay away from us? I would think my husband's disappearance would have been an opportune time to approach us again."

"I considered it, but I didn't want to appear too soon and arouse your suspicions. I had some business which took me away for several weeks, and when I returned you had already departed. Not too accommodating of you, cousin."

"Keeping you informed of our whereabouts was not one of my concerns," Emma replied.

"It wasn't necessary; your sister did an admirable job of that very thing," said Albert, eliciting another sob of remorse from Charlotte.

"I returned to the inn where I had stayed and found a letter from her explaining what had happened and where you were going. By the time I caught up to you, you were at Melbourne Park. I knew my task would be much more difficult while you were living in the earl's household. However, I did have special knowledge that I used to help me get you alone.

"After Edward had shown me the locket, and suggested he use his cousin's name to court you, we spent several long nights developing our plan. Edward told me more about the Tremayne family than I ever wanted to know, but one tale did help. He said he had heard that Adam had one stallion he prized above all others, and that Lord Melbourne had vowed to keep him safe until his brother returned from war.

"I was certain that the earl would go to any lengths to keep his promise. And while he was too shrewd to fool for long, I thought I might be able to keep him distracted long enough to allow me a chance to get close to you. So I stole the stallion knowing that Lord Melbourne would most likely take a personal part in searching for the horse.

"When the animal disappeared, the earl reacted in just the manner I had imagined," said Albert, looking pleased with himself.

"Dammit! I feel like a fool," whispered Lord Melbourne

"Anyone in your position would have done the same," said Adam.

"That does not excuse my gullibility," replied the earl, his knuckles showing white as he gripped his reins.

"With Lord Melbourne out of the way," continued Albert, "cutting the girth was easy. It was too bad he was with you when it gave way. If you had been alone when the fall didn't kill you, I could have finished the job then. After that I was too hasty in attempting to shoot you. I should have planned better, for you became too wary after that for me to get you alone again."

"I'm sorry to have inconvenienced you," replied Emma, but her sarcasm did not cause him to pause in his recitation.

"I met Charlotte again hoping to use her in some way, but she had become a watering pot, and pleaded for me to call on you and make everything right. In my mind, the only thing that would make things right would be your death."

A chill went down Emma's back at his words. If something didn't happen soon, her fate would be the same as Edward's.

"I finally convinced Charlotte to keep our meetings secret a little longer. Success was within my grasp and I couldn't have the chit ruin it for me." He glanced at Charlotte's tear-stained face, not bothering to hide his disgust of her. "I will put a stop to her sniveling once we are married," he promised.

Emma realized his story was finished. She glanced up and down the road searching for help, but saw no one.

"There is no one to save you today," said Albert, seeming to read her mind. "Lord Melbourne is probably just now drawing near his home; it will be longer before he hears of your departure and, even then, he will probably think nothing is amiss.

"Your entire party, except for Charlotte, will be found here. It will look as if you had an accident and, before you could get help, were attacked by highwaymen and killed. Before it's determined who you are, and that you have a sister missing, we'll already be man and wife."

Emma could not bear to think of Albert married to Charlotte. "Lord Melbourne will not allow you to get away with this. He knows everything."

"He has no proof of any of the things you've told him. Edward Tremayne is dead, and I will make certain that Charlotte will not speak against me. That is, if she wants to live," he said with a smirk.

"And if you want to live, you should drop your pistol immediately," said a voice from behind him.

Albert whirled around and stared directly into the barrels of two pistols held by Lord Melbourne and Adam.

"I'm not a patient man," warned the earl. "I will give you one more chance to give up, or it will be you who joins my unfortunate cousin."

Albert tossed his pistol into the dust of the road. "You'll never be able to prove anything," he blustered.

"I think we've heard everything we need to know," said Lord Melbourne, dismounting, and leaving Adam to hold his pistol on Nestor. He retrieved a length of broken leather from the overturned coach and bound Albert's arms tightly behind him, then pushed him to the ground and tied his feet. "That should hold you until we're ready to leave," he judged.

"Is everyone all right?" he asked, turning toward the women.

"Laura has a cut, but the coachman has not moved at all," answered Emma. Now that it was all over, her voice would not hold steady, and she fought back tears of relief.

"I'll check on him," said Adam, and the earl joined him at the man's side. He was still breathing, but they discovered a large bump on his head.

"We'll need to get him back to the inn and have a doctor attend him," said Lord Melbourne. "But he's breathing easy, and will probably be all right."

Just then a curricle approached them. Lord Melbourne gave a brief explanation to the men who were aboard it, and asked that they send two coaches from the inn to transport the ladies and the injured driver. In a very few minutes, the men were charging down the road in the direction of The Oak and the Acorn.

While Emma had followed the earl and Adam to the driver's side, Laura and Charlotte had stayed where they were. After the curricle left, Adam could stay away from Charlotte no longer, and moved past Lord Melbourne and Emma to the overturned coach.

* * *

Lord Melbourne wanted nothing more than to take Emma in his arms and never let her go. However, he did not think she would welcome his touch after all of his suspicions and the harsh words that had passed between them.

She looked very small standing in the dust of the road. Her bonnet must have been lost when the coach turned over, and her hair was falling loose from its pins. Her dress was rumpled and, although she did not acknowledge it, her eye was swollen and would most likely turn to purple within the day.

The question about Emma's husband had been answered, yet it brought the earl no joy. The information had come too late to keep him from insulting Emma to such a degree that he wondered whether he had also ruined Adam's chance with Charlotte. If that were the case, it would mean two more people who would never forgive him.

He tried to rouse his anger because Emma had been so secretive with him, not entrusting him with the full truth, but he could not even do that. He had not believed the part of her story that she had told him; why should she continue to confide in him? If he had been in her place, he would have done the same and kept his business to himself. No, he could blame no one for his unhappiness but himself.

"I'm afraid I can't offer you a chair," he said, with an encouraging smile, "but there is a rock at the edge of the road where you could sit until we're rescued."

Emma looked down at the coachman.

"There's nothing more we can do for him until we get him back to the inn."

She nodded, and Lord Melbourne guided her to the side of the road where she perched tentatively on a large gray rock.

"Now, let me look at you," he said, putting a finger under her chin and tilting her face upward. "Does your eye hurt?"

"I haven't had time to notice until now, but I suppose it does," she answered indifferently.

"I'm afraid it will be discolored for a few days."

"A small inconvenience compared with being dead forever," she retorted.

Lord Melbourne laughed. "I want you to come back to Melbourne Park," he said suddenly serious.

"I cannot do that, my lord." Her words were precise and unemotional.

"All of you will be sore and bruised. Laura has a cut and your eye will be none too good for at least a sennight. And Charlotte—I'm certain Charlotte is bruised more in spirit than in body. She'll need someone to help her through this."

They both looked toward the coach where Adam was kneeling by Charlotte's side. Her face was buried on his shoulder and his arms encircled her.

"And you think Adam should be that person?" Emma asked.

"I know he should," the earl replied confidently. "And so do you if you will only admit it."

"Only yesterday, you were eager enough to see the last of me. How can I rest easily under your roof again? If Laura and Charlotte are in such a fragile state, how can I expose them to such hostility?"

"There will be nothing like that, I promise you."

"And it only took all of our near deaths to convince you of my innocence," she said, beginning to regain a bit of her spirit. "No, I think we will stay at the inn and continue our journey once we are able."

"The inn does not have the conveniences Melbourne Park has to offer," he argued. "If you will not think of yourself, consider Laura and Charlotte. And there's the coachman, too. He would get much better attention there."

Emma looked toward the man who lay in the road, a blanket under his head. "All right. We will accept your hospitality."

"Good."

"But only for as long as it takes for us to recover enough to return home."

The earl felt a great deal of satisfaction that she would once again be at Melbourne Park.

* * *

It had been a fortnight since the accident and Albert's revelation of his sinister intentions. Edward's body had been found in the grove of oak trees near Dover, and Albert had been charged with his murder.

Laura's cut was minor and she had resumed her walks in the garden with David Whitney. She had confided to Emma that David had asked her to marry him, and that she had agreed. Emma would be sad to leave her behind, but knew that her well-deserved happiness lay with the man she loved.

Charlotte had been quiet since the incident. A haunted look lingered in her eyes, and she spoke only to apologize again and again for being taken in by Albert. Finally, Emma insisted that she had done so quite enough, and that she should concentrate on forgetting about Albert and all that he had done.

Adam spent every moment possible with Charlotte, and the last few days, Emma had seen a glimpse of her sister she had not seen since before Albert entered their lives. As soon as he felt the time was right, Emma felt certain that Adam would offer for Charlotte.

As for herself, her eye was back to its normal color, and she looked as if nothing extraordinary had ever happened to her. And if she discounted the attempts on her life, an unfulfilled marriage that had ended in murder, and falling in love with a man who held her in total contempt, she supposed nothing had.

Emma rose and walked across the drawing room to gaze out the window. She had the room to herself, and was taking advantage of the solitude to consider what she should do next.

John Coachman was fully recovered and assured her he was able to drive again without any discomfort. She would talk with Charlotte and they could decide on when to leave Melbourne Park and travel home. She would repeat her invitation to Adam to visit them, for if he and Charlotte were serious, they would not want to be parted for long.

She heard the door open and turned to see Lord Melbourne standing just inside. When they had returned to Melbourne

Park, he had been away a great deal of the time. She had assumed it had to do with Albert, but had not inquired.

The past week he had been at home more often, but they had been quite stiff and formal with one another when meeting. She would tell him they would be leaving soon; the news should bring a smile of relief to his face.

"My lord."

"Baroness Randolph," he replied in acknowledgement.

Emma smiled. "How strange that sounds."

"You think I would not do you the courtesy of using your title?" he asked, appearing offended.

"Not at all," she said. "It's simply been a long time since anyone has addressed me so."

He frowned, then crossed the room until he stood in front of her. "There is something I wish to say."

"I was ready to come looking for you," she said. "I wanted to let you know we'll be leaving soon."

"I don't want to discuss that just yet," he replied stubbornly.

"It wasn't meant to be a discussion," she snapped back, annoyed that he must always have his way. "I wished only to thank you for your hospitality before our departure. There is nothing that will repay you for saving our lives. To merely extend thanks seems trivial; however, I know nothing else to do."

The earl held up his hand. "Please, you can repay me by listening to what I have to say."

Emma lapsed into silence, and watched as his lips firmed into a resolute line. His dark blue gaze settled on her and she nearly shivered under its intensity. She did not know what he had on his mind, but he was determined to say it.

"There was a time when you told me your family was an honorable one. You said you expected an apology from me when I found out the truth."

She could not help but chance his ire and interrupt him. "Please, my lord, this is entirely unnecessary. So much has happened since then."

"It is necessary," he said, taking a step closer and looking down at her, an odd expression in his eyes. "I always keep my word, Baroness, and I am here to apologize."

"My lord—" she began to protest.

"No," he said, laying a finger across her lips, and leaving it a moment too long before removing it. "I will have my say."

She would not argue any longer. His touch had sent an odd feeling through her, and she only wanted to get the interview over with and be gone before she revealed her feelings toward him.

"I was wrong about you," he said. "And I apologize for everything I've said or done to insult you or your family."

"Thank you. Now shall we put it behind us?"

A smile curved his lips and lit his eyes. "I would be happy to. Now, about your leaving; I don't think it would be a good idea. At least, not in the near future."

Emma's goodwill vanished. "And why not, my lord?"

"There is too much left undone for you to go running off. David is determined to marry Laura as soon as possible. You would no sooner get home than you would need to return for the wedding. You wouldn't want to miss it, would you?"

"No, of course not, but—"

"There, I knew you would be reasonable," he said, spreading his hands wide.

"But it could be done," she commented, not wanting to give in so easily.

"Then there's Adam," replied Lord Melbourne.

"What of him?"

"Why, he's in love with Charlotte. Surely, you've seen that for yourself these past two weeks. I don't think they will want to be parted."

"I've already invited Adam to visit with us. He can stay as long as he likes."

"And take him away from his mother so soon after he has returned?" Lord Melbourne's expression was one of astonishment that she would do such a thing; however, there was a twinkle in his eye that he could not completely disguise that made her think he was doing it up a bit too brown.

"Lady Melbourne is more than welcome to accompany him," she replied obstinately.

The earl stood a moment watching her. "And what about me?" he said quietly. "Would I be welcome, too?"

"You will always be welcome, my lord. I will be eternally grateful for your saving our lives. If I can return your hospitality at any time, I shall be happy to do so."

"Dammit, Emma! I don't want your thanks, nor your gratefulness."

"Then what do you want?" she demanded, wishing the conversation over with so she could get away from his disturbing closeness.

"I want you, Emma." He moved close to her, and framed her face with his large hands. "But not without your love," he said softly. "I could not bear it if I did not have that."

Her pulse raced and her breath seemed too short for her to speak. "What do you mean?"

"I'm asking you to marry me. I know I've said despicable things to you, but I regret every one of them more than you'll ever know. I found myself falling in love with you, even though you were married; perhaps even to my brother.

"I fought my desire for you with everything I had, but I still lost. I turned my anger and frustration on you, and I was wrong." He leaned his forehead against hers and closed his eyes a moment.

Emma felt his breath against her face, and tilted her head until her lips touched his. He was as still as a statue, and she moved her mouth on his, searching for a way to bring him to life.

It was only a moment until he accepted her gift and enclosed her completely within his arms. He took control of their kiss, taking it deeper until Emma thought she could no longer stand. But she didn't need to do so, for he lifted her against him, holding her closer than she thought possible.

Her softness yielded to the hardness of his body until she did not know where one began and the other left off. Yet she still yearned for a closer bond that continued to elude her, no matter how hard she pressed against him.

With a groan, he pulled his mouth from hers, trailing kisses across her cheek and down to the pulse beating erratically in the curve of her throat.

"You tempt me beyond all belief," he murmured, against her skin.

"I'm glad," was all she could manage to get out.

"I hope this means you're accepting my proposal," he said, moving back a little in order to look down at her.

"Yes, I suppose it does," she said, still dazed from the effects of his kiss.

He smiled at her bewilderment. "Not an overenthusiastic response, but more than I had hoped."

Emma began to regain her composure. "Oh, no. I did not mean to sound so disinterested."

"There's no need to explain," he said, placing a light kiss on her lips. "There is one thing I'd like to know. Do you love me, Emma? It's all right if you don't," he rushed on before she had a chance to answer. "After all my suspicion I can understand, but at least give me a chance to hope that someday you might return my love."

Emma's eyes filled with tears. "Oh, Richard, of course I love you," she admitted, throwing her arms around his neck, and pulling his head down to hers.

Some time later, Lord Melbourne was seated in a wingback chair, Emma in his lap.

"What if someone should come in?" she asked, snuggling closer to him.

"I locked the door behind me when I entered," he said. "I was hoping we would need some privacy."

"You are probably known as a rake in London," she accused him playfully.

"No longer." His smile was smug as his hand wandered over the thin muslin of her gown.

"Richard," she feebly protested, while lifting her lips for another kiss.

He willingly obliged her, then said in a mildly disapproving tone, "You know, we've never discussed your leaving here so abruptly without so much as one outrider to guard you."

"It's too late to take me to task over that," she objected. "There was no reason to stay since you didn't believe anything I said."

"Until it was too late, to my everlasting regret," he admitted, pulling her closer for a moment. "When I realized what was happening, I hurried back as quickly as possible, but you were already gone. I never want to experience that feeling again, my love. I don't think I'll let you out of my sight again for a very long time."

Her life had gone wrong for so long that Emma wondered whether the last hour had been a dream. She placed her fingers on Richard's lips, thinking they might disappear. Instead, he nibbled gently on her fingertips, sending shivers of delight though her.

"You know, I must go home eventually," she said, attempting to carry on a practical conversation. "The estate means too much to me to leave it unattended."

"I believe there might be a solution to your problem," he replied. "I have no doubt that Charlotte and Adam will wed before long. He would take good care of her, and your estate, if you would entrust them to him."

"That would be perfect," agreed Emma. "Charlotte has said time and again that she does not want to leave home."

"David tells me he and Laura have an agreement that hinges on you and Charlotte being settled first. I suggest we hurry with our marriage so we won't keep them waiting."

"I made one marriage in haste and it was a disaster," Emma said.

"I promise you will never regret marrying me, my love. Besides, you will be able to fulfill your dream and wear your mother's wedding dress."

"You remembered," she said, her eyes filling with tears.

"I never forget anything important, and at the moment that is my love for you—now and for always."